THE
SUMMER
of
ME

Also by Angela Benson

Delilah's Daughters
Sins of the Father
Up Pops the Devil

THE
SUMMER
of
ME

ANGELA BENSON

wm

WILLIAM MORROW
An Imprint of HarperCollinsPublishers

THE SUMMER OF ME. Copyright © 2016 by Angela Benson. All rights reserved. Printed in the United States of America. No part of this book may be used or reproduced in any manner whatsoever without written permission except in the case of brief quotations embodied in critical articles and reviews. For information address HarperCollins Publishers, 195 Broadway, New York, NY 10007.

HarperCollins books may be purchased for educational, business, or sales promotional use. For information please e-mail the Special Markets Department at SPsales@harpercollins.com.

FIRST EDITION

Designed by Diahann Sturge

Library of Congress Cataloging-in-Publication Data has been applied for.

ISBN 978-0-06-200272-3

16 17 18 19 20 OV/RRD 10 9 8 7 6 5 4 3 2 1

*To all the Facebook friends
who prayed this story into existence*

Chapter 1

SEATED IN A SALON STYLING CHAIR IN THE BASEMENT OF Destiny Madison's townhouse-style apartment, Bertice Brown turned and looked directly at her friend. "Are you crazy, Destiny?" she asked.

Destiny tugged on her friend's braid with her hands and used her foot to pump the lever to lock the movement of the styling chair. "How do you expect me to make this straight and tight if you keep turning your head and moving around?"

"Forget my hair for a minute," her longtime friend said. "You're about to make a big mistake."

"You don't know what you're talking about, Bertice," said Destiny's other friend Natalie, who sat in the recliner across from the styling chair with her feet up. "You don't even have kids."

Bertice huffed. "Neither do you. Besides, you don't have to be a fireman to know how to put out a fire."

Destiny laughed at the banter of her two best friends.

"What the heck are you talking about, Bertice? There's no fire here."

"You know what I mean," Bertice said. "It's not smart for you to let your kids go off for the entire summer with that fat Mary Margaret. Let them go for the weekend, not the whole summer."

Natalie rolled her eyes. "What do you think the woman's going to do, Bertice? She's not a serial killer or a child abductor."

"Not that we know," Bertice said.

"Now you're really talking crazy," Natalie said. "What's your problem with the woman? She hasn't done anything to Destiny, the kids, or you."

"I don't trust her," Bertice said. "If she wants kids, she and Kenneth need to have them and leave Destiny's alone. There's something sneaky about that woman. Nobody is as good hearted as she pretends to be."

Destiny had her own suspicions about her ex-flame's wife. It was a sore spot for her, so her friends rarely brought it up, but Kenneth had been dating Mary Margaret when Destiny became pregnant. Destiny had known about the woman, but she'd foolishly believed Kenneth when he'd told her it was over between him and his high school sweetheart. "To be honest, I thought about not letting them go," Destiny said.

Bertice nodded. "That would have been the smart move. You're too bright not to see through Mary Margaret."

"No, that wouldn't be the smart move," Natalie said. "This trip will be good for the twins. They need to see the world outside Georgia."

Bertice huffed again. "They have," she said. "Destiny took them to Disney World in Orlando last year. That's outside Georgia."

Natalie shook her head. "There's no reasoning with you." She turned to Destiny. "You're doing the right thing, girl," she said. "I know it's difficult but you have to think of your kids first. Besides, Mary Margaret is not that bad."

Destiny swallowed hard. It was difficult to hear her friend spout positive words about the kids' stepmother. She enjoyed their jabs at the woman more than she acknowledged. "You two are so focused on Mary Margaret that you're forgetting something: the kids are spending the summer in Los Angeles with their father and their father's wife," she said. "This is not about Mary Margaret. It's about the kids and their father."

"Keep telling yourself that," Bertice said. "I've always thought Mary Margaret needed some tips on how to stay in her lane. She's too much in your business and the business of your kids."

"She's married to Kenneth, Bertice. She's involved because he is."

Bertice snorted. "Okay, Ms. Baby Momma of the Year. You sure have softened toward Mary Margaret. I can remember the day when you couldn't bear to hear her name."

Natalie eyed Bertice. "People grow and change, Bertice. At least, most people do," she added with a not-so-subtle dig.

"As usual, you're always on the side of Mary Margaret," Bertice said to Natalie, lifting her arms in frustration. "When did my two friends become saints right here on earth?" She cut a glance to Natalie. "I blame it on Gavin. We never should have let you marry that preacher. That's when you two began to change on me."

Natalie laughed. "Like you could have stopped me."

Destiny let the playful exchange between her friends wash over her as she considered the truth of Bertice's words. There had been a change in their friendship since Natalie married Gavin, one of the pastors at the church they all attended, three years ago. Destiny had watched her friend change from a selfish, sometimes vindictive witch with a *b* to a model pastor's wife. Natalie still had her same spunk but it was now couched in a genuine concern and love for others. Destiny didn't know much about miracles but she believed the change in Natalie was as close to one as she had seen. Natalie's compassion had been a strong factor in helping Destiny develop a cordial relationship with Kenneth and Mary Margaret. Bertice was right. She hadn't always been accepting of Mary Margaret. She wasn't wholly accepting of the woman now, but she was doing her best for the sake of her kids.

Destiny continued to listen as her two closest friends debated whether she should trust Mary Margaret. Bertice expressed the fears that Destiny felt about letting the woman into her children's lives, while Natalie presented all the good that could come out of a positive stepparent relationship. "The decision is made, Bertice," she said when she grew weary of all the talk. "The kids are leaving on Saturday."

Bertice opened her mouth as if to say more, but she wisely closed it.

"Are they excited?" Natalie asked.

Destiny sighed. "Too excited. They're bouncing off the walls. You know, they've never been on an airplane before. The entire summer is stacking up to be a big adventure for them. I wish I could experience it with them. I can't bear to think of the *firsts* I'm going to miss."

Natalie lowered the footrest on the recliner and leaned toward Destiny. "You're doing the best you can do right now. The important thing is that you love your kids and your kids love you. That's all that matters."

"I know," Destiny said, "but I want to do more for them, more than my financial situation will allow. I hate that Kenneth and Mary Margaret can give them more than I can."

"You'd have more money if Kenneth and Mary Margaret stepped up those child-support payments," Bertice said. "I know fat Mary Margaret gets a fat paycheck from Turner Entertainment each month, so they can more than afford it."

Destiny cut Bertice a glare. Both of her friends knew she didn't want or expect Mary Margaret's money.

"I'm just saying," Bertice said. "They seem to be adding to your expenses, so I don't see why they can't chip in a little bit more. You know it's more expensive to live in Gwinnett County near them than where you live over here with the folks in South DeKalb."

Destiny sighed. "That may be a moot point now," she said. "I may not be moving to Gwinnett after all."

"What?" Natalie asked. "I thought it was all set."

Destiny shook her head. She hadn't been able to bring herself to tell her friends that her grand plans for the summer had fallen apart. As she looked at the concern and questions on their faces now, she knew she had to tell them. "They rescinded the job offer, so I'm not going to have the money to move into the house."

"What happened?" Bertice asked.

Destiny shrugged. "They said it had something to do with funding but I'm not sure I believe them. It doesn't matter really. There's nothing I can do about it anyway."

"Well," Natalie said, "you'll just find something else. We'll help you look, won't we, Bertice?"

"That's right," Bertice added. "In fact, I may have the perfect business opportunity for you. Recently, my life between paychecks has gotten considerably better."

Natalie rolled her eyes. "I don't know if I want to hear this. Please tell me the police are not going to come rolling up to your house anytime soon. If you get in trouble, you're going to end up with a public defender and a life sentence."

Destiny laughed. "Stop it, Natalie."

"It's the truth and Bertice knows it. We've heard about her *business ventures* before. They range from sorta shady to really shady." She stared at Bertice. "Pyramid schemes are not legal. Please tell me this isn't one of your pyramid schemes."

Bertice shook her head. "My ventures were network marketing opportunities, not pyramid schemes. There is a difference. Amway is network marketing and the guy who founded it now owns a basketball team. I bet he had his naysayers, too. Besides, this opportunity is not network marketing."

Casting a wary eye at Bertice, Natalie got up from the recliner. "I'm leaving," she said. "I don't want to know about your harebrained scheme. That way, I can honestly tell the police that I don't know anything. I would hate to have to testify against you."

"Oh, ye of little faith," Bertice said, laughing.

Natalie picked up her purse. Then she leaned over and brushed a kiss on Destiny's check. "Don't get yourself in trouble listening to this crazy woman. Braid her hair and get her butt out of here."

Destiny laughed. "I won't let her lead me down the wrong road."

Natalie stared down at Bertice. "You need to be more careful of what you get caught up in, Bertice. One day things are going to go really bad for you."

Bertice stood and gave Natalie a kiss on the cheek. "You worry too much, Miss Preacher's Wife. I'm not going to get into any trouble."

"I'll be praying for you," Natalie said to Bertice.

The concern in Natalie's voice raised alarm bells in Destiny's mind, but she pushed them aside as she walked her friend up the stairs and to the front door of the townhome she shared with her twins.

"I worry about Bertice," Natalie said, after they were upstairs. "And you, too."

"Don't worry about me," Destiny said. "I'm not going to get caught up in any of Bertice's crazy schemes."

"It's not that," Natalie said. "Kenneth is not going to take the kids from you."

Destiny closed her eyes briefly as she let the words that captured her greatest fear settle over her. When she opened them, they were damp. "He's going to try," she said. "He already convinced me the kids needed to go to school in his district since it has the better schools. Now he's harping on all the shuttling back and forth of the kids between school, his house, and here that we do each week. He makes a good point about it being more convenient if the kids just stayed with him and Mary Margaret during the week, but I don't want that. I want my kids with me each night. I'm their mother."

Natalie brushed at a tear that fell down Destiny's cheek. "Of course you want them with you, which is where they're going to be. We're going to work this out, Destiny. When the kids get back from California, they'll come back to a new home in Gwinnett County close to their school just the way you'd planned. I'm believing God for it. Can you believe with me?"

Destiny nodded, silently thanking God for good friends like Natalie and Bertice.

"Then dry those tears and give me a hug. I have to get out of here."

Destiny leaned into her friend's embrace. When she pulled back, Natalie gave her a sheepish smile.

"What?" Destiny asked.

Natalie sighed. "Because Gavin and I know how much you're going to miss the kids this summer, we want to give you a trip to California to visit them as an early Christmas gift.

Destiny shook her head. She couldn't take such an extravagant gift, even knowing her friend was coming from a place of love. "It's sweet of you to offer and I love you for even thinking of it, but I can't let you do it."

Natalie lifted her brow. "What do you mean you can't let us? It's our idea. We want to do it."

Destiny's heart warmed. "I know, but you do enough for me already. More than enough really. You and Bertice both help out more than you know by paying me to do your hair. I hate to take money for something I enjoy doing for my friends. No, you're both doing enough. Please don't treat me as a charity case. Besides, with my second-job situation up in the air, I have no clue what my schedule will be."

"Okay," Natalie said, though the look in her eyes told Destiny the conversation was not closed for good. "Call me tomorrow and let me know what crazy scheme Bertice has gotten herself involved in."

Destiny laughed. "You can count on it."

"And don't forget I want you to meet Gavin's old friend Daniel Thomas, who's moving to town. He's a great guy. You two will hit it off."

"I'll think about it," Destiny said, though she already knew the answer. She wasn't ready to dive back in the dating pool, despite Natalie's determination to push her back in there.

"Don't think about it," Natalie said. "Come to dinner one night so you can meet him. It doesn't have to be a big deal. Just some friends getting together for a meal and some good conversation."

"I don't know, Natalie. I can't see myself going out with a preacher. I'm no saint."

"Neither is he," Natalie said. "And neither am I, but look who I married. Forget Daniel is a preacher and think of him as someone who has the same kind of hole in his heart that you have in yours."

Destiny closed her eyes briefly and then opened them. "I doubt that."

Natalie looked as though she wanted to say something more, but she just pulled the door open. Before she stepped through it, she pressed another kiss against Destiny's cheek and whispered, "You're not the only person in the world recovering from a broken heart. It'll heal if you allow it. God wants to heal it."

Destiny leaned against the closed door after her friend stepped out into the night air and let her parting words wash over her. Was her personal pain that obvious? Kenneth had broken her heart and the recovery was taking longer than she expected. The twins were six and her heart still ached. How sad was that? Destiny pushed the thoughts away as she moved away from the door and made her way back to the basement where Bertice was waiting for her.

"Natalie is too uptight," Bertice said when Destiny reached her. "She never should have married the preacher."

Destiny took a seat on the stool behind Bertice's chair and picked up her comb. "Gavin's a great guy."

"He's not bad, for a preacher," Bertice said, fidgeting in her chair.

"If you want me to braid your hair, you'd best be still."

Bertice looked up at her with a grin on her face. "So do you want to hear about my business opportunity?"

"I'm sure I shouldn't," Destiny said with a chuckle, "but tell me anyway."

Chapter 2

"FEELING SAD?" PATRICIA MADISON ASKED, PEERING OVER her cup of coffee at her daughter, who sat next to her on the couch.

Destiny put her cup on the ottoman that served as a coffee table in her mother's living room. "Am I that obvious?"

Patricia grunted. "You're a mother. Your kids are leaving for the summer and you'll be separated from them for the first time. It's not a matter of being obvious. What you're feeling is what any mother would feel."

Destiny leaned back, picked up a pillow from the couch, and pressed it against her chest. "They're growing up too fast, Mom. Pretty soon they won't need me anymore."

Patricia leaned over and pressed her forehead against her daughter's. "Now you know how I feel."

Destiny smiled. "I still need you," she told her mother.

Patricia leaned back. "It's not the same."

"No," Destiny said. "It isn't the same. My kids are getting ready to leave for three months and they'd rather spend the days before their trip with their friends instead of their mother. That hurts."

Patricia chuckled. "I can now officially welcome you to the Old Mom's Club since you've already passed the initiation."

"Well, I don't feel as though I've passed anything."

"I know, sweetheart, but you have. You've learned that kids are the source of your greatest joy and also the source of your greatest sorrow. You love them more than they'll ever know until they have their own kids, and sometimes you feel as though they wish you'd just disappear." She eyed her daughter. "I know you've always thought I was too hard on you, Destiny, but I hope you can see now that you have your kids that everything I did was because I loved you."

"I know you love me, Mom," Destiny said. She was sure her mom loved her, but she wondered if her mom knew the best way to show that love. If she did, Destiny might feel more comfortable sharing her problems with her. As it was, she didn't dare for fear her mother would attack her decision making or try to tell her what to do. Her mother had no idea she'd been planning to move to Gwinnett. She'd planned to tell her when it was a done deal because she didn't want to open herself up to any negative comments. Given that the job had fallen through, she was glad she hadn't told her.

"I push you hard, Destiny, but I do it only because I love you and want the best for you. I named you Destiny because you were special. You still are. And I want you to reach your destiny." Patricia put her hand on her daughter's knee. "I know you're going to miss the kids, but you can make good use of the time they're away by going back to school."

Destiny groaned. "Not again, Mom."

"Yes again," her mother said. "You're only a few credits short of getting your degree. You've put it off too long as it is. With the kids away, this summer is the perfect time to knock out a few courses. Then you should be able to finish up over the next year or so by taking a class or two each semester. The kids are in school now and are beginning to have their own interests. It's the perfect time, Destiny. Don't let this opportunity pass you by. You know I didn't like it when you left school because you were pregnant, but you were so determined to do what you wanted."

Destiny heard her mother's unspoken "and you see how that turned out" rebuke. She accepted that she'd used her pregnancy as an excuse to leave school. She'd wanted out long before the doctor had given her the news that had changed the trajectory of her life. There had been a time when she'd thought about going to New York or Los Angeles and trying her hand at modeling or acting. That dream may have still been achievable with one child, but giving birth to twins had closed all those doors. Her priority at that point became the health and care of her children. So she'd taken an entry-level job at Marshalls and reached the highest position she could reach without a degree, manager of the cosmetics department.

"I don't know," Destiny said, hedging even though she had absolutely no interest in school. Her mother was a teacher with a graduate degree, so the importance of education had been drilled into her since childhood. But she'd never really enjoyed school, something she attributed to her mother's unrelentingly high standards. It wasn't enough for Destiny to be a good student; she had to be a great student. As a result, Destiny had felt more inadequate in school than she did at home. "School is not for everybody, Mom. You should know that by now."

"It may not be for some people, but it is for you. You're a smart girl, Destiny. You just have to apply yourself. I don't think you ever applied yourself when you were in school before. You'll be surprised by how well you do when you give it your all."

Destiny nodded, but she didn't agree with her mother. She had been an average student at best. All the evidence pointed to that conclusion, but her mother refused to see it.

"There are no guarantees in life, Destiny, but a degree will increase the likelihood of your getting a better job. You need to let those executives at Marshalls know that you're not content with the position you have. Show them that you're willing to work hard to move up. That's the way it works in corporate America."

Destiny resisted the urge to point out that her mother had never worked in corporate America. Besides, she knew what the older woman said was true. She just didn't want to go back to school.

"Get that degree because you need the credential. Your managers will view it as a sign you're committed to your future. Then when an opportunity presents itself, they'll know you're ready for it."

"I hear you, Mom" was all Destiny could say. Well, she could say more, but it would do no good.

Her mother sighed. "It's still not too late to get your teaching degree."

Destiny began shaking her head, effectively cutting her mother off. "We agreed a long time ago that teaching was not the road for me."

"You should reconsider now that the twins are in school. Teaching is the perfect lifestyle for a single parent. You're at work when your kids are at school and you're off when they're off. The pay may start a little lower than in industry, but over time you can make a good living."

"I hear what you're saying, Mom, but teaching is not for me. I'm not you. I'm not like you. We've been through this."

Patricia leaned forward and picked up her cup of coffee. "No need to get upset. It was just a suggestion."

Destiny didn't buy it. Her mother rarely gave suggestions; she gave orders and she made points that she wanted others to adhere to.

Patricia gave another long sigh, clearly exasperated with Destiny. "If you don't want to go to school, what are you going to do? You don't talk much about it, but I know your finances are tight. What are you going to do about it? Don't you want to own your own home someday? Don't you want to be able to buy a new car for once rather than a used one? Don't you want to be able to afford vacations for you and the twins? And I don't even want to think about funding the kids' college educations."

Yes, Destiny wanted all those things and her mother knew she did. This was Patricia being her overbearing, unyielding self. Since arguing with her did no good, Destiny kept quiet. It was a tactic she'd learned as a child.

"If you don't go to school this summer," her mother continued, "what are you going to do while the kids are away? Sit around and mope? That wouldn't be too smart."

Destiny could feel herself shutting down. She knew her mother meant well but she poured it on too thick sometimes. "I'll do something productive," Destiny said, wanting to end the conversation. Now was not the time to tell her mom about her failed plans to get a second job so she could move herself and the kids to Gwinnett to be closer to their school.

"Like what?"

"I don't know yet, Mom," she said. Then she decided to test the waters. "Maybe I'll take on a second job," she added and held her breath while she waited for her mother's reaction.

Patricia began shaking her head. "A second low-paying job is only going to leave you exhausted. Think long term, Destiny. Finish that degree and start thinking about a career rather than a job."

"Okay, Mom," Destiny said, accepting that the test had failed. "I hear you. I'll think about it."

"What's there to think about, Destiny? I don't understand you. Wake up, girl, and smell the coffee. Who did the man of your dreams marry? An educated career woman, that's who. Do you think Mary Margaret and Kenneth worry about money the way you do? And look at the two of them living in that huge house while you and the kids are in that cramped apartment."

"We live in a spacious, townhouse-style apartment and it is not cramped," Destiny said, taking offense at her mother's choice of words. There were a lot of negative things to say about her home but size wasn't an issue. It had three bedrooms, two and a half baths, and a basement, which was all the interior space she and the kids needed. The outside space was another matter; she'd love for her kids to have a big backyard. The house she wanted in Gwinnett had a perfectly sized backyard. The twins would have loved it.

"That Mary Margaret may be fat but she's got a career and a man," Patricia went on. "What do you have?"

Destiny glared at her mother. "I have two beautiful children," she said defiantly.

Patricia sighed. "What kind of example do you want to be to those kids? Do you want them to get a job like the one you have or do you want something better for them? Don't you want them to get an education so they can live a full life and not worry about money all the time? Don't you want them to reach their potential?"

"You know I do," Destiny said, becoming more annoyed now that her mother was repeating herself. "I always want the best for my kids. They know how important education is and they know the sacrifices they have to make to get the best education possible. It's not lost on them that they get up earlier than all their friends and travel much farther to get to school. They're bright kids."

Patricia sighed again. "That may be true, but they also know that their mother works at a department store where they can get a ten percent discount. What they know is that they live in a small apartment and their mom drives them around in an old car. What they know is that the better schools are in their father's neighborhood, not yours."

Destiny didn't like what she was hearing. Her mother was hitting below the belt by talking about her ability to provide for her kids. The words hurt even more because Destiny felt there was some truth to them.

"Do you know what else they know?" Patricia asked. Not waiting for an answer, she said, "They know that their father and stepmother live in a huge house on the better side of town. They know their stepmother's job is sending her to glamorous Los Angeles for the summer. They can't help but think that Mary Margaret is somebody important. You don't want Kenae to come home one day and say she wants to be just like Mary Margaret, do you? And you don't want KJ to say that he wants to live with his dad who has that big game room with the seventy-two-inch television and enough gadgets and toys to impress any kid."

Destiny felt her mother's words as if they were blows to her midsection. Her greatest fear was that her kids would compare their life with her to their life with Kenneth and Mary Margaret and find their life with her lacking. That fear had her planning to take on a second job so she could enter into a rent-to-own agreement to purchase a house in Gwinnett County near Kenneth and Mary Margaret. That fear had almost made her nix their summer trip to California.

All the trip was going to do was magnify for her kids the difference in her lifestyle and that of their father's. That was not a comparison she welcomed.

"Well, do you?" her mother asked, not letting up.

"Of course I don't," Destiny said. "I don't even know why you're asking me something like that."

"I don't want you to let this opportunity pass you by, Destiny. For years, you've used those kids as an excuse for not going back to school. Well, you no longer have that excuse. This summer is the time for you to get your life on an upward trajectory. Do you want to spend the rest of your life working long hours at that department store every day and spending all your free time doing hair in your basement? Don't you want to take your kids on vacation? Don't you want to buy a house one day?"

Her mother continued to talk, asking the same questions over and over, so Destiny tuned her out. Her mother had made her point. Destiny knew she had to do something productive this summer. She wasn't yet ready to give up on her plans for a second job and moving to Gwinnett. She'd have to redouble her efforts to find work. And if she didn't find something soon, she'd see if Bertice could hook her up with her part-time gig. She wouldn't tell her mother her plans until she was ready to move.

Chapter 3

I KNOW YOU DON'T WANT TO HEAR THIS, BUT YOUR MOM IS right."

Destiny knew her ears were playing tricks on her. "What did you just say?" she asked Bertice.

Bertice got up, taking her paper plate with her. "You heard me. Your mom is right."

Destiny followed her friend to the kitchen of her four-bedroom ranch-style home in southwest Atlanta. "How do you figure that?" she asked, taking Bertice's lead and dumping her plate into the garbage can. She put her utensils in the sink. "You know what I'm trying to do this summer. How can you say my mom is right?"

"I'm thinking long term, Destiny, and so is your mother. What you're trying to do this summer is great. It just shows what a go-getter you are, but you have to face facts. Right now, you're only making ends meet because of Kenneth's child-support checks. When those stop, you're going to be in a world of hurt. You need to get a better hold on your financial future. And a second job is not the answer long term, not when you want more time with your kids, not less."

Destiny leaned back against the refrigerator. "I can't believe you're saying this to me. You're not exactly Suze Orman yourself. You're closer to Al Capone."

Bertice chuckled, not taking offense. "Look, I get my hustle on and I'm not ashamed to admit it. But I also take care of my business. I moved out of my apartment and bought this house last year and you're still living in an apartment. A very nice townhouse-style apartment, but it's still an apartment. And you couldn't pay for that without Kenneth's child support. And you're going to need Kenneth's child support to pay for this house you're taking on a second job to get. A second job can't be your answer all the time; at some point, it has to be a better job. And, in today's economy, that's probably going to require a degree."

Destiny blinked her burning eyes, praying she could keep the tears welling up in them at bay. "Wow. Tell me how you really feel."

Bertice put her hands on Destiny's shoulders. "I'm saying all this because I love you. You know that, right?"

Destiny turned her head away, not meeting her friend's gaze. "You certainly don't sound as though you do right now."

Bertice sighed, dropped her hands. "I know this is tough to hear, Destiny, but it needs to be said. Natalie is too goody-goody to go there, but she knows it's true as well. Why do you think she's so busy trying to get you hooked up with every eligible man she knows?"

Needing to get away from the intensity of the moment,

Destiny slid around her friend and made her way back to the sink. "You're out of dish detergent."

"Look in the cabinet under the sink."

Doing as she was told, Destiny found the detergent and began washing the few utensils that were in the sink.

"You're not going to get out of this conversation that easily," Bertice said.

Destiny looked over at her friend, sure her pain showed in her eyes. "I don't see what you can possibly add to what you've already said."

Bertice propped her hands on her hips. "Don't you want to know why Natalie's always trying to fix you up?"

To be honest, Destiny didn't want to know. "I don't have to ask," she said. "Natalie's still in newlywed mode. She's in love and she wants everybody else to be in love. She wants me to find my Gavin the way she found hers. She wants that for you, too."

Bertice reached over and turned off the faucet. "That's just part of it. The real driving force is that Natalie doesn't think you can take care of yourself. She thinks you need a man to take care of you. No, that's not right. She thinks you don't want to take care of yourself, not really, and that you'd rather depend on a man to do it for you."

Destiny took her friend's words as body blows. "Natalie doesn't think that. Why would she?"

As if seeing how much her words had shaken Destiny, Bertice took her by the hand and led her away from the sink and toward the living room. "We can finish up in the kitchen later. We need to talk this through."

"I don't think there's anything to talk through. You've shared some pretty eye-opening truths about the way you and Natalie see me."

"I'm not trying to hurt you, Destiny," Bertice said after they were seated on the couch. "I love you like a sister but you've got to do something to change the status quo. It's as though you've put your life on hold since you had the twins. I know you had this picture of how life would be with you, Kenneth, and the kids as the perfect little family. And I know how hard it was for you when Kenneth decided he didn't want to get married. Heck, it was hard for me. And in some ways, it still is. But then Kenneth stepped up and has been a good parent, financially and emotionally."

"That's what he's supposed to do. He is their father."

"I know that, but he's no longer your boyfriend, lover, or whatever he was to you. And though it pains me to say it, he's another woman's husband. While he's providing financial support to your household now, that's going to stop as soon as your kids come of age. Then where are you going to be?"

Destiny didn't want to think about the answer to that question. She knew her financial situation wasn't strong, but she was doing the best she could, wasn't she? "Look, I have a lot of years to figure that out."

"Not that many. Suppose something happened to Kenneth?"

Destiny gave a dry laugh. "He has a life insurance policy for the kids. We'd be in good shape if something happened to him, better shape than we're in now."

Bertice shook her head. "Do you hear yourself? If something happened to Kenneth that money should be reserved for the kids and their future needs. It's not for you to make ends meet every day."

Destiny shot hard eyes at her friend. "Are you saying I'm not a good mother?"

Bertice sighed. "That's not what I'm saying at all. You're deliberately misunderstanding me. You're a great mother, Destiny."

Destiny snorted. "Well, thanks for the compliment."

Bertice slumped back into the couch. "Just forget I said anything. Let's talk about something else."

That was fine by Destiny. She welcomed a change in topic. Unfortunately, what seemed like several minutes passed and there was nothing but silence between her and Bertice, who sat with her head down, twiddling her thumbs. Destiny couldn't come up with anything to talk about because she was still stuck on the notion that her friends saw her as some weak woman unable and unwilling to take care of herself. She cleared her throat. "Is that really what Natalie thinks of me?" she was forced to ask.

Bertice looked up. "It's not that simple, Destiny. She just wants better for you, and she believes you can do better. She doesn't want you to struggle the way you do."

"I'm not struggling that badly. We make do."

"Yeah, but we all want more for you than making do. And that we includes me, Natalie, and your mom."

Destiny chuckled.

"What's so funny?" Bertice asked.

Destiny wiped her hands down her face. "I was just thinking that we got into all of this because I was telling you my mom was trying to convince me to go back to school. I thought she'd been harsh last night, but she was comforting compared to you."

Bertice turned sad eyes to her. "I didn't mean to hurt you."

Destiny met her friend's eyes and knew that wasn't her intent even if it had been the result. "I know you didn't," Destiny said. "Maybe I needed to hear what you had to say. Maybe I do need to take a closer look at myself and my future."

"That's all I'm saying. Go to school the way your mom suggests or take me up on my business opportunity or do both or neither. It's up to you. You just have to get started in some direction. You can't depend on child support forever."

Chapter 4

DESTINY HUNG UP THE PHONE AFTER PLACING THE order for pizza delivery. When she turned to Natalie, her friend said, "You're a gem for doing my hair tonight, Destiny. I know it would have been easier to do it the night you did Bertice's."

"No problem, girl," she said as she took her seat on the stool in her makeshift salon. "You knew I'd do it for you."

"I know, but this is a busy day for you with the kids leaving tomorrow. How are you holding up?"

"I'm getting anxious. I keep reminding myself of what a great experience this is going to be for them. Not only are they going to see the California sights, Kenneth and Mary Margaret are planning to take them to the Grand Canyon and Hoover Dam, to Pearl Harbor, and they're even going to make a trip down to Tijuana. They plan to take in the entire region while they're on the West Coast. They may even get to Washington state and Canada. Their passports arrived yesterday so they're ready for it all. The kids may not fully appreciate it now, but I know they'll look back on this summer as a very special one. My only regret is that I won't be able to share it with them."

Natalie squeezed her hand. "But you'll have a great surprise for them when they get back—a new house."

"I haven't found that second job yet," Destiny said, "but I'm not giving up. Bertice has offered to hook me up with the temporary service that she used to find her part-time gig. I'm going to take her up on it." Needing her friend to see her as someone who wants to stand on her own two feet, rather than depending on some man, she added, "The second job should help me with my immediate need to get in the house in Gwinnett, but I'm also considering school and finally finishing up my degree as a long-term solution to getting myself in a better financial position."

"That's a wise idea," Natalie said. "I think you're making a good choice."

"You're not the only one."

Natalie smiled. "Your mom?"

"How'd you guess?" Destiny deadpanned. "She's been lecturing me about it ever since I dropped out, and she thinks with the kids away, this is a great time."

Natalie started laughing.

"What's so funny?"

"You. You've turned into your mom; you realize that, don't you?"

"Not hardly." Destiny was surprised by how much Natalie's characterization hurt her. She did not want to ever become her mother. She would never become her mother.

"You saw how beneficial this trip could be for your kids and you encouraged them to be excited about it. Left to their own devices, they would have stayed home where everything is familiar rather than taking on this life-changing experience. That's a parent's lot. To think about what's best for the kids and then to point the kids in that direction, even as the kids kick and scream to go in another direction. Your mom's doing it with you and you're doing it with your kids. That means you've turned into your mom."

Destiny tugged on one of Natalie's fresh braids. "Stop saying that. I get your meaning but your words leave a bit to be desired. They're making me queasy."

Natalie laughed. "Well, you were right about your kids and your mom is right about you. This summer is the perfect time for you to take some time and focus on Destiny. And it can't be all about work. You should be getting back out on the dating scene."

"Oh no, not again."

"Come on, Destiny. Daniel is a great guy. I know you two will hit it off."

"I don't know if I'm ready to start dating."

"Then don't think of it as a date," Natalie offered. "Think of it as making a new friend. If there are no sparks between you, so be it. You can never have too many friends."

Destiny saw the logic in her friend's words but she knew Natalie was counting on a romance blossoming between her and Daniel despite her words to the contrary. "You're not going to give up on this, are you?"

Natalie shook her head. "All I want you to do is meet him. Is that too much to ask?"

"I guess not," Destiny said, pushing away thoughts of the negative perceptions Bertice had planted in her mind. She would accept Natalie's gesture as a loving act from one friend to another, not as an act of pity. "So tell me some more about this guy."

Natalie started shaking her head. "He's a great guy. That's all I'm going to say. You'll have to find out about him by talking to him. That's what dating is for."

"You have to tell me more than that. What does he know about me? Does he know I have kids?"

Natalie nodded. "Yes, he knows you have kids and he knows you're a great person. I relented and told him that much."

Destiny rolled her eyes. "Please tell me you didn't tell the man I had a great personality."

"Of course I did," Natalie said.

"Then he probably thinks I look like a man."

Natalie laughed. "Don't worry. Gavin cleared that up for him. He told him you were a younger version of Gabrielle Union."

Destiny slapped Natalie on the shoulder. "No he didn't."

"Yes he did."

"You're both crazy."

Ignoring her words, Natalie said, "So what if you come over for our cookout tomorrow after you drop the kids off at the airport? Daniel will be there, along with a lot of other people, so there won't be much pressure for the two of you to entertain each other."

"Okay," Destiny said.

Natalie's eyebrows drew together. "That was too easy and too quick," she said. "You're not humoring me, are you?"

Destiny laughed. "You're unbelievable. I said I'd be there, so I'll be there." Probably I'll be there, she added to herself.

Natalie glanced down at her watch. Then she jumped up from her chair. "Time has gotten away from me. Let me get out of here so you can do what you need to do for tomorrow."

Destiny inclined her head toward the stairs. "The twins should be finished packing their backpacks by now. I should go upstairs and check that they've gotten everything. I figured I'd wait until the pizza came. They can eat while I'm double-checking everything. Thank goodness I packed their suitcases and dropped them off at Kenneth's when I picked them up the other day."

"Smart woman," Natalie said, slipping her arms into her light jacket.

The doorbell rang as they walked up from the basement. "Perfect timing," Destiny said. She grabbed her wallet off the table at the top of the stairs and continued toward the door. When she opened the door, Natalie gave her a quick hug and scooted out past the pizza delivery guy.

After pulling some bills from her wallet and handing them to the delivery guy, Destiny took the pizzas and called out to her kids, "Pizza's here." Then she headed to the kitchen. Soon after, she heard the footfalls of her kids as they trotted down the stairs.

"Are you guys hungry?" she asked when they reached the kitchen.

"I am," KJ said, reaching for a slice of pizza. He wore a Dodgers cap and shirt with Matt Kemp's number. Her son was already in California mode.

"What's to drink?" Kenae said, after she pulled her earphones out of her ears.

"There's soda in the fridge," she said to her daughter, who seemed to have earphones in her ears 24/7 since watching the Kids' Choice Awards and deciding she wanted to be the next Selena Gomez, Rihanna, or Katy Perry. Well, Kenae and her headphones would be Kenneth's problem this summer. She grinned at the thought. "Why don't you get some for us?"

Kenae took three cans of orange soda from the fridge and handed a can to her mother and another to her brother.

"Thanks," Destiny said.

KJ could only nod since he'd just stuffed half a slice of pizza in his mouth.

Kenae took a slice of pizza. "This is good," she said after the first bite.

Destiny smiled. "I wanted you to have your favorite the night before you left. I can't believe you guys will be gone the entire summer. I want you to have a great time."

KJ shrugged. "I'll be talking to my friends on Facebook and we're going to do video Skype and FaceTime. They think going to California is pretty neat. I promised to send pictures. I really want one with Matt Kemp and Magic Johnson. Dad said Mary Margaret might be doing some work with Magic, so she can hook it up for me."

"Me too," Kenae said. "Mary Margaret said we could go to the studio where Rihanna makes her records. I might even get her autograph."

"I want to go to Disneyland," KJ said. "And Mary Margaret said I could film the trip to the Grand Canyon so I can show it at school next year. I already talked to my teachers about it. That will be cool."

Destiny forced her smile to remain in place as she listened to her kids though she wanted to grind her teeth at every mention of Mary Margaret's name. She knew her kids were going to grow closer to the woman during this trip; she just didn't want them to get too close and forget who their mother was. And she didn't want Mary Margaret to even think about trying to take her place in their lives. She'd make that clear to the woman when she saw her at the airport in the morning.

Chapter 5

DESTINY TOOK A QUICK GLANCE IN THE MIRRORED walls of the airport as she and the kids made their way through the double doors on the lower level. She'd taken special care with her appearance this morning, as she always did when she was going to cross paths with Mary Margaret. The woman may have the better job and she may have the man, but Destiny had the upper hand in the looks department. She had deliberately worn a form-fitting dress and heels, something she knew the chubby Mary Margaret could never pull off. Though she knew she was being petty, Destiny still felt good knowing she was getting the best of the woman in some small way.

"You both have your phones, don't you?" she asked her kids.

"I got mine," KJ said. Then he leaned his shoulder into his sister's, causing her to glare at him.

"What do you want?" Kenae asked, pulling her earphones out of her ears.

"Don't speak to your brother that way," Destiny said. "I asked you a question. Do you have your phone?"

"Duh, Mom," Kenae said, holding up the earphones. "How do you think I'm listening to music?" With those words, Kenae put her earphones back in.

"Kids," Destiny muttered to herself as she followed her kids onto the escalator and up to the ticketing area. This summer break might be just the thing she needed. It might also be good for Kenneth and Mary Margaret to experience what it means to be a full-time parent over an extended period of time. This summer could put an end to their desire to have the kids live with them full-time during the school year.

"There's Dad," KJ said, breaking into a trot and heading in his father's direction.

Destiny resented the flutter she felt in her belly when Kenneth turned in their direction and smiled. It was as though the years between them fell away and she remembered only the boy she'd loved more than she loved herself. She'd accepted long ago that Kenneth would always have a part of her heart. He was her first and only love, the father of her children, and the second man to break her heart.

"Hey, champ," she heard Kenneth say to KJ. "You ready for your big adventure?"

KJ bobbed his head. "More than ready," he said. "I can't wait to meet Matt Kemp. We're still going to the Dodgers game on Friday, aren't we?"

Destiny smiled at her son's excitement. Though basketball was his favorite sport and the one he played and his father coached, he was a big baseball fan and Matt Kemp was one of his favorite players. She knew that seeing Kemp play in the famed Dodger Stadium would be one of the highlights of KJ's summer.

"I already have tickets," Kenneth said. He turned to Kenae. "Got one for you, too, pretty lady," he said to her.

"I don't like baseball."

Kenneth pressed a kiss against her forehead. "Well, that's going to change after you attend your first game in a stadium. You're going to love the game as much as your brother and I do." He tugged on her earphones and pulled them out of her ears. "And you won't need these when we're there."

"I'm listening to Rihanna," Kenae said, putting her earphones back in.

"Nice to know you're excited about the trip, Kenae," Kenneth said, pulling her earphones out again.

"Dad," Kenae wailed. "Stop doing that."

"Doing what?" Kenneth teased.

Destiny watched, taking joy in the easy way Kenneth interacted with his children. Whatever issues lay between them, she had to admit he was a good father to KJ and Kenae. Before Kenae could answer her dad's question, Destiny interrupted, "Where's Mary Margaret?"

Kenneth inclined his head to the left. "She went to the bathroom." He stepped closer to Destiny. "Go easy on her, Destiny," he said softly. "She's anxious about this trip."

"What's she anxious about?" Destiny asked, though she knew. A part of her was happy the woman wasn't too confident about the summer.

"She wants to do right by the kids and make this a great trip for them. It's important to her, to both of us."

"What do you think I'm going to do to the woman?" Destiny asked, feigning ignorance. Unfortunately, there was too much bad history between her and Mary Margaret for her to fake out Kenneth.

He looked her up and down, from toe to head. Then he tilted his brow. "You know how to push her buttons; we both know that. I'm just asking that you not do it today."

"I don't know—"

"Here she comes now," he said, interrupting her. "Be nice, Destiny."

Destiny watched as Kenneth extended one of his hands and pulled Mary Margaret close to him. "I thought you had gotten lost in there," he said to his wife.

Mary Margaret slapped him playfully on the shoulder. "Silly man." Then she turned to Destiny. "It's good to see you, Destiny."

Destiny didn't believe her. "Good to see you, too," she said with a forced smile. She and Mary Margaret tolerated each other to the point that they could be cordial, but Destiny doubted it would get any further than that. It was hard to build a relationship after sharing a man. It was even more difficult when one woman had the babies and the other one had the man. Mary Margaret got the man Destiny wanted but Destiny had his kids and a hold on him that would last their lifetimes. So the women had to deal civilly with each other, if they wanted any peace. She was glad they both did.

Turning her attention to the kids, Mary Margaret asked, "KJ, Kenae, are you ready to see Los Angeles?"

"I am," KJ said. "We're going to the Dodgers game on Friday. When are we going to the Grand Canyon?" He turned to his dad. "Are you still going to get me a video camera so I can film the trip for school?"

Kenneth tugged on his son's baseball cap. "Sure, sport. We can pick one out after we get settled."

"What about you, Kenae?" Mary Margaret asked.

Kenneth tugged on his daughter's earphones. "Mary Margaret's talking to you."

"Hi, Mary Margaret," Kenae said, finally looking up at the older woman.

"Are you ready to see Los Angeles?"

Kenae nodded. Then she turned to her mother. "Why don't you come with us?"

Destiny's heart warmed. She leaned down and pressed her forehead to her daughter's. "We've talked about this, sweetheart. This trip is for you, KJ, your dad, and Mary Margaret. You're going to have a big adventure. I've seen the itinerary Mary Margaret put together. It's going to be a great trip."

"What are you going to do all by yourself?" Kenae asked.

Destiny smiled. "I'll work on a big surprise for you and KJ when you get back."

Kenae's eyes widened. "A surprise?"

"What kind of surprise?" KJ asked.

Destiny stood straight and rubbed her hands across KJ's head. She chuckled. "It wouldn't be a surprise if I told you what it was, would it?" She tapped Kenae on her nose. "You two better send me pictures every day so I can see what you're up to. You can use that phone for something other than music. Okay?"

"Okay, Mom," Kenae said.

"I'll send a video," KJ added.

"That'll be great, KJ."

Mary Margaret looked up at Kenneth. "We'd better head for the gate. We still have to go through security and that line is pretty long."

"Okay, babe," he said. "You guys got all your stuff?" he asked the kids. "Do you need help with anything?"

The kids shook their heads.

"Okay, then," Destiny said. "Come and give your mom a hug big enough to last the entire summer."

"Mom," KJ whined, but he did as she asked.

"You be good," she whispered in his ear. "I love you and I'm going to miss you. I'll be looking for your video updates. They'll be the highlights of my summer."

"Okay, Mom," he said.

"Bye, Mom," Kenae said, giving her mother a big hug. "I'm going to miss you."

"I'll miss you, too, baby," she said. "But you're going to have a great time. Just make sure to take time out of your busy schedule to call your old mom."

"I will," the young girl said.

"Okay, gang, let's head off." Kenneth pointed to the security line. "That line is calling our names."

While Kenneth was busy with the kids, Mary Margaret stepped closer to Destiny. "We'll take good care of them,

Destiny," she said. "They're going to miss you, of course, but we'll try to make the trip a fun and educational time for them."

Destiny took a deep breath. Though he was engaged with the kids, she could sense that Kenneth was waiting to hear how she would respond. "I know you will, Mary Margaret," she said, and felt Kenneth relax. "And if they give you any trouble, I'm just a phone call away."

"I'm sure it won't come to that," Mary Margaret said. "I'm looking forward to having the time with them. I enjoy having them around. They're good kids."

Given that Mary Margaret and Kenneth wanted the kids to spend more time with them by living with them full-time during the school year, Destiny wasn't sure how to take that comment. "Well, you can enjoy them for the summer," she said, using what she hoped was a light tone to restate her own case. "Just be sure to bring them back to me."

Chapter 6

DESTINY HAD STAYED AT THE AIRPORT UNTIL THE flight to Los Angeles departed. Though she didn't accompany her kids to the concourse, she took comfort in sitting in the airport until she knew they were safely off the ground and en route to their destination. While she waited, she'd changed out of her dress and heels into a pair of form-fitting jeans more suited for a cookout and sandals that showed off her recently painted toenails. She was dressed more casually, but she knew she still looked good.

By the time she pulled into Natalie's driveway, three things had become very obvious to her. First, she had to keep herself busy or she'd go crazy worrying about her kids; second, there was no way she was going to go the entire summer without seeing them; third, now that she'd told them about the surprise, she had to make the move to Gwinnett happen or come up with something equally exciting.

As she checked her face in the rearview mirror, Destiny acknowledged that making Mary Margaret uncomfortable wasn't the only reason she'd taken special care with her appearance today. She also wanted to make a good impression on this Daniel character that Natalie was so high on her meeting. She hadn't really dated since before the kids were born, so this was all new to her, new and a bit uncomfortable. The guy had better be worth the anxiety she was feeling. If it turned out he wasn't, she'd make Natalie promise to give up on her matchmaking efforts. She didn't think she could go through this again and again. Her emotions couldn't take it.

Satisfied with how she looked, Destiny climbed out of the car and followed the sounds of laughter, chatter, and music to the back of the house.

"Destiny," Natalie called out, as soon as she rounded the corner. "I'm glad you came." She leaned in and gave her friend a brief hug. "Did your kids get off all right?"

Destiny nodded. "I came here straight from the airport."

Natalie rubbed her hand down Destiny's arm. "How are you holding up?"

"Let's just say I'm glad I had somewhere to go after leaving the airport. Returning to that empty and much-too-quiet townhouse would be a bit much right now."

Putting an arm around her shoulder, Natalie said, "Come on then. There are some folks I want you to meet."

Destiny chuckled. "Some folks, huh?"

Natalie rocked her hip against Destiny's side. "Okay, one person first, but I promise there'll be other folks later." Natalie stopped when she reached her apron-wearing husband and an attractive bronze-skinned man in jeans and a pale blue polo shirt. "Food ready?" Natalie asked to get her husband's attention.

When Gavin looked up and saw them, he said, "Speak of the devil."

"You two are the only devils I see here," Natalie said, grinning. "What have you been saying about me?"

Gavin inclined his head toward Destiny. "Not you. We were talking about Destiny."

"All good, I hope," Destiny said, meeting Daniel's gaze. He was a tall guy, about six feet two, with a killer smile. So far so good. If he passed the conversation test, she'd have to tell Natalie she'd done a good job.

Gavin leaned over and kissed Destiny's check. "What else could it be?" he asked. "I was just telling Daniel here that he needed to be on his A game if he wanted any chance at winning your heart."

"My heart?" Destiny repeated, glancing again at Daniel. "I'm thinking of keeping my heart to myself."

Gavin turned to the man next to him. "She's everything I said she was, isn't she?"

Daniel extended his hand to Destiny. "I'm Daniel Thomas," he said. "You'll have to forgive my buddy here."

"I feel your pain," she said, taking his hand. "My girl here is just as bad."

"Well," Natalie said, with fake upset, "I guess that's our cue to leave, Gavin. These two seem like they were made for each other."

"I'm right behind you, babe." He winked at Destiny as he passed her. "I can tell where I'm not needed or wanted."

Destiny chuckled. "They mean well."

Daniel laughed. "I know, but haven't they heard of subtlety?"

Destiny laughed with him. "Apparently not."

"Despite all their plotting and scheming," Daniel said, "I'm glad to finally meet the mysterious Destiny."

"Mysterious?"

"It was like pulling teeth to get any information about you. They only told me that you were wonderful, and the rest I'd have to find out on my own."

Destiny chuckled. "Well, that makes you the mysterious Daniel because Natalie has told me very little about you."

He flashed that killer smile at her. "That's easily corrected. I'm in need of a meal companion. If you're hungry, we can get some food and then sit and get to know each other."

"Sounds good to me," Destiny said.

After they filled their plates, Destiny followed Daniel to one of the empty tables for two. "I wonder if Gavin and Natalie set this table up just for us."

Destiny chuckled. "I wouldn't put it past them."

He put their plates down and pulled out a chair for Destiny. After she was seated, he went to get drinks for them. When he returned, he sat in the chair next to hers. "It really is nice to finally meet you," he said again. "Gavin and Natalie had me intrigued."

Destiny picked up her fork and dipped it in the potato salad on her plate. "I don't know if I can live up to the hype."

Daniel smiled. "You already have."

Destiny met his eyes briefly before looking down at the

food on her plate. If this was flirting, she liked it. It had been so long since she'd engaged in such banter that she wasn't sure. She glanced back up at Daniel, thinking again that flirting was not bad at all.

He gave her another smile. "So, mystery Destiny, what's the first thing you want me to know about you?"

She met his eyes. Since she knew he already knew about her kids, she said, "I'm the mother of six-year-old twins, KJ and Kenae."

"They were tighter with information than I'd guessed. I knew you had two kids but I didn't know they were twins. Do twins run in your family?"

She shook her head. She hadn't wanted the conversation to turn to past relationships this early. Even though she had very little recent dating experience, she knew that talking about old flames was a big dating no-no. "That comes from Kenneth, their father. There are three sets of twins on his mother's side of the family."

"Well," Daniel said, "this is not where I wanted the conversation to go."

"That's all right," Destiny said, heartened by his sensitivity. "As their father, Kenneth's a part of their lives, which makes him a part of mine."

"So you two have a good relationship?"

She considered before answering. "We make it work because we both love the kids," she said in all honesty.

"Good for you. With names like KJ and Kenae, I assume they're named after him."

She nodded. Her kids' names were a harsh reminder of

how much she had loved Kenneth and wanted to have a life with him. "What can I say? KJ is Kenneth Junior and Kenae is a feminine version of Kenneth. It seemed like a good idea at the time."

"It's nothing to be embarrassed about," he said. "I think I'd be honored to have kids named after me—DJ and Danielle. It has a nice ring to it."

"Those are great names," she said, appreciating his attempt to put her at ease. He was beginning to convince her that he was one of the good ones. "Do you have kids?"

He shook his head. "My wife and I wanted kids but we weren't blessed. She died a couple of years ago, breast cancer."

"I'm sorry," she said, recalling what Natalie had said about Daniel suffering from heartbreak the way she was. "Breast cancer has touched my family, too. My mother is a survivor."

"I'm sorry to hear it but glad your mother is well," he said. "It's a scary disease that affects people in such different ways. I think it was scarier for me than it was for Gloria, my wife."

"I know what you mean," Destiny said. She remembered how she had clung to Kenneth during that time. Even with the demands of being a scholarship college basketball student, he'd been there for her when she'd needed him. She'd already started falling in love with him but his support when her mom was sick had sealed the deal. When she looked back on it, she realized she had gotten pregnant during the time her mother had been going through her surgery, chemotherapy, and radiation treatments. A part of her still wondered if she'd done so on purpose.

"A penny for your thoughts," he said, bringing her attention back to him.

"I'm sorry," she said. "I was just thinking about all the folks who supported me when my mom was sick and going through various treatments. Natalie was one of them," she said, not seeing a need to mention Kenneth again. "We go way back. We grew up together. She's been a very good friend to me for a very long time."

He nodded. "It's the same with me and Gavin. We didn't grow up together; we met in college and became fast friends our freshman year. He and two other college friends were there for me. I don't know if I could have made it without those guys. God never fails to put the right people in our lives."

"Amen to that," she said, understanding that she knew he was including her among the *right people* and agreeing with him. "So you're a minister and Daniel's a minister. Are the other two friends you mentioned ministers as well?"

He chuckled. "No way," he said. "They're good guys but they serve in other ways. Only Gavin and I chose this path. And Gavin chose it before I did."

"If you don't mind me asking, how did you come to this place? Did God speak to you, like in a dream, or did you just make a decision based on your interests? I've always wondered, but I've been too much of a chicken to ask Gavin."

"There's nothing wrong with asking," he said. Then he seemed to consider her question before answering. "It was a little of both. I believe that this is the path God planned for me, but I didn't hear His voice speaking to me the way you and I are speaking. It was more a strong feeling in my spirit that was confirmed by people I trusted, people like Gavin and, even more strongly, Gloria."

"Your wife?"

He nodded. "I didn't come to this path easily or directly. I started out in a small business with my two other buddies. It was only after Gloria became ill that I accepted this path."

"Do you think—" she began, but stopped herself when she realized she was about to get too personal. She'd just met the man, for goodness' sake.

"It's all right," he coaxed. "You can ask. If I don't want to answer, I'll tell you."

She met his eyes, and seeing the sincerity there, she asked, "Do you think you would have chosen this path if your wife hadn't gotten sick?"

He nodded. "That's a question I've asked myself."

"And?"

"I think so. If not this, something else would have led me here. Gloria often teased me about it. When she became ill, we both realized that time was not something we could count on. We had to live today, plan for tomorrow, but live today. More than anything, that's what she taught me, both by the way she lived through the disease and how she died with it. She was incredible."

Destiny smiled at the way his love for his wife poured through his words and shone on his face. "You shared a special love, didn't you?"

He nodded. "We did. And losing her was very hard. She

spent the last year preparing me for life without her. She was that kind of woman."

"I wish I had known her. She sounds like someone I would have liked."

He smiled. "I think she would have liked you, too. She didn't really get to know Natalie that well, but she considered her a friend."

After a few moments of easy silence, he chuckled. "You can tell that I'm not good at this dating thing, can't you? I don't think I'm supposed to spend that much time talking about my wife."

She began shaking her head. "You're easy to talk to," she said. "I asked questions and you answered them. Honestly. I appreciate that. I feel that I'm getting to know you."

"Well, we've spent enough time on me. I know you're a mother, and I suspect you're a very good one. Do you have another calling beyond that?"

Destiny pressed her forefinger against her chest. "A calling? Me? Not hardly."

"Sure you do," he said. "We all do. Not everybody is called to be a minister in the pulpit, but we're all called to serve in some way. You're called to be a mother and that could be your primary calling, but there could also be something else. Do you work?"

She nodded. "I'm the manager of the cosmetics department at a local department store. I don't think that could be considered a calling."

"I don't know," he said. "It could be. It depends on how

you approach it. It's not what you do that makes it a calling; it's why you do it and how you do it."

She smiled. "You know, you're good at your calling."

"Getting too deep?"

"Just a little," she said.

"Do you like sports?" he asked.

She smiled more broadly. "Of course. I have a six-year-old son who adores his father. Did I tell you that Kenneth was a star college athlete who's now a middle school coach?"

Daniel laughed. "We can't get away from our past relationships, can we?"

"It sure does seem that way."

"We'll have to try this again," he said. "I've heard that practice makes perfect."

"Sounds like a plan to me," she said.

"The breast cancer walk is in two weeks. I'm planning to go with Gavin and Natalie. Will you and your mother be there?"

Destiny nodded. "We walk with the church every year. I'll be walking for me and my mom because she'll be out of town that week."

"Good. Let's plan to see each other there. You can show me the ropes."

"I'd like that," she said.

"So it's a date?" he asked.

She looked up at him. "It sure is."

Chapter 7

DANIEL THOUGHT ABOUT DESTINY WHILE HE WAITED for Phil Harris to return to his office. He smiled at the realization that he was so bad at the dating game that he had not even remembered to get her phone number. He was sure he could get it from Natalie or Gavin but he preferred not to go that route. He had hoped to see her at church on Sunday so he could ask her for the number, but either she hadn't attended or he'd missed her. He'd just have to wait to see her at church next Sunday or the following Saturday at the cancer walk. That was probably for the best. He was intrigued by her, attracted to her actually, but both of them were taking baby steps into the dating scene so there was no need to rush anything.

"Sorry about that," Phil Harris said when he returned to his office. "My meeting ran longer than I expected."

"No problem," Daniel said to the man who was now his client. "You have to keep to your regular routine. Nothing should change because I'm here and nobody can know the real reason I'm here. All anybody needs to know is that I'm new in town and we're associates from way back. Nobody in my circle knows either."

"I understand," Phil said. "William and George laid out the ground rules for me. Since I don't want to go to jail, I'm going to abide by them."

"Good," Daniel said. "As you know, we have a lot of experience with these kinds of investigations." He shook his head, marveling that Phil was again on the wrong side of the law. "How in the heck did you get yourself involved in something like this, Phil? You know better."

"I know, man," Phil said with a shrug.

"So what happened? After our last encounter, I thought you were going to stay on the straight and narrow."

"That was the plan," he said, "and then I met Margo."

Daniel shook his head. "You're not going to blame this on some woman, are you?"

"You asked," Phil said.

"So tell me," Daniel said.

Phil closed his eyes as he leaned back in his chair. He sighed deeply. "She took my breath away."

She took more than his breath, Daniel thought, she also took his brains. What else could explain the situation in which Phil found himself? Again. GDW Investigations, the cybersecurity company that Daniel founded with his college friends, George Campbell and William Harrison, had outed Phil in an insurance fraud scam about five years ago. Luckily, the man had gotten off without being prosecuted. Unfortunately, his pledge to stay out of trouble had not lasted. "So what was the setup this time?" Daniel asked.

"I met her at a New Year's Eve party given by one of my frat brothers. I thought I was lucky. Turns out she'd targeted me."

"It figures," Daniel said. A temporary services agency like Phil's HR Solutions was a prime conduit for money laundering.

"Well, we started seeing each other and, as you can imagine, she had very expensive tastes. More expensive than I was able to provide on my salary, which was hefty, but not hefty enough. She was a good sport about it though, which drew me to her even more. She wined and dined me, man! Do you know how it feels to have a beautiful woman pursue you? Most women like her would walk away from a brother with light pockets, but not Margo. She had me, man. I was thinking she could be the one."

"In a way she was."

Phil grunted and then folded his arms across his chest. "In the worst way. To make a long story short, she told me how she made her money and suggested I could get in on it. All I had to do was accept some wire transfers, take my cut, and transfer the rest to another account. It was easy."

Daniel clapped his hands together. "And just like that, you went for it? You put your job at risk. Heck, you put your freedom at risk."

Phil shrugged. "I was a fool for love."

Daniel thought Phil had been a fool all right but he wasn't sure what role love played in it. More like greed. Phil had a history of taking shortcuts, a history that had almost landed him in jail the last time their paths crossed. The man enjoyed playing with fire. "Do you still see this Margo?"

Phil shook his head. "We were strong while I was being integrated into the program, as she called it. She guided me every step of the way. The last step was expanding the network and bringing in others to do what I was doing. That's when we started funneling the money through HR Solutions. After I got the hang of it, she moved on to her next target."

"So you never see her?"

"I don't see anybody. All transactions are wire transactions. I get a new burner cell every month and every month I get an update phone call that sounds like an automated message."

"When did the threats start?"

Phil sighed. "After I figured out Margo had been using me, I decided to get out. Turns out it wasn't that simple. They threatened to report me to the police if I didn't keep up my end of the program. I don't have an electronic trail of crime on them but they have evidence of multiple counts of fraud on me. And these are federal crimes with mandatory sentences. They had me."

"So why did you make contact with GDW Investigations?"

Phil laughed. "Another woman. Can you believe it?"

"I believe it, all right."

"Bertice is different, special. She's not high maintenance like Margo. She's a hardworking sister trying to make the most of the cards she's been dealt. I've gotten her caught up in all this and I need to get her out."

"Does she know you're working to get out?"

Phil shook his head. "She's totally in the dark. She has no idea she's involved in fraud and George and William both think it best we keep it that way. She's a good woman, Daniel. She just made a bad choice."

"Because she trusted you?"

Phil nodded. "She needed some extra money and I hooked her up. I was still with Margo at the time, but I've gotten to know her since that ended. I don't want to see her hurt."

"She's going to be hurt, Phil, you need to resign yourself to that truth."

Phil met his eyes. "She could really be the one."

Daniel didn't know what to say. He could tell Phil had genuine feelings for this Bertice but he didn't see how there was any chance for them. When the woman found out the depth of Phil's deception, she was not going to be happy. "Who knows what can happen," Daniel said, seeking to give the man the hope he so desperately wanted. "Maybe you two can pick up the pieces and put all this behind you."

"I don't like lying to her," Phil said. "She's involving herself more and more each day. She's brought a couple of people to me, friends she wanted to help. She's bringing another one tomorrow. She's getting in deeper without knowing it and she's doing the same to her friends. I want to turn her friends down but that would be a case of me doing something differently."

Daniel nodded. "You hold some responsibility, Phil, but

this Bertice had to know what she was doing was illegal and so did her friends. If they didn't, they were willfully ignorant. You may have dangled the carrot but they willingly reached for it."

"I know," Phil said, "but that doesn't make it any easier. I want to tell her the truth."

"George and William are right. You can't. Not now. It's too dangerous. After we gather all the evidence, we need to make some key high-level arrests, and then you can sit her down and tell her everything."

"It'll be too late."

Daniel thought he was probably right, but he didn't rub it in. "There's always hope. This will surely test your relationship, but it could survive."

"That's the thing," Phil said. "We don't really have a romantic relationship. Not yet. I haven't gotten up the nerve to tell her how I feel. She sees me only as a helpful buddy. When she finds out the truth, even that will be gone."

Daniel had no response for the man. Phil was looking at multiple federal fraud counts and all he could think about was a woman he hadn't even taken on one date.

"Like I said, she's bringing another friend by tomorrow," Phil continued. "So we'll bring another person into this deceit."

"It'll all be over soon," Daniel said. "We'll do everything we can to make sure the net catches the big fish while keeping damage to the little fish to a minimum."

"I'm counting on it," Phil said.

Chapter 8

DESTINY TRIED TO FOCUS ON WHAT HER SON WAS TELL-
ing her, but her mind was on Kenneth. He had never
been late with his child-support payments until this month.
She hoped it was an oversight on his part because he'd been
distracted with planning the California trip. They didn't
have a child-support order from the courts, only an informal
agreement between the two of them that she found more
than generous. In fact, she thought Kenneth's contribution
was more than what the court would have ruled. After he'd
married Mary Margaret, to her amazement, he'd increased
what he sent to her. Though she could definitely use more,
she didn't have any problem with the amount he gave.

"Good night, sweetie," she said when KJ finally wound
down from telling her about his day. Any other night she
would have kept him on the phone just to hear his voice, but
tonight she needed to talk to Kenneth. "Put your sister on
the phone so I can tell her good night."

"Okay," he said.

"I love you, KJ," she added.

"Love you, too, Mom," he said before she heard him yelling for his sister.

"Mom," Kenae began as soon as she came on the line. "Me and Miranda are watching a movie."

"I'm not going to keep you," she said. "I just wanted to say good night and tell you that I love you."

Destiny knew by her daughter's deep sigh that she'd rolled her eyes. "You already told me," Kenae said.

"Well, I wanted to tell you again. Sue me."

Kenae laughed. "Okay, Mom."

"Now put your dad on the phone. I need to talk to him for a minute. And tell your cousin Miranda that I said hello."

"Okay," she said. Then she yelled for her dad.

Destiny would have to talk to her kids about using their indoor voices more often. All that yelling was too much.

"Hey, Destiny," Kenneth said when he came on the phone. "What can I do for you?"

Destiny cleared her throat. She hated to talk to Kenneth about money and she was glad she rarely had to do it. "It's about the child support. It hasn't arrived."

The ensuing silence was not a good sign.

"Kenneth," she said, "did you hear me?"

"I heard you."

"And?"

"Well, since the kids are with me for the summer, I didn't think I needed to pay child support."

"You didn't think—" Destiny began. She stopped so she could calm down. "And why would you think that?" she asked after she gathered herself. "Neither the rent nor utilities stopped because you decided to take the kids for the summer. What makes you think the child support should stop?"

"I'm taking care of the kids' day-to-day needs this summer so I figured I'd use the child-support money for their care."

"And you didn't think you needed to discuss this with me?" Destiny could feel herself getting angry. "You just made this decision all on your own."

"Mary Margaret and I thought—"

"I don't care what Mary Margaret thought. I'm asking you, not her. You can't just stop paying without discussing it with me, Kenneth. That's not fair to me or the kids."

Kenneth sighed. "Well, I'm discussing it with you now. I don't think I should pay child support this summer since the kids are with me full-time."

"Well, I think you should. It's not like you have extra expenses. I know Mary Margaret's job is paying for everything."

"I thought we were leaving Mary Margaret out of this."

Destiny took a deep breath. Losing her temper would not get her what she wanted. "You can't do this, Kenneth. I depend on that money each month to keep a roof over your kids' heads. It's not like I'm using it on extras for myself. You don't see me in designer anything. Do you expect me to move into a cheaper place for the summer? Come on."

Kenneth sighed. "So what do you want, Destiny? I don't think it's fair for me to pay the full amount since the kids are with us and we're paying for everything. I won't put Mary Margaret in the position of having to take care of all their expenses. It's already coming out of her pocket for the excursions we're planning to take. I have to contribute something."

"That's between you and Mary Margaret. All I want is what's coming to me."

Kenneth sighed again. "How much do you want, Destiny?"

"I want what you usually send."

"That's not going to happen."

"I knew I should have taken you to court," she mumbled. "Then you wouldn't try to pull some stunt like this."

"It's not a stunt, Destiny."

"Why didn't you discuss it with me earlier then? Why didn't you tell me you planned to stop the child support while the children were with you for the summer? You intentionally misled me. You and Mary Margaret both."

"We did no such thing."

"Well, it certainly seems that way to me. Why didn't either of you tell me then? Why did I have to find out this way?"

Silence was his answer to that question.

"Did you think I wouldn't let them go with you if you told me? Did you think I'd hold my kids hostage over some child support? Is that what you thought?"

Again, silence.

"Speak up, Kenneth. Now's your time to talk."

"Hold on a minute," he said. "I don't want the kids to hear this."

Destiny drilled her fingers on the counter while she waited

for Kenneth to get back on the line. She couldn't believe he had done this to her. She was a reasonable woman. If he had told her his plans for child support, they could have worked something out in advance. It wasn't fair of him to blindside her the way he had.

"Okay," he said, "I'm back."

Destiny thought the phone sounded different. "Do you have me on speakerphone?"

He cleared his throat. "Yes," he said. "Mary Margaret is with me. Do you mind?"

"It's a fine time to ask me," she said. Of course she minded, but she'd never let them know. "I don't care if Mary Margaret listens. Maybe she can explain why you two never thought to tell me you wouldn't be paying child support this summer. Can you tell me why, Mary Margaret?"

Destiny heard some mumbled words back and forth between Kenneth and Mary Margaret. Then she heard him take Mary Margaret off speaker.

"What?" she asked. "All of a sudden Mary Margaret doesn't want to listen?"

"This doesn't concern Mary Margaret."

"I agree," Destiny said, "but you put her on the phone, not me."

"Well, I shouldn't have. You and I will work this out. We always have, haven't we?"

Destiny had to agree. "Yes. That's why this thing surprised me. It's not like you, so I can't help but feel there was some manipulation involved."

Kenneth sighed again. "Look, Destiny, maybe I did worry

that you wouldn't let the kids come with me if you knew I was planning to stop the child-support payments."

Destiny sank back in her chair. "When did you start thinking so little of me, Kenneth? You, of all people, should know that I put the kids first."

"If that's the case, why are you arguing with me about the money?"

"Because you know as well as I do that I budget with that money in mind. If you were going to stop the payments, you should have discussed it with me so I could make the necessary adjustments."

"You're right," he finally said. "I should have discussed it with you. It was unfair of me to drop it on you this way. I apologize."

Destiny wasn't going to fall into that trap. "Does that mean you're sending the money?"

He sighed. "No, it means I'm sorry I didn't tell you earlier that I wasn't going to send it."

"That's not fair, Kenneth. What am I supposed to do? I was counting on that money."

"You can't tell me that your expenses aren't less now than they would be if the kids were with you."

"Yes, but not by that much. A major part of that support money goes for fixed expenses."

"So what do we do? Do you want me to cut the trip short and bring the kids back home?"

It was Destiny's turn to sigh. Of course that wasn't what she wanted. She wanted her kids to have the experience, but she also wanted the child-support money. She was beginning to realize she couldn't have both. "Is it what you want? Do you want to cut the trip short?" she asked. She could bluff as well as he could.

"You know it's not what I want but you have to be reasonable. You have to contribute something. Mary Margaret—"

"I thought we were leaving Mary Margaret out of this."

"These are our kids, Destiny, not hers. She's trying to be a good stepparent, but she can't be fully responsible for them. I won't do that to her."

Destiny sighed, knowing she had lost this round. Unfortunately for her, everything Kenneth said made sense. She hated when facts got in the way of a good argument. "Okay, okay," she said. "What if you keep half and send me half? Will that work?"

"That'll work," he said, much too quickly. She wondered if she'd given in too easily. "I'll have the money transferred into your account tomorrow."

"Thank you," she said.

"I'm not a bad guy, Destiny. I want to do right by you and the kids."

"I know you do, Kenneth. Just don't do anything like this again. You have to talk to me."

"I know," he said. "But you can be unpredictable. There was a time when you really would have held the kids hostage to get what you wanted."

"That was a long time ago. It's not fair of you to hold the things I did back then against me. I've been nothing but reasonable with you and Mary Margaret. I want only what's best for the kids."

"So do I," he said. "Are we clear on everything now?"

"Yes," she said. "Give Mary Margaret my regards."

"Right," he said, the word dripping with sarcasm.

She chuckled. "Good night, Kenneth."

When she hung up the phone, Destiny knew she had made the right decision to relent about the money. She also knew that, as a result, her plans to get the house in Gwinnett were even more in jeopardy. Not only did she need extra money to move, she also needed more money to maintain her current household. Her situation was growing dire.

Chapter 9

DANIEL SMILED AT THE WOMAN, UNABLE TO RECALL her name. He only knew she was a member of the matrons group at Faith Community. According to Gavin, the women brought him lunch on special occasions, but they had brought lunch every day since Daniel's arrival, with a different woman delivering the meal each day. "Thank you so much," he said. "But you-all really don't have to feed me every day."

"We don't mind, Brother Daniel," the woman said. "It's part of our ministry."

A knock on the open door interrupted their conversation. "Something smells good in here," Natalie said, walking fully into the office next to Gavin's where Daniel had been installed. "What do you have here, Eve?" she asked. "I hope there's enough for me."

Eve smiled, but Daniel noticed the smile didn't quite reach her eyes. "Of course, Sister Weston. We brought enough for you and the pastor. We'd never leave you out."

Natalie leaned over and brushed a kiss against the woman's cheek. "I knew you wouldn't," she said. "I was just teasing." Natalie rubbed her stomach. "Gavin loves your cooking, so you know he dived in as soon as you brought it to him. I stopped by his office before coming here to meet with Daniel so I dived in with him. You are the best cook I know. I've been meaning to talk to you about catering the upcoming regional pastors' wives luncheon. Not a big group, about forty women. Do you think you'd be interested? You'd make some great contacts."

Daniel watched as Eve's eyes brightened.

"I'm more than interested," she said. "Thank you so much for thinking of me. I really want to get my catering business off the ground. Every event helps me to do that."

"We have to help each other," Natalie said. "It's all part of belonging to the family of God."

"I'm glad to be a part of a church that lives those words rather than just saying them," Eve said to Natalie. Then she turned to Daniel. "Enjoy your lunch. I'm going to run along. I don't want to keep you two from your meeting."

Daniel stood. "Thanks again, Eve," he said. "You-all are certainly making me feel welcome here at Faith Community."

Eve waved him off. "It's like Sister Weston said, it's what we do in the family of God."

Daniel watched as the young woman walked out of the room. "You've got some great members," he said to Natalie.

Her eyes flashed amusement. "We've got some eager single women. They don't do this for everybody. You're special." She grinned outright. "And you're single."

"Don't you start," Daniel said.

Natalie chuckled. "You're a rarity. Single Christian men are hard to find."

"I'm not even going to comment on that," he said, reaching for the pad on his desk. "Let's sit at the table. I'm assuming Gavin told you about the personal finance program I want to start."

Natalie followed him to the table and took a seat. "He sure did. It's very generous of you to offer to use the proceeds from Gloria's life insurance to fund it, Daniel. More than generous. You really don't have to do it."

He nodded. "Yes I do," he said. "It's what she would want."

"Yes, she'd be pleased that you're using the money to help others, but she'd also want to know you'd taken care of yourself." She raised her question-filled eyes to his. "Have you?"

"Don't worry about me," he said. "I don't need much. Besides, I still get partnership checks from GDW Investigations and the company is doing well."

"If you're sure," she said.

"I'm sure."

She leaned toward him. "A personal money management program is exactly what this church needs. I can't believe we haven't already done one. I guess we were just waiting for you. How long has a program like this been in your heart? Why do you want to do it?"

"In the work at GDW, we see a lot of people who get themselves in bad situations because they're desperate for money. These people tend to fall into three categories: those who just did a poor job of managing what they had, those who never had enough in the first place, and those who were greedy and just wanted more. I wanted to do something to help the folks in the first two categories and maybe keep folks from compounding their money problems by doing something illegal. I'm not sure what we can do for those in the third category."

"And you saw a lot of that when you were working at GDW?"

"More than I care to remember," he said, thinking of Phil. A part of him wanted to tell Natalie and Gavin about him, but he knew the importance of secrecy when dealing with cases like this. He'd give them all the details once they closed the case. "It breaks your heart sometimes. If I can stop just one person from deciding to take a shortcut to financial well-being, the program will have been worth it."

Natalie smiled. "You have a big heart, Daniel Thomas."

"I guess I'm living up to the Faith Community standard then, since I'm just doing my part as a member of the family of God."

"Have I told you how happy I am that you decided to join us?"

He chuckled. "Several times."

She sat back in her chair. "Well, I am," she said. "We need you. I don't think we realized how much until you got here, but God knew."

Daniel agreed with her. His primary reason for being in Atlanta was to support Gavin and the church ministry, but working this case with Phil was also part of the reason he was here. He hadn't been able to balance the two in the past.

He hoped to do better going forward. "Enough about me," he said. "I got another idea listening to you and Eve talk about her catering business. What would it take to get something like that up and running?"

Natalie shrugged. "I have no idea, but I bet Eve does. You should have asked her."

Daniel shook his head. "I wanted to talk to you first. I had thought to use Gloria's insurance money to help folks get themselves out of personal financial binds, but maybe we can focus on helping folks start small businesses where they can employ folks in need."

Natalie's eyes lit up. "That's a great idea, Daniel, but I don't see why we can't do both things. You're starting with a good bit of money. There's no reason we can't help folks out short term and also help them long term with starting a small business. Of course, folks are going to need some education in what starting and running a small business entails but you're the perfect person for that. Look what you, William, and George did with GDW Investigations. You've come a long way since you started."

Daniel nodded. GDW had started with just the three of them working out of rented space above a Chinese restaurant on the outskirts of downtown Memphis. Today, they had a floor of offices in a major downtown business complex and employed more than fifty full-time staff. "The business certainly exceeded our expectations."

"So let's call the programs you're starting here the Ephesians 3:20 Project. This fund is going to be the answer to somebody's prayer in a way they never imagined. You think you're popular now. Just wait until folks find out what you're doing."

"The name works for me," he said, "but I don't want folks knowing that I'm funding the project. Let's keep the focus on what the project is doing rather than who is funding it."

"I understand you want to be humble about it, Daniel, but folks are going to figure it out since you're running the project."

He shook his head. "Then I won't run it. I'm sure you know somebody in the congregation who could do it."

"Yes, but you'd still need to be involved, especially with the small business education."

"I'm on board with that," he said. "I just don't want to be the face of the project. You can bring on somebody to do that."

Natalie smiled. "I think I have just the person. And you've already met her."

"Eve?"

Natalie shook her head. "Destiny."

Daniel eyed her. "This is not you matchmaking again, is it?"

Natalie chuckled. "Let's just say it's matchmaking plus. That you and Destiny would get to spend some time together as friends and coworkers is a bonus. The real truth is that Destiny could use the extra work and the money that goes with it."

Daniel hated to think of Destiny in need. He'd been raised by a single mother so he knew that finances could get tight. "So her ex-husband is one of those deadbeat dads?"

Natalie shook her head. "It's more complex than that," she said. "If you want to know more, you'll have to talk to Destiny. You are going to see her again, aren't you?"

Daniel grinned. "You don't give up, do you?"

"Never. Not when it matters. And you and Destiny both matter."

"Well, you and Gavin have done your parts. Now you need to step back and let us figure out the rest."

"Yes, sir," Natalie said, giving him a mock salute.

"I'm serious, Natalie," he said.

"So am I."

Daniel didn't believe she was going to give up her match-making, so he decided to let the topic drop. "If Destiny needs money, why can't she be one of the recipients of a fund award?"

Natalie's eyes widened. "She'd be perfect." She leaned closer. "She's trying to do something for her family this summer and her plans to get the money to do it fell through. This could be just the opportunity she needs."

"Well, that's great. Will you talk to her or should I?"

"Let me do it," she said. "Destiny can be prickly at times. Her pride rises up and makes her think she can't accept help from friends. She'd appreciate the work though, so I'd still like to talk to her about working with you on developing the programs." She looked at Daniel. "She'd have to know you're putting up the money for the programs. Are you okay with that?"

Daniel nodded. "I'm okay with her knowing. I don't think she'd announce it to the world."

"No, she can be discreet."

"Well," Daniel said, "then I think we need to pull her in on the planning as well. The two of us can rough out the broad parameters of both programs today but I'd like to get her input as well. I want her to feel a sense of ownership for the work we're trying to do."

"You're putting your heart into this, aren't you, Daniel?"

"It's Gloria's heart," he said. "I want this program to honor her. She lived a life of service so I know she'd be pleased to know she was still giving service, even in death."

Natalie covered his hand that rested on the table with her own. "She knows, Daniel. And we'll honor her every day. There's no reason we can't name the fund after her."

He shook his head. "She wouldn't want that. She was all about the work, not the recognition. Her joy will be in seeing how lives are changed because of what we do. That's enough."

Chapter 10

"ARE YOU READY TO DO THIS?" BERTICE ASKED DESTINY. They sat in the lobby restaurant of the building that housed HR Solutions, a temporary employment services firm based in Atlanta and with offices scattered all over the country.

"More than ready," she said. "I want that house in Gwinnett for me and the kids and, if I can swing it, I want to make a weekend trip to visit the kids while they're away. My summer plans are headed down the drain if I can't come up with the extra money. My situation is further complicated by Kenneth's decision to reduce his child-support payments for the summer. Girl, I need this job. Thank you for introducing me to your friend."

"Kenneth was wrong to do what he did," Bertice said. "I bet that fat Mary Margaret was behind it."

Destiny didn't want to go down that road again with Bertice. She almost regretted telling her friend about Kenneth and the child-support money. She didn't regret it though because she'd needed to talk to someone who understood. That left out her mother and Natalie. She couldn't bear to hear her mother's "I told you so" when it came to Kenneth and she didn't want Natalie offering to loan her money again. This was her problem and she had to fix it. "Hey," she said to Bertice, "I ought to blame you."

Bertice's eyes widened. "Me?"

Destiny nodded.

"How am I at fault?"

"You put it out there when you got on my case the other day about the instability of relying too heavily on Kenneth's child-support payments. And just like that"—Destiny snapped her fingers—"a few days later my child support is cut in half. That has to be more than coincidence. You put some bad mojo on me."

Bertice chuckled. "You're joking, right?"

Destiny wasn't so sure. Bertice had put the thought out there first. She believed in thoughts and ideas in the air taking shape in the world. "I'm kidding," she said to reassure her friend. "If I thought you were bad luck, I definitely wouldn't be down here with you trying to find work. You're more like my good-luck charm."

"Thanks for saying that," Bertice said. "Sometimes Natalie can be so negative about the things I do, but I'd never do anything illegal." She grinned at Destiny. "Nothing big, I mean. Besides, we aren't doing anything illegal, not really. This job is going to work for you for the summer just like it's worked for me for the last year."

"A whole year?"

Bertice nodded. "Off and on. When I need some extra cash for a special project or something, Phil hooks me up. Where do you think I got the money for all the new furniture in my new house? I saved up the down payment, but this job helped with all the extras."

Destiny rolled her eyes. "I believed you when you said you had a windfall from playing the lottery. I can't believe you lied to me and Natalie."

"I had to lie," Bertice said. "I told you about Natalie and her negativity. I know her. She would only find fault and try to make me feel guilty. She even tried to make me feel guilty about the lottery. She's gotten a bit too self-righteous for me."

"I don't think that's true," Destiny said.

Bertice turned to look at her. "Are you going to tell her that you're working with me?"

Destiny shook her head. "Not right away. She'd worry and I don't want her to do that. I'll tell her later in the summer when I finalize my moving plans."

"What about your mom?"

"You don't even have to ask; you know I'm not telling her until the last possible moment. I still haven't told her about my plans to move to Gwinnett."

"I think you're too hard on your mother," Bertice said. "She's not that bad."

Destiny just stared at her friend.

"Well, she's not," Bertice repeated. "And you are too hard on her."

"I'm in too good of a mood to even debate you on that

point. Besides, I've got some news to tell my mother that should keep her off my back this summer."

"What's that?"

"I'm going back to school."

"What? That's great news. When did you decide?"

Destiny shrugged. "I don't know. I guess I'm just tired of being afraid."

"Afraid?"

"Yes, afraid of going back to school. I wasn't that good a student the first time around. Who knows if I'll be any better now?"

"Well, I think it's a good decision. And I know Natalie and your mom will be all over it. You're going to have a full plate this summer."

"That's the point," Destiny said. "I want to fill up every minute of my day while the kids are away. If I don't, I'll go crazy with missing them. I miss them so much already and they've been gone only a couple of weeks. I welcome the challenge of school if it'll help keep my mind off the kids and what they're doing."

Bertice snapped her fingers. "Hey, I just thought of something. If you're going back to school, you'll be eligible for a loan. If you need to explain any extra money before you're ready, you can always say you took out a school loan."

Destiny glared at her friend. "You can't be serious."

Bertice shrugged. "Please. I know folks who live off student loans. A girl I work with bought a car, a used car, with her student loan money."

"And this is legal?" Destiny asked.

Bertice nodded. "You have to pay the money back, so it's legal."

"You're too good at this," Destiny said, studying her friend. "That's not a bad idea though. It has only one downside. I'd have to lie."

Bertice chuckled. "Well, there is that." Bertice lifted her glass of soda to Destiny. "Welcome back to college," she said.

"I'm excited about it, even though I don't know what I want to be when I grow up. Isn't that a shame?"

Bertice laughed. "It's a shame that you've had two kids and you still don't consider yourself a grown-up."

Destiny slapped her friend lightly on the shoulder. "That's not what I meant. I'm talking in terms of finding a career. I know more about what I don't want to do than I do about what I want to do."

"Well, that's a start. You should visit the career counseling office at the college. They probably have some assessments to help you figure out where your interests and skills intersect."

"You're just a fountain of information today, aren't you?"

Bertice winked at her. "Hey, I already have my BS degree, so just call me Encyclopedia Bertice. One day after you get your degree, you'll be as smart as I am."

Destiny rolled her eyes. "Oh please."

Bertice looked down at her watch. "It's about one. We need to head upstairs. Your appointment is for one fifteen. You have the application all filled out, don't you?"

Destiny patted the portfolio that rested in the chair next to hers. "I'm good to go."

Bertice led the way to the elevator. When they got off

at the fifth floor, Destiny followed her friend down a long hallway to a set of oak double doors with an HR Solutions placard on one of them. "This is it," Bertice said, turning back to look at her. "You ready?"

"As ready as I'll ever be."

Bertice nodded, pulled open the door, and walked to the reception desk. When she got there, she gave the receptionist their names.

"Yes, I see you have a one-fifteen appointment," the young woman said. "Please take a seat. Mr. Harris will be with you shortly. His earlier appointment ran over, so he's running a little behind schedule. Would either of you like something to drink while you wait?"

"No, but thanks anyway," Bertice said. "We just had lunch in the lobby restaurant. Great food, wasn't it, Destiny?"

"It was very good, much better than I expected."

"I'm glad you enjoyed it," the receptionist said. "The restaurant has been open only a couple of months, but they're doing great business. Everybody raves about them."

Destiny looked up when the door to the office behind the receptionist's desk opened and a handsome guy of average height walked toward them. When he reached Bertice, he leaned close and bussed her on the cheek. "You get more beautiful every day," he said.

Bertice gave him the full effect of her smile. "Thank you," she said. "You're looking pretty handsome yourself."

As Destiny watched the exchange, she wondered if there was something going on between her friend and Mr. Harris. Bertice hadn't even hinted at anything romantic between them but there were fireworks there. The kind that could be felt as well as seen.

"This is my friend Destiny Madison," Bertice said, finally getting around to introducing her.

Phil Harris extended his hand. "It's nice to meet you, Ms. Madison. Any friend of Bertice's is a friend of mine. Why don't you follow me into my office so we can get everything taken care of."

Destiny looked at Bertice, who said, "I'll wait here for you."

Destiny nodded and then followed Mr. Harris into his office.

"Have a seat," Mr. Harris said, pointing to a couple of office chairs in front of his desk. After she was seated, he walked around the desk and took his seat. "Let me see," he said as he opened his desk drawer and pulled out a binder. He opened it, pulled out the top sheet, and handed it to her. "The details of the job are outlined in this document. While you look it over, I'll look over your application materials. Did you bring them?"

Opening her portfolio, Destiny said, "I have them right here." She handed the papers to him.

"Thanks," he said. "I'll give this a quick review. If you have any questions about the job as described there, please ask."

Destiny read the paper and found the details to be pretty much as Bertice had explained. HR Solutions would offer her services as a consumer consultant to a variety of companies, small and large, who would pay her directly for services rendered. Services would typically be the review of a product or website or a comparison shopping task conducted online or in-store. The companies would pay her by direct deposit. She'd keep 10 percent of the deposited amount and transfer the remaining 90 percent to an HR Solutions account. Each job would net her from $500 to $750 and she was guaranteed a minimum of four jobs per month. It was pretty straightforward. When she looked up, she found Mr. Harris watching her.

"Do you have any questions?" he asked.

She shook her head. "Not really. This document is pretty clear. The work doesn't appear to be too difficult or too time consuming and the pay is very good. It's perfect for what I want to do this summer."

"It is a great opportunity for the right people," the man said. "Marketing is very important to our clients and they're willing to spend money to learn what consumers think about their products and services."

"It makes sense to me," she said.

"I didn't realize how big the market was until we here at HR Solutions got involved in it." He grinned at her. "Companies pay celebrities like the Kardashians thirty to fifty thousand dollars for a single tweet. Pro athletes make more money from their endorsements than they do for playing their sports. Here at HR Solutions we've found a way to capture a small chunk of those marketing dollars by providing companies contact with actual consumers."

"I guess it makes a lot of sense," she said. "You explained it very well. When Bertice first told me about this opportunity, I thought it sounded a little bit too good to be true."

Mr. Harris chuckled. "I'll bet Denzel thought that, too, the first time he made twenty million dollars for a movie role. In marketing, it's not about how much they pay you, it's about how much they're going to make because of you. Don't ever doubt your worth, Ms. Madison. We here at HR Solutions don't."

"That's good to know," she said.

"And you should also know that there are not a lot of openings for these jobs. We don't advertise broadly for them. We work primarily with referrals from people who are already working with us."

"The way Bertice referred me."

He nodded. "Exactly. We have to have a trust relationship with the folks on our team. We have that with Bertice and now we have it with you because of Bertice. If you have someone you'd like to bring on, I suggest that you talk to me before you talk to them because there's no use getting their hopes up when there are no openings."

"Okay," she said, clearly understanding the line that would start forming at their door if everybody knew the kind of money being paid.

"Well," he said. "If you don't have any questions, I'd like to unofficially welcome you aboard. Your application seems to be complete, but in order for us to process it, we'll need to do a background check. We can typically get that done in a couple of days and you'll get your first job within about a week. Your contact will be via an e-mail account that we set up for you.

As you read in the document I gave you, you are responsible for checking that e-mail at least every twenty-four hours, including weekends. If you're going to be away from e-mail for longer than twenty-four hours, you have to forward your mail to the designated address."

Destiny nodded. The more she talked to Mr. Harris, the more comfortable she became with the job. Her plans for the summer were officially back on track.

Chapter 11

THE MORE THINGS CHANGED, THE MORE THEY STAYED the same, Mary Margaret thought. Here she was in a beautiful beach house in Los Angeles and she still didn't know where her husband was. While she was glad that Kenneth had found a twelve-step meeting nearby that he liked, she needed him to be more considerate about his time. Why did he continue to stay out late like this when he knew it drove her crazy? He did it back at home and now he was doing it out here. She sometimes thought he did it on purpose.

"Mary Margaret."

She looked up from where she sat on the bed reading a company report to see KJ standing in her bedroom doorway. "What's up, KJ?" she asked, glancing at the clock. "Why aren't you in bed?"

"I was waiting for Dad," he said. "When is he coming home?"

Mary Margaret wished she knew. She put the report she

was reading aside and patted a space on the bed next to her. "Come," she said, "sit with me." After he was seated on the edge of the bed, she asked, "What do you need?"

"I wanted to talk to Dad about the video camera. It's not working right. He said he was going to help me learn to use it. We leave for the Grand Canyon on Saturday and I need to know how to use it by then."

Mary Margaret smiled. "What kind of problem are you having?"

The boy's eyes brightened. "I'll show you," he said. "Let me go get the camera."

Mary Margaret's smile grew wider. So far, the trip to L.A. had been all she expected and more when it came to KJ and Kenae. She could feel the bond between them growing, which made her happy and did a little to make up for her disappointment with Kenneth. She couldn't deny that having the kids around all the time had rekindled her desire to have a baby of her own. She hoped the trip was doing the same for Kenneth. She'd have to broach the subject with him soon. She loved seeing him in his kids and wondered which of his features a baby they created together would share. They'd been married four years now, so it was time to find out.

"Here it is," KJ said, running back into the bedroom with the camera and what she guessed was the instruction manual in his hands. He sat next to her on the bed and began to explain where he was having trouble. As he talked, she rubbed her hand across his head.

"Have you tried this?" she asked, twisting one of the knobs on the back of the camera to change a setting.

"Hey, it worked," he said, smiling brightly. "Thanks, Mary Margaret."

"No problem, buddy," she said, rubbing his head one more time. "I'm glad I was able to help."

"What's going on in here?"

Mary Margaret and KJ both looked toward the doorway. KJ hopped up from the bed, camera in hand, and ran to his dad. "Mary Margaret was helping me with the video camera. I'm good to go now."

With his hand resting on KJ's shoulder, Kenneth looked over at Mary Margaret. "Thanks, sweetie."

Mary Margaret steeled herself against his endearment. Kenneth wasn't going to get off that easy. "It's late," she said. "KJ should be in bed."

"But, Dad—" KJ began.

Kenneth shook his head. "No buts, young man. Off to bed. I'll be there in a minute to say good night. Is Kenae still up?"

KJ nodded. "She had those headphones on all night, Dad. You told her not to wear them so much but she still does."

Kenneth smacked his son lightly on the backside. "Mind your business, KJ. I'll take care of Kenae and her headphones. Don't you worry about them. Now get to your room."

"Night, Mary Margaret," the young boy said.

"Sleep well, KJ."

After the boy left the room, Kenneth closed the door. "Thanks again for helping KJ with the camera."

Mary Margaret picked up her report and pretended to begin reading. "He was expecting you to help him."

Kenneth kicked off his shoes and began to undress. "I was going to," he said. "I still will. We have plenty of time. We don't leave for the Grand Canyon until day after tomorrow."

"You know KJ," she said. "He's so excited about the trip. He wants everything to be perfect."

In only his boxers, KJ sat next to Mary Margaret on the bed. He planted a soft kiss on her lips. "Now that was perfect. How was your day?"

Mary Margaret could feel her displeasure with Kenneth slipping away. He was such a charmer that it was hard to stay angry with him. "Nothing special," she said. "It was a normal workday."

Kenneth pulled back and looked at her. "Still upset with me?"

Mary Margaret kept her eyes on her report. "I'm not upset."

He pulled the papers out of her hand. "Yes you are."

She folded her arms across her chest. "What do I have to be upset about?"

He leaned in and brushed his lips across hers again. "From where I sit, nothing. You have a perfect husband so you have nothing to be angry about."

She fought the smile that was bubbling up in her. "Not quite perfect."

Kenneth pulled back, eyes wide, as if he couldn't believe what she was saying. "Which husband are you talking about?"

The laughter she was holding in erupted.

"That's my girl," Kenneth said. "Life's a lot better when you're happy. You are happy, aren't you, Mary Margaret?"

Mary Margaret leaned into Kenneth and he pulled her closer. "For the most part."

"You aren't still mad at me about the miscommunication with Destiny about the child support, are you?"

She was more upset because he'd stayed out so late after his meeting ended, but it was easier to complain about his lie to Destiny. She much preferred being the righteously indignant stepmother to the insecure wife. "It wasn't a miscommunication, Kenneth. We agreed that you would talk to her about stopping the child-support payments for the summer and you didn't. You even told me you had spoken to her about it. I don't understand why you lied."

Kenneth sighed. "You know how unpredictable Destiny can be. She may not have let the kids come if I'd told her before we left."

"Maybe, maybe not," Mary Margaret said. "It's just that when miscommunications like that happen, I become the bad guy. Destiny thought I was behind the deception, which couldn't be further from the truth."

"She doesn't blame you."

Mary Margaret challenged him with her eyes. "Then why did you take her off speakerphone?" She knew the reason, so she didn't wait for him to answer. "I don't want to go back to those drama-filled days of the first couple of years of our marriage."

"Neither do I," he said.

Then don't start drama of your own, she thought. After

a few moments of strained silence, she asked, "Have you thought any more about inviting Destiny out to visit the kids? You know they would enjoy seeing her."

Kenneth shrugged. "It's not like this is the first time they've been apart from her."

"I know," she said. "But it's the first time they've been this far away and the first time they've been away so long. They may get homesick if they don't see her and I'd hate to have to cut their trip short."

"Well, she may not be able to afford it. You know money's tight for her."

Mary Margaret had already considered Destiny's finances. "Maybe, maybe not. We don't really know the state of her finances, we can only guess. It doesn't matter anyway. We still need to let her know she's welcome to come. Besides, you could give her the full child support one month and that would cover the trip. It would be worth it and she'd appreciate the gesture."

He pressed another kiss on her lips. "I'll think about it, babe." He got up from the bed. "Let me go say good night to the kids. Otherwise, they'll be up all night."

Mary Margaret nodded. She knew Kenneth didn't want Destiny to come visit. Sometimes she thought he wanted full custody of his kids. Since he had convinced Destiny to enroll the kids in a school in their district because it has a stronger school system, he'd been angling for them to spend their weekdays at their house and weekends at Destiny's. If he had his way, she was pretty sure he'd go for full custody. She wasn't ready to support that position. From what she could see, Destiny had grown as a parent over the years. She didn't see a need to take her kids; she just wanted to maintain the cordial relationship they had developed over the last couple of years. When she and Kenneth did have a baby, she wanted the environment to be drama free. She'd have to watch her husband and make sure he didn't do anything to undermine the progress they'd made in creating a functional extended family with Destiny and the kids.

Chapter 12

"Dᴵᴰ ʏᴏᴜ ᴍᴀᴋᴇ ᴀɴ ᴀᴘᴘᴏɪɴᴛᴍᴇɴᴛ ᴛᴏ ᴍᴇᴇᴛ ᴡɪᴛʜ ᴀ counselor at the university?" Bertice asked from the passenger seat of Destiny's Ford Fusion.

Destiny glanced briefly at her friend dressed in her ᴛʜɪɴᴋ ᴘɪɴᴋ tank top and matching leggings before turning her eyes back to the interstate. The downtown exit was coming up so she navigated the car into the far-right lane. "I made one. After I get off work on Monday."

"In the evening?"

"Surprised me, too," Destiny said. "Things sure have changed since I was last a student. According to the website, they want to accommodate the working student."

"And that's you."

Destiny nodded. "I guess it is."

"Have you told your mom yet?"

Destiny shook her head. "Not yet. I have to prepare myself for her gloating."

Bertice laughed. Then she sobered. "What a difference a few days make, huh?"

"You're right about that," Destiny said. "And I have to thank you again for the hookup at HR Solutions. It's a better job than the one that was rescinded. I wouldn't be able to go back to school if I was doing the other job, so I guess it all worked out."

"I'm glad," Bertice said. "Now that you've got your professional and financial life in order, you can focus on the personal. You haven't told me much about this Daniel character that Natalie wanted you to meet. How did it go? What do you think of him?"

"He's a nice man," Destiny said. "Natalie did good with this one."

"Well, I need to meet him."

Destiny glanced over at her. "You will. He'll be at the walk today. He's coming with Gavin and Natalie," she said as she turned her car into the Omni parking deck.

"I can't wait," Bertice said. "These parking prices are too high. We should have taken the train," she added.

"Too late now," Destiny said, taking the parking ticket. When the gate opened, she navigated the car to a parking space on the third level. After she and Bertice got out of the car, they took the stairs down to the main level. When they exited, Destiny turned at the sound of her name.

"Perfect timing," Natalie, flanked by Gavin and Daniel, said. "I was just about to call you two."

"You three look like triplets," Gavin said, a big grin on his face.

"Hello, Destiny," Daniel said with a simple smile.

Destiny smiled back. "Hi, Daniel," she said. "I'm glad you made it."

"No place else I'd rather be," he said.

"Stop flirting, Daniel," Gavin said. Then he gave Destiny a peck on the forehead. "I'm glad you two hit it off," he whispered.

Destiny wanted to tell him that he was getting ahead of himself, but he pulled away from her and turned his attention to Bertice.

"It's been too long since I've seen you, Bertice," he said, pulling the woman into a big hug. "Where have you been hiding? I've missed you at service."

"I've been around," Bertice said.

Destiny cast a quick glance at Natalie. Both women knew Gavin made Bertice uncomfortable. She couldn't get past the fact that her best friend had married a pastor. In fact, her church attendance had dropped steadily since Natalie and Gavin's marriage.

"You haven't been around me," Gavin said. "I was about to start thinking you didn't like me."

Bertice began shaking her head. "It's not that. I've just been busy. You know I moved and everything."

"Yes, I heard, Ms. Homeowner," he said. "Congratulations. I'm still waiting on the invitation to see your new place. But I guess it's not so new now."

"Your wife has been there," Bertice offered.

"That counts for something, I guess," he said. "We still miss you at service. When you don't have time for church," he continued, "you're too busy." He tugged her hand and pulled her toward Daniel. "You've been so busy that you haven't met my good friend Daniel."

"It's nice to meet you, Bertice," Daniel said, extending his hand to her. "What a lovely name."

"Thank you," Bertice said, taking his hand. "And it's nice to meet you, too. Welcome to Atlanta. Natalie's told us a lot about you."

"Hey, guys," Natalie said, "let's move as we talk. The walk starts in ten minutes and we are a couple of blocks from the starting point. I knew we would be late when we missed the church van."

Destiny released a breath she hadn't realized she'd been holding, very thankful Natalie had interrupted before Bertice said something that would embarrass all of them. Her friend had a knack for doing that.

"Yeah," Daniel said, "what's up with that? I can't believe they left the pastor behind."

Natalie smirked. "I can. He was late. They were right to leave him."

Gavin grinned. "They were right to leave *us*. I wasn't late by myself or because of myself."

As they walked, Daniel fell in step next to Destiny, while Natalie and Gavin flanked Bertice.

"It's good to see you again. I would have called," he said, smiling down at her, "but I realized I didn't ask for your number."

"I noticed that myself," she said, returning his smile.

His smile grew wider. "What can I say? I'm out of practice."

Before Destiny could respond, Natalie glanced back at them. "What are you two whispering about?" she asked, a sly grin on her face.

Destiny knew her friend was hoping for a love connection between her and Daniel but she wasn't even ready to think that far into the future. The idea of getting to know him better appealed to her. For now, that was enough.

"Whatever it was," Gavin said, "you're going to have to hold it till after the walk. They're lining up the runners first, so Daniel and I have to get a move on."

"We're not finished," Daniel whispered to her. Then more loudly, he said, "I'll see you at the finish line."

Natalie dropped back and put her arm through one of Destiny's. "You two seem to be hitting it off. I knew you would."

"Don't go marrying them off yet," Bertice said. "Let them have a summer fling first."

"It's too early to talk marriage or a fling," Destiny said.

"But you do like him?" Natalie prodded.

"He seems like a nice guy," Destiny said, not wanting to give away too much at this point.

"Has he asked you out yet?"

Destiny shook her head. Meeting at the walk wasn't actually a date, was it? She wasn't sure she was ready to start dating anyway. Not yet. There was also a small part of her that didn't want to give Natalie the satisfaction of knowing her matchmaking efforts were working. The things Bertice had shared with her about the reasoning behind Natalie's efforts still stung a bit.

"Doesn't matter," Natalie said.

Destiny was taken aback by Natalie's reaction. Given the things Bertice had told her about Natalie's determination to find her a man, she was surprised her friend had given up on her matchmaking so quickly.

"Doesn't matter?" Bertice repeated, voicing Destiny's concerns. "I can't believe you're giving up your matchmaking efforts."

"Who said I was giving up?" Natalie said.

"Uh-oh," Bertice said. "What do you mean by that?"

Natalie shrugged, a smile tugging at the corners of her mouth. "Daniel's such a great guy. We're so lucky he chose to move here and make Faith Community his church home. You'll never guess what he wants to do for the church."

"Something tells me you're going to tell us," Bertice said, grinning.

Natalie rocked into Bertice with her hip. "And you'd better not say anything to him or anybody else about it."

"Spill," Bertice said.

Natalie looked at Bertice again. "He wants to start two financial assistance programs, one for folks in a short-term bind and another for folks looking more long term. It's awfully generous of him to want to give of himself this way."

"Is he a financial whiz or something?" Bertice asked.

"Not exactly," Natalie said, "but he's had some good success in business."

"Well, you didn't tell me he was rich," Bertice said with a wry smile. "You should have introduced him to me instead of Destiny."

"I didn't say he was rich," Natalie said.

"So where is the money coming from for these programs? Is the church providing the funds?"

"In a way," Natalie said.

"You may as well tell us," Bertice said. "I can tell you want to."

Natalie lowered her voice. "He doesn't want everybody to know, but he's donating the insurance money he received after his wife died."

"That's pretty generous," Destiny said, her esteem for him growing.

"It's more than generous," Natalie said. "Daniel really has a heart to help people. He knows some folks are having a hard time and he wants to do more than pray about it."

"A man of action," Bertice said. "I like that."

Destiny liked it, too. She had been one of those folks having a hard time, so what he wanted to do was even more special to her.

"It gets better," Natalie was saying. "We're going to need somebody to serve as the face of the programs and Daniel doesn't want that person to be him."

"Who's it going to be?" Bertice asked.

Natalie turned to Destiny. "I thought of you," she said.

"Me?" Destiny repeated.

"Yes, you," Natalie said. "It's a part-time job, so it won't pay a lot, but it has flexible hours and you'll be doing some good. Besides the money, there's the added bonus that the extra work will keep you from missing your kids so much."

Destiny shot a hopeful glance at Bertice, counting on her

quick-thinking friend to come up with a reasonable response. She couldn't take on another job now, could she? Not with the HR Solutions gig, school, and her day job already on her plate.

"Destiny's summer schedule is filling up fast," Bertice said.

"What's Bertice talking about?" Natalie asked Destiny.

Destiny shrugged. "I've decided to go back to school," she said, withholding the information about HR Solutions.

Natalie hugged her friend. "I'm so happy for you, Destiny. I think it's a good choice for you." When she pulled back, she added, "This job is so flexible that it shouldn't interfere with school or your day job. It's perfect."

"I don't know," Destiny said, sending a silent plea to Bertice for help. "School is going to keep me plenty busy."

Natalie put a hand on Destiny's shoulder. "Come on, Destiny. This job is perfect for you. Your pride won't let me help you in any other way, so let me do this. I know you still want that house in Gwinnett. This job can help with that."

Destiny glanced from one friend to the other. These two women loved her and wanted to help her. She'd taken help from Bertice, so how could she turn down help from Natalie? Besides, there was the added benefit of getting to know Daniel without the awkwardness of dating. "Okay," she told her friend. "I'll do it."

Chapter 13

DANIEL AWOKE THE NEXT MORNING TIRED AND REST-
less. Though he had done a good job of hiding his reaction, meeting Bertice at the cancer walk had shaken him.
Bertice was the woman who had unknowingly captured
Phil's heart. Phil said she was innocent, but how innocent
could she be? And what about Destiny? Did she know her
friend was involved with Phil? Was she involved herself? She
didn't strike him as the kind of woman to fall for something
like this. But Natalie had hinted that her friend's financial
situation was shaky. Destiny was involved with Phil's scam.
He knew it in his gut. What was he going to do? He couldn't
talk to Gavin or Natalie because of the promise of secrecy
he'd made to William and George before agreeing to take on
the case. There was no point in calling them either since he
knew they would tell him to keep quiet and let the situation
play itself out. He just wasn't sure he could sit by and let the
women get themselves in deeper. That's why he was seated at
this Waffle House waiting for Phil. He had a plan.

"Hey, man," Phil said when he joined him at the table. "What's so urgent that we had to meet this morning? Nobody's up for breakfast this early on Sunday except preachers, lovers, and truck drivers."

Daniel didn't even smile at Phil's teasing words. "Thanks for meeting me," he said.

"No problem," Phil said, taking a seat. Almost immediately, the waitress came over, poured him coffee, and took his order. Unlike him, Phil didn't settle for coffee. No, he also ordered the Hungry Man breakfast of pancakes, eggs, and sausage.

"That's a heavy breakfast," Daniel said.

Phil took a long swallow from his cup of coffee. "I'm sure you didn't get me down here this early in the morning to discuss my breakfast caloric intake."

"No, I didn't," Daniel said. "Did you sign up a Destiny Madison in the last few days?"

Phil nodded. "Bertice brought her in. She's one of her friends. I didn't want to do it but you told me I had no choice. I had to keep doing things the way I'd always done them."

"Yeah, I remember," Daniel said. "But we have a problem, so we have to make some adjustments."

"What kind of problem?" Phil asked.

"I know Destiny. She's a close friend of close friends of mine and so is Bertice."

Phil sat back in his chair. "You're joking, right?"

Daniel shook his head. "I wish I was but I'm not."

"So are you going to tell them what's going on?"

"You know I can't," Daniel said. "If they knew what they'd gotten themselves into, they'd want out and right now they can't get out. If we're going to catch these guys, we need to keep the status quo."

The waitress brought Phil's food and then returned to the table and refreshed both their coffees. After nodding his thanks to her, Daniel said, "We're going to have to keep a close eye on them. If they find themselves in trouble because they were victims of the identity theft part of the scam or some other scam that we don't know about, I need to know."

"And how do you propose we keep an eye on them?"

Daniel met his eyes and smiled. "You're going to ask Bertice out."

Phil's eyes widened. "No I'm not. I can't."

Daniel nodded. "Yes you can."

Phil shook his head. "I can't date her while I'm lying to her. I'd been holding out some hope of us getting together once your team gets to the bottom of all of this."

"It's not ideal, I know," Daniel said, understanding the man's reluctance, "but it's our only option right now. We have to watch out for them."

"You may be right," Phil said. "But my asking Bertice out after all this time is going to seem odd."

"Not if she knows you've been interested in her for a long time."

Phil's eyes widened. "And how's she going to know that? I'm not going to tell her."

"I'll mention it to Destiny," Daniel said. "I'll suggest that the four of us do something together. My friend and his wife have been trying to fix me and Destiny up since I arrived in town, so she won't suspect anything out of the ordinary."

Phil forked some pancakes into his mouth. "What makes you think she wants to go out with you?"

Daniel smiled to himself. "I feel pretty sure she will. We hit it off when we met. But if she won't do it for me, she'll do it for you and Bertice. I'll tell her that you're trying to find a way to get to know Bertice better and you need her help. She'll go for it. Women like that kind of stuff."

Phil's lips curved into a frown. "You realize we're not teen-agers, right? Your plan is sounding very high school to me."

Daniel agreed that the idea wasn't particularly sophisti-cated, but it was the best he could come up with on such short notice. Besides, just because it was a simple idea didn't mean it wasn't a good one. "The matchmaking my friends are doing with me and Destiny is straight from high school and it hasn't stopped them. Besides, like I said before, women go for this kind of thing. Believe me, it will work."

Phil took another swallow of coffee. "I'm not so sure it would work with the women I know."

"Let's hope Destiny and Bertice are not like the other women you know," Daniel said, thinking of Margo, who had initially gotten Phil involved in this scam, but deliberately not throwing her name in the man's face.

Phil gave a wry smile. "Good point, well stated."

Daniel finished off his coffee. "I'll be meeting with Des-tiny sometime this week on another matter. I'll lay the groundwork then. I'll also tell her that I'm trying to get you to come to church. You and Bertice both. That might work even better than a traditional date. Don't make any plans for Sunday. If things work out the way I hope they will, you and Bertice will be joining me and Destiny at church."

"Church?"

"Yes, church," Daniel said. "You do know what that is, right?"

"Funny," Phil said. "It's just been a while since I've been to one. You sure did get hooked up with one quickly. You've been in town only a minute."

Daniel realized he hadn't told Phil much about what he was doing in Atlanta, other than this case. "I'm one of the associate pastors at the church."

Phil's eyes widened. "You're a pastor? When did that happen? You weren't a pastor the first time our paths crossed, were you?"

Daniel shook his head. "A lot's happened since then."

"A whole lot. So you're a pastor and an investigator. What a combination."

"I've given up the investigator title. I'm just helping out on this one last case. I was reluctant at first, but I can see now why I was chosen to work on it. I needed to be here to protect Destiny and Bertice. And you, of course."

"I hear you," Phil said. "But this whole thing gives me a bad feeling in the pit of my stomach. Forgetting about Bertice for a minute, how do you think Destiny is going to feel when she finds out you've been lying to her? Heck, you're a minister. How can you lie to either of them?"

"I'm not lying to them," Daniel said, though he knew

technically he would be lying by omission. "Besides, I'm doing it for their own good. They got themselves into this mess. We're only trying to get them through it with the least amount of scarring."

Phil laughed. "You haven't dealt much with women lately, have you?"

Daniel's thoughts naturally went to Gloria. "No, not much."

"It doesn't sound like you have. This plan of yours could really blow up in our faces."

"Stop being so negative," Daniel said. "You wanted to get closer to Bertice and now you get the chance. Don't think it to death."

Chapter 14

DESTINY WAS LATE LEAVING WORK ON MONDAY, WHICH meant she was going to be late for her five-thirty appointment with the campus career counselor. She checked her watch as she pulled her car into the parking lot of the Career Center. It was already 5:30. She grabbed her purse off the passenger seat, opened the driver's-side door, and got out. As she half-trotted to the Career Center front door, she realized she didn't remember the name of the person she was supposed to meet or the meeting room number. She slowed her pace while she rummaged around in her purse looking for her appointment card. She found it just as she reached the revolving glass entry doors.

She greeted the receptionist and handed her the appointment card. "Sorry I'm late," she added.

"No problem," the young woman said. "You don't meet with Mrs. Robinson until six fifteen."

"I thought my appointment was at five thirty."

"It is, but you're scheduled to complete some computer

assessments before meeting with the counselor." The young woman stood. "If you're ready, I can take you to the computer lab."

Destiny took a deep breath. "I'm as ready as I'll ever be."

"Good," the girl said, "then follow me."

Destiny followed the young woman, who she guessed was a work-study student, down a short hallway to a computer lab with about twenty workstations.

"You can take a seat at any computer," the girl said. "If you press the space bar, a page with the words *Career Assessment* will appear. After that, just follow the on-screen instructions."

Destiny did as the girl directed. "Well, I got the career assessment screen so I guess everything is all right."

The girl nodded. "The on-screen instructions are really clear," she added. "If you have any trouble, just ask me. I'll be back at the front desk. We usually have a student working back here who answers questions but she's out sick today, so I have to cover both the front desk and back here."

"No problem," Destiny said, already making her way through the on-screen instructions.

"Oh yes," the girl added, "these tests are not like entrance exams, so you're free to go to the bathroom or to get some water as needed. When you're finished, you can come back out front and I'll get Mrs. Robinson for you."

When the girl left, Destiny took a deep breath. She didn't like tests because, in the past, she hadn't been good at them. As she read through the items on the career assessment, she relaxed a bit. All she could do was her best, so she committed to doing that. After what seemed a short time, she reached the final screen that signaled the completion of the assessment. "That wasn't so bad," she said aloud, feeling pretty good about what she had just accomplished. It was a start, she thought, as she got up and made her way back to the reception area.

The young girl turned as Destiny made her way back to reception. "Perfect timing," she said. "Mrs. Robinson is ready for you." She pointed down a hallway to the left. "Her office is down that hall, the second door on the right. Good luck!"

"Thanks," she said, finding the girl's enthusiasm contagious. Destiny was beginning to feel a bit excited herself. Who knows? she thought as she made her way down the hall. Maybe she'd enjoy college a lot more the second time around.

Destiny stopped outside Mrs. Robinson's office, took a deep breath to fight back her returning anxiety, and then cleared her throat to make her presence known. She could do this, she told herself.

An older woman with graying hair looked up from the desk where she was seated. "Come on in," the woman said with a smile. "Welcome to Hillman, or maybe I should say welcome back."

"Thank you," Destiny said. Calmed by the older woman's warmth, she took a seat in the chair in front of the woman's desk.

Mrs. Robinson turned her attention to the computer monitor on her desk. "The results from your assessment were sent directly to my computer. Let me print a copy for you and one for me. It will take a couple of minutes. The printouts go down the hall. Somebody will bring them to us when they're ready."

Destiny nodded and back came her anxiety. She reminded herself that she'd taken a career assessment, not an achievement test. There was nothing to worry about.

"I like to use this time before we get the paperwork to get to talk a bit more informally," Mrs. Robertson said. "Are you okay with that?"

The warmth in the woman's smile did it again. Destiny felt herself relax. "It's fine with me."

"Okay, then tell me a little about Destiny."

Destiny shrugged, unsure where to begin. "What do you want to know?"

"You can start by telling me why you want to come back to school and why now?"

Destiny breathed a sigh of relief. She could answer those questions easily. "I'll start with the why now. I have six-year-old twins who are out of town for the summer so I had some free time."

"I gather you're raising your kids alone?"

Destiny shook her head. "I have custody of them but I coparent with their father. They're spending the summer in California with him and his wife."

"Do they go there every summer?"

Destiny shook her head again. "Oh, no, their father lives here in Atlanta. His wife is on a work assignment in L.A. for the summer and they wanted the kids to go with them for a long vacation."

The older woman smiled. "I admire you for letting them

go. I know it has to be hard being without them, especially at that age. The good news is that school will definitely help you fill up some of the time."

"So I've been told," she said.

Mrs. Robinson lifted a questioning brow.

"To be honest, school wasn't high on my list of things to do this summer," Destiny continued, surprising herself at how open she was being with the older woman. "My mother and my friends encouraged me to do it."

"Sounds like you have a strong support network of people who care about you. That's good."

Destiny nodded. She was blessed in that way even though she often took it for granted.

"What was the source of your reluctance about school? Why did you need a little push from your friends and family?"

Destiny gave a sheepish grin. "You've seen my records. I wasn't a very good student when I was here the first time. And I was much younger then. My brain probably worked a lot better back then than it does now."

Mrs. Robinson met her gaze. "Grades tell only a part of the story," she said. "I find that students do well when they're passionate about their subject area, if they see a purpose in the learning. And it's been my experience that older students, like you will be, tend to do well because they come here with a purpose. They're not here because their parents sent them; they're here because they want to be here, because they see the education, the degree, as valuable for their life's plans."

Destiny wasn't sure where school fit in her life's plans. Her mother thought of a degree as a credential to get her to the next level in her job at Marshalls. Her friends, like most people, just knew that people with degrees ended up in better financial condition than people without them.

"What are you passionate about, Destiny?" Mrs. Robinson asked. "What do you enjoy doing?"

Destiny thought for a few long seconds before answering. The older woman's question reminded her of one that Daniel had posed about her calling. She hadn't been able to answer him then and she wasn't sure she'd do any better this time. "Let's see. I enjoy my children. And I actually enjoy my job at Marshalls. A lot."

"What do you do there?"

"I manage the cosmetics department."

"You're a manager and you don't have a degree. That's impressive."

Destiny wasn't sure how that was impressive but she smiled anyway.

"What about the job do you like?"

Destiny thought about the young girl she had taught to apply makeup today. Today had been a very good day at work. "I like making people feel better about themselves. The best days are when somebody comes in for a makeup session who has never used makeup or who rarely uses it. I like the way their eyes light up when I give them the mirror and they look at themselves. That look of joy makes me happy. I feel good knowing I helped put it there."

"And you should feel good about it. You're helping to make a difference in folks' lives. What else do you like about the job? You're a manager. How do you feel about the managerial tasks?"

Destiny shrugged. "To be honest, I do them because I like the manager's paycheck. The enjoyment comes from working with customers. The good thing about my job is that I get to do both. Our department is so small that it wouldn't work any other way."

"You're fortunate, you know. There are a lot of people who find no enjoyment or fulfillment in their work."

"Excuse me," a man's voice said. Destiny turned and saw a young man, about the same age as the receptionist, standing in Mrs. Robinson's doorway. "I have your printouts, Mrs. Robinson."

"Thank you, Larry," she said, extending her hand toward him.

He put the papers in her outstretched hand. "You're welcome," he said, backing out of the room.

Mrs. Robinson glanced down at the papers and then back at Destiny. "Before we get into these assessments, is there anything else that you enjoy or are passionate about?"

Destiny was quick to answer this time. "I also enjoy doing hair," she said. Daniel's words came back to her and she began to wonder if she was identifying her calling.

Mrs. Robinson's eyes seemed to brighten. "You do? What's your specialty?"

"I can do a little bit of everything—chemicals, pressing—but my passion is natural hair styles. I'm pretty good at it, too," she said confidently. Whether she'd be a good student this time around was a big question, but she was confident in her skill with hair and cosmetics.

Mrs. Robinson smiled. "You want to know what I think, Destiny?"

Destiny nodded. She wouldn't be there if she didn't want the woman's opinion.

"I think you're going to be a great student the second time around because we're going to relate your schoolwork to your passion. You're going to be as passionate about school as you are about makeup and hair, or close to it."

Destiny wasn't sure she agreed, but she hoped Mrs. Robinson was right. "You really think so?"

Mrs. Robinson shook her head. "I know so."

A part of Destiny believed her.

Chapter 15

DESTINY WAS SO PSYCHED AFTER MEETING WITH Mrs. Robinson that she didn't want to spend the evening alone. Instead she called Bertice and arranged to meet her at her house for dinner. It didn't matter that she had to pick up takeout from Dreamland Bar-B-Que. Her friend had a lot of talents but cooking wasn't one of them.

"You're a good cook," Bertice said, licking her fingers.

Destiny chuckled. "Yeah, well, I have to give all credit to my American Express card."

Bertice laughed. "You're a trip."

"Hey, I'm about to be a college-educated trip, so treat me with some respect."

Bertice lifted her glass of tea in the air. "That deserves a toast."

Destiny lifted her glass and tapped it against Bertice's.

"To my best friend and soon-to-be college graduate. You go, girl!"

Destiny took a swallow from her glass and then placed it

back on the table. "You have to meet Mrs. Robinson," she told her friend. "She was so motivating. I really felt like she believed in me."

"Why wouldn't she?"

"Yeah, but why would she? All she knows of me is my record and, believe me, it's not that impressive."

"She knows more than that," Bertice said. "She met you, talked to you."

"Well, yeah, still."

"Still nothing," Bertice said. "I don't know when you lost your self-confidence but you need to get it back in a hurry."

"I'm confident about some things," Destiny admitted. "Just not school. When I was talking to Mrs. Robinson and answering all her questions, I realized how much I enjoy my work at the cosmetics counter and how much I enjoy doing hair. I also realized how good I am at it." She shrugged. "I guess I never really thought about it before."

"Well, you need to keep thinking about it. You are good, Destiny. Better than good. Keep listening to Mrs. Robinson. She's good for you."

"I'm beginning to think so. Did I tell you that she owns a salon?"

"A salon? I thought she was a career counselor."

"She is. She's worked at the college for almost twenty years but the salon is her passion. She says it also generates income for her retirement."

"I see why you two hit it off. You have a common interest."

Destiny nodded. She had felt an almost instant connection with the older woman. Her warmth drew Destiny in and made her feel safe. Learning about their shared interest in hair care had solidified that connection. "She got me to thinking about what I want to do with my degree. Maybe I could open a shop one day."

"I don't see why not," Bertice said. "Now you're talking."

"Not right now, of course," Destiny said. "It's just something for me to think about as I go through my classes. Mrs. Robinson said I needed to look at my degree as something that will help me achieve my goals." Destiny chuckled. "But first I have to come up with some goals."

"Sounds like you had a very productive session. I'm glad it's working out for you, Destiny."

"Let's not get too carried away. Classes haven't started yet. I could still flame out."

"Don't say stuff like that. You've got to stay positive."

"You're a good friend, Bertice," Destiny said, remembering Mrs. Robinson's comment about her support system. "I don't say it enough, but I really do appreciate you and our friendship. I can't imagine my life without you and Natalie. You're like the sisters I never had."

"Same here, girlfriend," Bertice said. "You've been there for me, too. We've been there for each other. That's what friends are for."

Destiny chuckled. "Please don't start singing. I love you but you're no Dionne Warwick."

Bertice laughed. "Don't hate."

Destiny got up and got some more potato salad from the bowl on the counter. "You want something?" she asked Bertice.

"Nah, I'm good," she said, licking the barbecue sauce off her fingers. "So when do classes start?"

After Destiny was seated at the table, she said, "Monday of next week. It's perfect timing. Can you believe it?"

"Yeah, I can believe it. It was meant to be."

Destiny was feeling the same way. "Of course, it's too late for me to get financial aid, so I have to pay for the two courses I'm taking."

Bertice chuckled. "Well, since you have three jobs, I guess you can afford to pay."

Destiny shook her head. "Three jobs and school. Can you believe it?"

"I believe it," she said. "But I don't envy you. When does your job at the church start?"

"I'm not sure," Destiny said. "I meet with Natalie and Daniel tomorrow after work. I guess they'll tell me then."

"Girl, you're going to have money and a man. Somebody upstairs must really like you or you're living a charmed life."

"I don't know about all that," she said. Thinking about all the good things happening to her made Destiny want to pinch herself. Her summer had gone from bust to a bevy of riches in no time.

"You just don't know how to accept when good things happen to you," Bertice said. "You'd better learn. You're going to miss out on something special if you keep up the negative thoughts."

"I hear you," Destiny said.

"I'm serious, Destiny," Bertice said. "You have a great life and this summer things are only getting better. You'd better appreciate these days and everything you have."

"I do," Destiny said, and she did. She wasn't taking anything for granted.

"Then stop looking for the negative. Believe you're going to do well in school. Believe Daniel could be the start of something good, a solid relationship. Believe your financial needs are going to be met, and then some, this summer. It's all lining up for you, Destiny. You and the kids will soon be moving into that house. Don't mess it up."

"Okay, Mom."

Bertice chuckled. "At least you didn't frown when you said it this time. What I wouldn't give to be there when you tell your mom about school and the job at the church."

"That can be arranged, you know?"

Bertice shook her head. "I was only kidding. Ms. Patricia likes me better in small doses."

Destiny wished she could tell her friend she was wrong, but she couldn't. Her mother had always had problems with her friendship with Bertice, though she'd become a little more tolerant after learning Bertice had bought a house. She'd had problems with her friendship with Natalie as well but all of those seemed to fade away after Natalie became a preacher's wife. Though she'd deny it until the cows came home, her mother was something of a snob.

Destiny looked at her watch. "I'd better get home," she said, clearing the table of her plate, glass, and utensils. "I want to get there and get settled before the kids call."

"How are they doing?"

"So far, so good. They're enjoying themselves, which is good for them. And they haven't forgotten me, which is good for me."

"There you go again," Bertice said. "Your kids are not going to forget you."

Destiny stood behind the chair where she had been seated. "I know," she said, "but I still worry."

Bertice stood and gave her a hug. "We'll have to work on that worrying another day. Just try to be happy today."

Destiny pulled back. "I'm gonna try," she said. "I'm really gonna try."

Chapter 16

DANIEL WATCHED THE INTERACTION BETWEEN NATalie and Destiny and concluded that their bond was similar to what he shared with Gavin, William, and George. The only wrinkle was the secret he knew Destiny was keeping about her work at HR Solutions. On second thought, maybe that was another similarity. He, William, and George were keeping a secret from Gavin in much the same way Destiny and Bertice were keeping a secret from Natalie. Of course, the men were keeping a secret about a crime they were trying to solve, while the ladies were keeping a secret about a crime they were committing, even if they didn't know it. Significant difference.

Daniel took a quick glance at Destiny out of the corner of his eye. He wasn't quite sure how he was going to pull this off. He was about to perpetrate a fraud on Destiny and he didn't like having to do so. But he didn't see any other way to protect her and Bertice. He wished he did.

Daniel caught the sly glance that Natalie exchanged with

Gavin before his friend cleared his throat. "I think Natalie and I have contributed about as much as we can to this project," he said. "The two of you will have to take it from here."

"You're leaving?" Destiny asked. "We're just getting started."

Natalie stood when her husband did. "We've hashed out your salary and established the general parameters for both programs. You and Daniel can work out the details without us, can't you?" She glanced at her watch. "We had hoped to drop by the hospital and see Deacon Jones before it got too late."

Daniel tried to catch Gavin's eye but his friend wouldn't look at him. Daniel began to wonder if this Deacon Jones even existed. He let it go. A quick glance at Destiny revealed that she wasn't buying the couple's act either.

"You two can handle it," Natalie said, repeating her husband's words before giving Destiny a brief hug. "We have all the confidence in the world in you."

Gavin turned to Daniel. "I know you don't want to hear it, but thanks again for what you're doing. These programs are going to make a difference in a lot of lives."

"Ephesians 3:20," Natalie said. "'Now to him who is able to do immeasurably more than all we ask or imagine, according to his power that is at work within us.'"

"What's that?" Destiny asked.

Natalie turned to her. "It's what this program is going to mean to people and it's the name Daniel and I thought about giving it. What do you think?"

"It works for me," she said.

"Good," Gavin said. "Now all we need is a roll-out schedule, and some materials that describe the programs and its applications."

"That's all?" Daniel said, his words dripping with sarcasm.

Gavin grinned. "I'll see you tomorrow, Daniel." Giving Destiny a hug, he told her, "I'll see you when I see you, which should be pretty often now that you'll be working around here."

Daniel watched as the couple left his office. Destiny's laughter made him turn to her.

"If they weren't so obvious, this wouldn't be so funny," she said. "They are the absolute worst matchmakers ever."

Daniel smiled. "They mean well."

"We have to give them that," she said.

"To be honest," Daniel said, "I appreciate their efforts. If it were not for them, we would not have met. And that would have been a loss for me. A big loss."

Destiny responded to the sincerity she saw in his eyes. "Okay, they did good, but that doesn't mean we have to tell them."

Daniel chuckled. "I'm with you. Gavin's head would be too big to fit through the door."

Destiny laughed with him. "So would Natalie's."

He stopped laughing and sobered. "In all seriousness, how are we going to handle working together and whatever else may be happening between us?"

She met his eyes. "I'm open to suggestions."

"Let's agree that we want to get to know each other. That can start here at work and it can continue after work with our friends."

"Natalie and Gavin?"

He shook his head. "No way," he said. "We're staying clear of them. A buddy of mine is interested in your friend Bertice."

Destiny chuckled. "What? Who? Is it somebody from church?"

Daniel shook his head. "No, he doesn't go here now but I hope he will start soon. He's somebody I met a while back and ran into since I've been here. All he could talk about was this Bertice woman who'd stolen his heart. Even though Bertice is a fairly unique name, when I met your friend at the cancer walk and heard her name, I wasn't sure your Bertice was Phil's Bertice. Turns out she is."

"Talk about a small world," Destiny said. "Who is this friend anyway and how does he know Bertice?"

"His name's Phil Harris. Apparently, he met Bertice through his work. He runs a temp agency downtown, HR Solutions. Do you know it?" he asked, even though he already knew she did. For some reason, her answer was important to him.

She nodded. "I've heard of it and him, too. In fact, Bertice recently introduced me to him. How do you know Phil?"

"I met him several years ago in my old job," he said, pleased she hadn't lied about knowing Phil. He wanted his instincts about her to be right. He much preferred to think of her as a needy person who'd gotten caught up in a scam, rather than as a greedy person who'd been ensnared by her own greed. For him, intent made all the difference. "I wouldn't say that Phil and I are close friends but our lives seem to keep crossing."

She looked up at him. "And Phil has this thing for Bertice?"

He nodded. "He's got it bad."

She smiled. "I'm not surprised. I thought I detected some heat between them when she introduced us, but so much was going on that I forgot to follow up with Bertice about it. I can't believe my friend has been keeping this a secret."

"She doesn't know how Phil feels. I know he hasn't told her."

Destiny began to laugh. "So you're telling me that Phil has a crush on Bertice?"

He nodded, though she made the idea sound as high school as Phil had told him it was. He hoped she wasn't about to squash it before giving it a chance. He really didn't have a backup plan if this one didn't work.

"Phil has a crush on Bertice," she repeated. "I can't wait to tell her."

"Hold on," Daniel said. "Let's not get ahead of ourselves. Has she said anything about him?"

"Not to me," she said. "Like I said, sparks were flying between them when she introduced us, but that's all."

"If she introduced you to him, she must be interested in him, right?"

Destiny lifted her shoulders in a slight shrug. "All I know is that he's helped her out with some part-time work in the past and she thought he might be able to help me out this summer."

"Was he?"

She nodded. "Yes, he was able to find something that paid well and didn't conflict with my day job. And it won't interfere with my work here at the church either."

"I just counted three jobs. When are you going to sleep?"

She chuckled. "It's not that bad. The job and the HR Solutions job are very flexible with working hours. That's the only reason I'm able to handle the three jobs."

"Okay," he said. "I can see how you can handle three jobs, but why would you want to? That's a lot."

"I have some big goals this summer and I need money to achieve them. It's that simple."

Daniel waited for her to tell him what her goals were. When she didn't, he changed the subject. "Well, it looks like God worked it out for you."

"He definitely did. I had another well-paying part-time job lined up at the beginning of the summer but the offer was rescinded about a week before the job was to start. I thought my plans were going to die, but I've been given a second chance to make them come true. I'm more than blessed."

"That you are," he said. "That's the way I feel about this project. I didn't come to Atlanta with a plan to start these programs, but I believe God knew we'd be doing them. It was all part of his plan."

"Is this matchmaking project of yours also part of a plan?"

Daniel chuckled. Sensing that she wanted to change the subject, he asked, "How about it? Do you think Bertice will go out with Phil?"

"I can't answer for her. He'll have to ask."

Daniel tapped her on the shoulder. "Have a heart. Phil's sorta nervous about it. What if the four of us got together and did something? That way, it wouldn't be a big deal. Just four friends having a nice night out together. If something develops between them, so be it. If it doesn't, well, that's okay, too." Daniel realized his words also applied to him and Destiny. The light in her eyes told him she saw the connection as well.

"I'm game," she said, after thinking about it. "But it'll have to be on Saturday or Sunday. With work and school, my weekdays are booked solid."

"School?"

She nodded. "Yes, school."

He grinned. "You really are a wonder woman, aren't you? You may not have any time for going out." Shaking his head, he said, "Your schedule is fine with me. Let's try for lunch on Sunday, after church. That way I can kill two birds with one stone. I've been trying to get Phil to come to church; I think I've found the appropriate inducement. If Bertice will come, he'll come too."

"I'm not sure," Destiny said. "All I can do is ask her. She doesn't attend as regularly now as she did a few years ago."

"What happened to make her stop coming?"

"What makes you think something happened?"

"There's usually a reason folks stop attending church."

She looked at him as though she were debating what to tell him. "Well, she has her reasons, but it's time for her to put them aside. This double-date idea might be a good thing after all."

Daniel put his hand to chest. "I can't believe you doubted my idea."

She smiled. "It's just that I know you don't have the best role models when it comes to matchmaking."

He smiled back, knowing she was talking about Gavin

and Natalie. "The good news is that we can't be worse at it than they are. So are you willing to help get the two love-birds together?"

She nodded. "I'm in. It's about time Bertice came back to church anyway."

"Good," Daniel said. "Now that we've got that settled, how about we finish up the plans for these programs."

She nodded. "Sounds good to me. I just want to agree with Gavin and say again how great it is of you to do this."

"It's not me," he said. "It's all Gloria. It's what she would want."

"I think she's looking down from heaven with a smile on her face."

"I hope so," he said, thinking of the first time Gloria had come into his office at GDW Investigations for help with a financial adviser who had conned her nonprofit out of a hundred thousand dollars. Her visit had changed the trajectory of his life in ways he could not have imagined when he first met her.

"I promise you I'll do everything in my power to see that these programs live up to her memory," Destiny said, as if sensing how much he loved his wife and wanted to honor her. "She'll be proud of the work the money is doing."

"Thank you," he said, "for understanding."

She nodded. "I do have a question though."

Daniel braced himself for a question about Gloria or their marriage.

"Which program do you want to start with—the small business development one or the personal finances one?"

He relaxed at the softball question. "Any chance we could launch them around the same time? If you're up for it, I can take the lead on the small business development one and you can take the lead on the personal finances one."

Destiny wasn't sure she was the right person to take the lead on anything related to personal finances, but she guessed she was better equipped for that one than she was for the small business development one. "No problem. I have all the notes from our meeting with Gavin and Natalie. I'll sort those out and e-mail them to you by tomorrow. When should we plan to meet again?"

"We each have a lot of legwork to do, so let's say next week. You're welcome to come here to the office to work anytime you like. We don't have any extra space but I'm willing to share mine. I've asked Gavin about putting a second desk in here and he plans to get it done by next week. Until then, we can share my desk."

Destiny began shaking her head. "I don't want to put you out."

"You're not putting me out," he said. "For now, this office is the home base for the two programs, so this is your space as much as it's mine. If we find sharing doesn't work, we'll come up with another option, but for right now, let's just go with it. Okay?"

"But it's your space," she said again.

He put his hands on her shoulders and smiled down at her. "It's our space now. I want to hear you say it."

She smiled back. "You win. It's our space now."

Chapter 17

DESTINY CHECKED HER BANK BALANCE ONLINE AT THE kitchen table while she waited for her kids' nightly call. She couldn't help but feel some relief at the numbers. Her check from Marshalls had been deposited, of course. She'd gotten a totally unexpected deposit from Faith Community even though she hadn't yet worked a full week. That had to be Natalie's doing. She'd have to thank her friend for looking out for her. And her first deposits from the HR Solutions work had been made. Though those deposits caused a hefty increase in her balance, she felt a little guilty at the small amount of work she had done to earn them. She'd filled out ten surveys, each taking less than an hour, and gotten ten checks. Upon getting the checks, all she'd had to do was keep 10 percent of the money and forward the balance to the HR Solutions account number Phil had given her. The old adage, *If it's too good to be true, it probably is,* rang in her ears, but she pushed it away. She was giving up the negative and focusing on the positive. This job was a gift from God and she'd continue to treat it that way.

The sound of her doorbell interrupted her thoughts. "Who could that be?" she asked herself as she got up and headed for her front door.

When she peeked through the side curtains, she saw her mother standing outside. With a sigh, she opened the door. "Hi, Mom," she said. "What brings you by?"

Patricia Madison walked fully into the house. "It's good to see you, too, sweetheart."

"I'm glad to see you, Mom," Destiny said, following her mother back to the kitchen. "I'm just surprised at seeing you so late."

"It's not that late," her mother said. "I had choir practice tonight. Don't you remember?"

Destiny did remember, but that still didn't explain her mother's presence.

"I hope I didn't interrupt anything," her mother said, looking at the papers spread out on the table. "What were you doing?"

Destiny quickly walked around her mother, gathered up the papers, and moved them away from the older woman's prying eyes. "I was catching up on bills."

Her mother pulled out a chair and sat at the table. "Where are your manners, Destiny? You haven't even offered me anything to drink."

Destiny rolled her eyes as she headed toward the kitchen. "What do you want? I have diet soda and tea."

"Tea, please," her mother called out.

Destiny brought her mother the tea and then sat at the table across from her. "You still haven't told me what brings you by."

Her mother took a long swallow of tea. "That's good," she said. "Exactly what I needed."

"Mom!"

Her mother looked at her. "What's your problem, Destiny? Do I really need a reason to visit my only daughter? Maybe I should have called first. Are you trying to rush me off? Do you have a date or something?"

Destiny rolled her eyes. "I'm not trying to rush you off and I don't have a date."

"Well, how am I supposed to know? I haven't seen you or talked to you since the kids left town. A lot can happen in a month."

Destiny began shaking her head at her mother's exaggeration. "The kids have been gone only a few weeks."

"Three weeks to be exact," her mother said, "though it seems like much longer to me."

"I know," Destiny said. "Kenae and KJ can be a handful when they're around, but this place is too quiet without them. Too quiet, too big, and too empty. I've been trying to keep myself busy so I don't miss them so much. It's not working."

"I know what you mean," her mother said. "I miss those little rascals, too. And you becoming a stranger has not helped."

"I'm sorry, Mom," she said. "I'll do better. I promise."

"I hope so," her mother said, running her finger down the

side of her glass. "I hate hearing news about my daughter secondhand."

Now they were getting to the real reason for her mother's visit. "What are you talking about? What news have you heard?"

Her mother shrugged. "Oh, this and that."

Destiny fought hard to keep from rolling her eyes again. She didn't want to play games with her mother. She'd tell her what she wanted to hear and let her gloat. "You must have heard that I'm back in school."

Her mother looked up at her, eyes full of surprise. "School? You're back in school? That's great, Destiny. You should have told me." She reached out and covered Destiny's hand with her own. "I'm so proud of you."

Destiny took little joy in her mother's praise for she knew all too well how fleeting it was. "There's nothing to be proud of yet," she said. "Classes don't start until Monday."

Her mother pulled her hand back. "That doesn't matter. The important thing is that you took the initiative and enrolled. This is a great move for you. Things are really shaping up for you on all fronts."

"All fronts?" Destiny asked, wondering who had been talking to her mother about her and what they had been saying. "What are you talking about?"

Her mother smiled. "Your going back to school is great news. A little bird told me that something else good was happening for you. I don't know why you're being so close-mouthed about it."

Destiny saw no use holding out on her mother. Experience told her the older woman would win. "You must have heard about my job at Faith Community."

Her mother's eyes widened and again Destiny saw surprise in them. "Job?"

Destiny nodded. "It's been a little over a week now. I'm planning and administering two new church programs."

"This is a paying job?"

Destiny smiled. "Yes, Mom, it's a paying job. A paying part-time job."

"Which is about all you can handle with school and your day job. I must say I'm impressed, Destiny. You're really making the most of your summer without the kids."

"I'm just trying to keep busy."

Her mother shook her head. "You're doing more than that," she said. "You're taking charge of your life, making moves that will positively affect your future and the future of your kids. They're going to be as proud of you as I am. You just wait and see."

"Well," Destiny said, uncomfortable with her mother's praise, "I may not have to wait long. I'm going to treat myself to a long weekend trip to visit the kids in a few weeks. I'd love to stay longer, but my summer schedule won't allow it."

"What a great idea! It's going to be hard going through the entire summer without seeing them. I just may join you on this trip. Would you mind?"

Destiny hadn't thought of her mom joining her but she couldn't tell the woman she couldn't come. "Of course, you're welcome to go with me, Mom. The kids will love to see you."

"And I can help with expenses."

"You don't have to do that," Destiny said. "I had planned to cover the trip myself. I have it all budgeted. Your going won't add that much. I can cover you."

Her mother began shaking her head. "I'm going to pay my own way, Destiny. If you have extra money, spend it on gifts for the kids or use it to stay in California longer. It's up to you."

Destiny considered her mother's offer. She would be crazy to turn it down. "Thanks, Mom," she said.

"Don't thank me," the older woman said. "I should be thanking you. The summer was looking pretty bleak without the kids and with seeing you so little. Now I have something to look forward to."

"Just don't mention it to the kids when you talk to them. I want the visit to be a surprise."

Her mother nodded. "Have you told Kenneth and Mary Margaret that you plan to come? Have you agreed on a date?"

"No," Destiny said. "I wanted to make sure my money was right first."

"Well, let me know as soon as you decide on dates. My summer is wide open," her mother said. "Another perk of being a teacher. It's a great field for someone with children. It's still not too late for you to think about joining the teaching ranks."

Destiny didn't bother to respond to that statement since she'd made her feelings clear on the matter several times before. "School and my job at the church were surprises to you, so what did your little birdie tell you about me?"

Her mother smiled. "What you told me is better than the gossip I heard, so let's just forget it."

Before Destiny could respond, her cell phone rang. Looking down at the phone, she said, "It's the kids." Then she handed the phone to her mother. "You answer it. They'll be surprised to hear your voice."

Smiling, her mother reached for the phone.

Destiny sat back and listened while her mom spoke first to KJ. She appreciated the easy way her mother had with her children. She wished the relationship she had with her mother was as positive as the one her children had.

Chapter 18

WE HAVE TO HAVE A REAL LADIES' NIGHT OUT ONE DAY soon," Natalie said as Destiny twisted her hair.

"Sounds like a plan to me," Destiny said.

"I'm all for that," Bertice said. "I'm just surprised you two sticks in the mud are up for it."

Natalie rolled her eyes. "Just because we don't want to go clubbing every weekend does not make us sticks in the mud."

"Well," Bertice said, "I don't consider going to Red Lobster a real ladies' night out."

Destiny chuckled. "I don't know, Bertice. Red Lobster sounds pretty good to me. An exciting night out for me is any night I don't have to cook." She turned to Natalie. "Maybe we are sticks in the mud."

As Destiny and Natalie laughed, Bertice began shaking her head. "You two are pitiful. When did you lose your interest in fun?"

"I haven't lost mine," Natalie said.

"I lost mine soon after giving birth to the twins. Raising two kids slows you down some."

Bertice threw her hands in the air. "I give up. You two are hopeless. But since I love you, I'll go for a group meal. But Red Lobster is out. We're going to that new place downtown, Five."

Natalie chuckled. "Gavin took me there a couple of weeks ago. I guess I'm not such a stick in the mud after all."

"Okay, smarty-pants," Bertice said. "I'll have to find another place. If we're going to do a ladies' night out, we have to do something that's new for all of us. When are we having this evening of female bonding and adult fun, anyway?"

"With school and work, weekends are best for me," Destiny said.

"Gavin has a speaking engagement in Cincinnati on Sunday so we'll be out of town this weekend," Natalie said. "How about one day next weekend?"

"Sounds good to me," Destiny said. She turned to Bertice.

"I'll clear my calendar," Bertice said. "Unlike you two, I prioritize my girlfriend time."

"Please," Natalie said, "you just don't have a date that weekend."

"You got me," Bertice said. "My social life has slowed down a bit recently. Too bad I don't have a friend trying to set me up."

"Oh no you don't," Natalie said. "It's not like I haven't tried before."

As her friends bantered, Destiny realized she had the perfect opening to tell Bertice about Phil's feelings for her. She passed on it though because she preferred to speak with Bertice when they were alone, after Natalie had gone. She didn't want to give her friend any more matchmaking ideas and she didn't want to discuss the connection between her, Bertice, Daniel, and Phil. Keeping the secret about her work at HR Solutions from her friend was making her feel more uncomfortable each day. She really didn't like hiding things from Natalie. Shaking off her discomfort, she handed Natalie a mirror and said, "I'm done."

Taking the mirror, Natalie said, "I don't have to look. I know you did a good job. You always do." She looked anyway. "You hooked me up, girlfriend. Just like always."

"I'm glad you like it," Destiny said.

"Like it? I love it. You're so good at this, Destiny. It's a gift."

"According to Mrs. Robinson, doing hair is my passion."

"Who's Mrs. Robinson?" Natalie asked.

"The career counselor she talked to at the college," Bertice offered.

"We need that ladies' night out more than I realized," Natalie said. "We have a lot of catching up to do. So school is going well?"

Destiny nodded. "Let's just say the meeting with Mrs. Robinson got things off on the right foot."

"She and Destiny are kindred spirits," Bertice said.

"How's that?" Natalie asked.

Destiny glared at Bertice, who just shrugged her shoulders. "She owns a salon," Destiny explained.

"I think Destiny wants to be her when she grows up," Bertice said.

Destiny shot another glance at her friend. Bertice was right though. The thought of owning her own shop like Mrs. Robinson had crossed her mind. That was way down the line though.

"Good for you," Natalie said. "You're really good at what you do, Destiny. There's nothing wrong with turning it into a real business. Who knows? You could be the next Madame C. J. Walker."

Destiny chuckled. Her friends didn't know it but Madame C. J. Walker, the orphaned daughter of slaves who became the first black millionaire, was one of her idols. Marshalls had given away copies of *On Her Own Ground*, her biography done by her great-great-granddaughter, as part of a cosmetics promotion during Black History Month a few years ago. Destiny had read the book several times, developing a strong affinity for the woman who shared her belief in the importance of pride in appearance. Madame Walker had turned her passion into one of the largest black-owned manufacturing companies in the world. While Destiny admired her, it never occurred to her that she could be her.

"Now you're talking," Bertice was saying. "Just don't forget your friends when you become rich and famous. We'll put you in charge of all ladies' nights out. For our first trip, you can fly us to France, first class of course, for real French food."

Natalie gave Bertice that "Not now" look before turning to Destiny. "I'm serious, Destiny," she said. "You should talk to Daniel about opening a salon. He has a lot of experience with small business start-ups. Heck, you should even consider applying to the church's small business development program." She winked. "I'm sure you'd get in since you have the inside track."

"Slow down, Natalie," Destiny said. "I'm not ready to open a salon."

"Not today," Natalie said. "But it's never too early to start learning and preparing. You know, I thought you and Daniel could be a love match but maybe God had a different idea. Maybe he and Mrs. Robinson were brought into your life to serve as mentors."

"Now you're reaching," Destiny said, though the idea of Mrs. Robinson as her mentor did appeal to her. She wanted more than mentorship from Daniel.

"Don't do that, Destiny," Natalie said. "I'm not reaching. Look, you go back to school and your counselor tells you to follow your passion. Then you learn she shares that passion and owns a salon. Then you end up working part-time at the church with a man who not only built his own successful business but who is also starting a small business development program to help others start businesses. All of that is more than coincidence."

"She may be right," Bertice said. "A lot of things are lining up for you this summer."

Destiny wondered if her friends were right. Were all the things happening to her this summer—the kids going away, Kenneth stopping the child-support payments, going back to school, and the job at the church—God at work in her life? And where did HR Solutions fit? Was that also part of God's plan? "Well, first things first," she said, pushing the questions aside. "Let me make it through these summer classes before I become a business mogul."

Natalie chuckled. "Okay, I hear you," she said. "But I'm going to nag you about it. I don't want you to miss out on your blessing."

"I won't nag you," Bertice added. "I'll just keep reminding you of how much I'd like to have a rich and famous friend. I really do want to go to France."

"France will be first on my list," Destiny deadpanned. She really didn't know how else to respond. She looked at her friends and realized again how blessed she was to have them in her life. She felt the flutter of excitement bubbling in her stomach at the thought of someday owning her own salon. Was it possible? Could she really do it? The smiling faces of her two friends told her that they believed she could.

Looking at her watch, Natalie got up. "I've got to run," she said. "Gavin and I are going to a reception for one of his friends." She leaned over and pressed a kiss against Destiny's cheek. "Thanks for doing my hair, Madame Destiny."

"Okay, now you're going too far."

Bertice laughed. "No, I like the sound of it. Madame Destiny."

"Madame Destiny," Natalie repeated, "entrepreneur extraordinaire."

"Actually the name sounds more like a fortune-teller,"

Bertice said. "Miss Cleo. Madame Destiny. They both have a certain ring to them."

Natalie brushed a kiss across Bertice's forehead. "You're too much, but I love you anyway."

"Back at you," Bertice said.

"Are you heading out, too?" Natalie asked Bertice as the three of them made their way upstairs from the basement. "I can give you a ride home."

Bertice shook her head. "I'm going to hang out here a little while longer. Destiny, I mean Madame Destiny, will take me home later."

"If you don't stop calling me madame, I'm not taking you anywhere." She turned to Natalie. "Drive safely."

Natalie nodded. "I will."

After Destiny closed the door behind Natalie, Bertice asked, "You don't mind me hanging out with you tonight, do you?"

"You know I don't," Destiny said, turning to follow her friend back downstairs. "I appreciate the company. I told you this place is too quiet without the kids."

"I'm thirsty," Bertice said, walking past the basement stairs and heading toward the kitchen.

Destiny followed her friend. When they reached the kitchen, she took a seat on one of the bar stools at the counter, while Bertice opened the fridge and grabbed herself a can of diet soda. "Well, just make yourself at home."

"That's what I'm doing," Bertice said, dropping down on the bar stool next to hers. "We really should go out clubbing one night this summer while your kids are away. Don't you want to let your hair down and have some fun?"

Destiny grinned at her friend, seeing another opening to bring up Phil. "That may be a good idea."

Bertice's eyes widened. "You're really going clubbing with me? Don't tease me."

"A low-key club could work."

"We're on," Bertice said. "We're going to have a great time."

"Somebody wants to come with us."

"Who?" Bertice asked. "I know you don't mean Natalie. No way is she going clubbing with us or anyone else for that matter."

Destiny shook her head. "Daniel."

Bertice's eyes widened. "Daniel? He asked you out? Why didn't you tell Natalie? She'd be over the moon to know that her matchmaking efforts were paying off."

"Hold on a minute. He did more than ask me out."

"What? I don't understand."

"He asked us out."

Bertice scrunched up her nose. "He wants to go out with both of us? The guy is sounding kinda freaky. I knew there was a reason that pastors as dates made me uncomfortable. I can't believe you're going along with the idea."

Destiny began shaking her head. She was making a mess of things. "Daniel doesn't want to go out with both of us. He wants to go out with me and Phil wants to go out with you. He wants us to double-date."

"Phil? A double date? What are you talking about?"

"Daniel says that Phil has a crush on you."

"Crush? We're not in high school, Destiny."

"Well, let's just say Phil is very attracted to you and he wants to take you out."

"He hasn't asked me."

"Daniel says he's really shy."

"He doesn't seem shy to me."

Destiny agreed. "After all that flirting you two were doing, I didn't think he was shy either."

Bertice waved her off. "Oh please, that meant nothing. Phil flirts like that with every woman he meets."

"Well, maybe it's you who makes him feel shy."

Bertice eyed her skeptically. "Are you sure this isn't just a slick way for Daniel to get you to go out with him?"

"Why would he go to such lengths?" Destiny asked, though the thought had briefly crossed her mind.

Bertice inclined her head toward the door. "Because of that woman who just left your house."

Destiny shook her head. Subterfuge wasn't Daniel's style. "I don't think so. I really do think this is about Phil."

Bertice smiled, showing off her pearly white teeth. Then she rubbed her palms together. "All right then. Why don't we make a little wager? If Daniel is interested in you, I'll treat you to dinner on our ladies' night out. If Phil is interested in me, then you can treat me. Deal?"

Destiny nodded. "How would we settle this wager?"

"Like grown-ups," Bertice said with a smirk. "I'll call Phil and see if he wants to go out."

"Just like that?"

"Just like that. I'm not much for double-dating, to be honest. If Phil wants to take me out, then he can take me out."

"I guess that's easy enough, though Daniel was thinking of us going to lunch after attending church together."

"I'll bet he was," Bertice said. "No, I'll handle Phil on my own. And since he wants to impress me, he'll be open to answering any questions I have about you and Daniel."

"There is no me and Daniel." Yet, she added silently.

Bertice wagged her finger at Destiny. "But there could be. Let me see what I can find out from Phil."

Chapter 19

DESTINY SMILED AS SHE LOOKED AT THE YOUNG WOMAN, Leslie, seated on the stool in front of her. "So what do you think?" she asked.

"Is it really me?" Leslie asked, looking up at Destiny with wide eyes.

Destiny nodded. "It's really you."

Leslie looked back at her reflection in the mirror. "It is me, isn't it?"

Destiny's heart filled. These were the moments that made her job so much more than a job. Leslie had called a week or so ago saying she needed a makeover because she had to have some professional photographs taken. She was a first-time author and her publisher wanted a picture for the back cover of her book. She had been very anxious when she'd sat down. The difference in her now was magical.

Leslie gave a self-deprecating smile. "It's amazing what some face paint will do, isn't it?"

Destiny shook her head, unwilling to feed the woman's

insecurity. "The makeup only brings out what's already there. You were beautiful when you sat down in this chair, Leslie. The makeup just makes that beauty obvious to everybody else."

Leslie didn't look as though she believed her. "I'll never be able to do this on my own," she said.

"Oh yes you will," Destiny said. "I'll make sure of it. If you stop back by here after you have your pictures taken, we'll wash it all off and you can reapply it."

Leslie began shaking her head. "No way am I washing this off today. No way. After I finish having pictures taken, I have to go show my new look to my mom and a few friends. I sure do wish I had somewhere to go tonight." She smiled up at Destiny. "I just may have to invite some folks over for dinner."

Destiny chuckled. She'd seen this kind of excitement before, so she wasn't really surprised. She handed Leslie one of her business cards. "Okay. Call me when you want to come back for a lesson. We can do this multiple times until you get the hang of it."

"Thank you so much, Destiny," she said. "I'm going to have to dedicate my next book to you."

"That's not necessary. I didn't do anything to help with the book."

"You did a lot to help with the author photo that's going to be on the book. I'm probably going to sell a few thousand copies on looks alone."

Destiny could only shake her head. Leslie was getting carried away now. "You're going to sell a lot of books because you're a good writer. You don't have to dedicate your next book to me, just make sure I get a copy of this one."

Leslie slid off her stool. "You'll be one of the first people to get one. I'll autograph it and everything."

"You'd better."

Leslie looked at her watch. "I need to get to that photo session upstairs, but first, why don't you put one of everything you used on my face in a bag for me."

Destiny laughed. "You don't have to buy everything."

"Oh yes I do," Leslie said. "I want to look like this all the time."

Destiny held back her laughter this time. "Maybe not all the time."

Leslie looked at her, a smile tugging at the corners of her lips. "Most of the time?"

"That's more like it," Destiny said, collecting the requested items. After she rang up all the purchases and bagged them, she said, "I have a card on you that I'll keep here at the counter so anytime you need something, I can look at your card and make sure we're consistent with the shades and colors."

Leslie handed Destiny a credit card. "You'll never know how much I appreciate it, Destiny," she said. "Writing a book comes naturally to me. I find it easy to sit around my house and make up characters. How I look really doesn't come into play. But having my picture on a book, going on a book tour, meeting readers, those things are out of my comfort zone. I'll still be self-conscious and nervous but at least I know I'll look good in the process."

"Now that's what I like to hear," Destiny said, tucking the

receipt in the bag and handing it and the credit card back to Leslie. "Here you go."

Leslie glanced at her watch again. "I really do have to go," she said, "but I will call you next week about coming in for a practice session. In the meantime, I'll see what kind of magic I can work up on my own with the goodies you've sold me."

"That's a great idea," Destiny said. "And stop by anytime you're in the mall. You don't need an appointment to visit."

"I'll do it," Leslie said, backing away from the counter. Waving she said, "I'll be back."

Destiny looked after the young woman with a smile on her face.

"So this is what you do every day?"

Destiny turned around and faced the other side of the makeup counter. "Mrs. Robinson?"

The older woman shook her head. "We're not at school," she said. "I'm Annie."

Destiny wasn't sure she'd feel comfortable calling the older woman Annie. Her southern upbringing had been pretty thorough. "I'm surprised to see you," she said. "Are you out shopping today?"

Mrs. Robinson nodded. "And I remembered that you worked here. I decided to drop by and see how you are doing. I hope you don't mind."

"Not at all," Destiny said, feeling the same easy rapport she'd felt when she first met the woman. "Thanks again for helping me get all set up with my courses."

"How are they going?"

"So far, so good. I've only been to the first class for each of them, but I think they're going to be okay. My old brain seems to still be functioning at a high enough level that I can keep up."

Mrs. Robinson eased down on a stool. "Of course you can keep up. You're going to do well. You'll be one of the better students. I can tell."

"You can?" Destiny asked. "How?"

Mrs. Robinson nodded. "I've been watching you."

"You have? When?"

"Just now. I watched you with that young woman." She picked up one of the lipstick samples and, looking in the mirror on the counter, applied some to her lips. "You've got a way with makeup and you also have a way with people. That's a great combination. Have you thought about opening a salon or a beauty spa of your own?"

Destiny's mouth opened but no words came out. Maybe God was trying to tell her something.

"How's that?" Mrs. Robinson asked, looking up at Destiny after rubbing her lips together to smooth out the lipstick.

"That's a good color on you."

Mrs. Robinson looked in the mirror again. "It is, isn't it?" she said. "Why don't you ring me up two tubes?"

"You don't have to buy anything," she said, her thoughts still on the woman's comment about her opening her own salon. First, Natalie and Bertice, and now Mrs. Robinson.

Mrs. Robinson turned to her. "This is a business, Destiny. You always want the customer to buy. Always."

"Always?"

Pulling out her credit card, Mrs. Robinson added, "You

always want to make the sale but you want to make sure the person being sold to is getting what's best for them. So, yes, you want to sell lipstick to everybody but you don't want to sell every shade or color or brand to everybody. The only reason you shouldn't want to make this sale to me is if you don't think the color or shade or brand is good on me. If it is, you make the sale. If it's not, you find the color, shade, and brand that works and you make that sale." She tapped her finger to her temple. "Running a business is not that difficult. Consider that a tip from Salon Basics 101."

Destiny rang up the sale and handed Mrs. Robinson her bag. "Thank you," she said. "For the sale and the tip."

Mrs. Robinson took the bag and handed Destiny a card. "You should drop by my salon one day and see the setup."

"I appreciate the invitation," Destiny said, "but no way am I ready to open a salon."

"You may not be ready today," Mrs. Robinson said, "but who knows about some day in the future. You remind me of me, Destiny," she said. "You see the value in personal grooming, you know that people feel better when they look their best, and you get some level of joy and personal satisfaction in knowing that you've helped somebody put forth their best self. The business plan for my salon started with little more than that."

Things were going too fast for Destiny. She didn't know what to say.

"Just come by the salon one day," Mrs. Robinson said again. "I can already see you as a salon owner but you need to see it for yourself. Will you come by?"

Destiny looked down at the card she'd been handed, and then she looked up again. "I'll come by," she said.

"Saturday?"

Destiny couldn't see a reason why sometime during the day on Saturday wouldn't work. "I'll stop by on Saturday."

"That's great. It'll be hectic but I think you'll like the frenzy."

Chapter 20

DANIEL GLANCED UP FROM STUDYING THE PLAN FOR the financial program that Destiny had provided to him and found her yawning. Her full-time job, school, working with him, and the nonjob she was doing for HR Solutions seemed to be taking a toll.

"Excuse me," she said, covering her mouth.

"Tired?"

She shook her head. "Not really."

"That yawn says otherwise." He tossed the stack of papers he'd been reading on the table. "I know you have a lot on your plate. We don't have to do this today."

"No, today is fine. I was up late last night doing homework." She shrugged. "I'm trying to stay ahead. Completing assignments near the due date got me in trouble the first time I was in school so I'm trying a different strategy."

"Good for you," he said.

She inclined her head toward the papers she had given him. "So what do you think?"

"I think you've been doing more than studying. This is a pretty extensive plan. I really like the idea of using the Dave Ramsey materials."

"You don't think the series will be too long? It shouldn't be a burden for folks to participate."

He shook his head. "I think eight weeks is about right for us. The twelve-week version would be too long. And I like the idea of holding two sessions—one during the day and one in the evening."

She nodded. "I followed the pattern of how Gavin does Bible study. He holds a Wednesday-midday service and a Wednesday-night service. Both have good turnouts, so it seemed we should do the same."

"Great idea. Do you think we should take the same approach with the small business development program?"

She shook her head. "I thought so at first."

"But—"

"The programs are so different. It seems to me that everybody in the church would want to go through the personal finance class, but only select folks would be interested in the small business development class. I was thinking we could have those interested folks complete applications and we'd select a group of twenty to twenty-five for the first class. Instead of arbitrarily picking a day, we'd come up with the day after looking at the availability of the interested folks."

"Makes sense to me," he said. "I've pretty much laid out the curriculum in the materials that I gave you, but I haven't worked on an application."

"No problem," she said. "I can do that. I ran across a good

template for one when I was looking for the personal finance materials. I can pull something together for you by next week."

"Sounds good," he said. "In the meantime, I'd like to get moving with the personal finance class. We're going to need at least two teachers. I'd prefer a man and a woman colead each class."

"A married couple?"

"Maybe one married couple and two singles."

"I like that," she said. "It can be awkward for singles when everything is catered to married couples."

"I know what you mean," he said. "There are probably more of us than there are of them anyway."

She laughed. "Singles united."

Daniel's thoughts went back to Gloria. In all honesty, he'd enjoyed being married much more than he enjoyed being single. Now that he was considered single again, he began to see all the challenges that came with the status. The world seemed to be a much easier place to navigate married than it was single.

"You're thinking about your wife," she said.

Though he knew it wasn't a question, he nodded.

"Did she love you as much as you loved her?"

Though he'd never thought of their love in comparative terms, he knew what he felt for Gloria had been returned, so he nodded.

"Then you're fortunate."

He knew without her saying it that she'd loved before but

that love hadn't been returned. He guessed it was her kids' father but he didn't dare ask. "I was more than fortunate," he said. "I was blessed. Don't think I don't know it."

"She was a lucky woman."

He shook his head. "I was the lucky one."

"Let's just say you two were fortunate enough to love each other."

Since she seemed to have opened the door, he said, "He was a fool."

She looked up at him, eyes wide. "What did you say?"

"The man who didn't love you well was a fool."

She nodded. "Yes," she said. "He was."

Daniel thought he saw another layer to Destiny in those few words. Instead of deflecting his question, she'd been forthright in her answer though it was obvious the topic was still painful for her. Understanding that pain, he moved the conversation back to the work at hand. "Do you have any recommendations for the personal finance workshop leaders?"

"Not really," she said. "Let's open it up to the church and see who's interested. Then we can select the best folks from those who express interest."

"It's going to be a couple of months before we can start on this, isn't it?"

She nodded. "At least. The leaders are going to need training and that's going to take a couple of months."

He frowned. "I had hoped that we could get these programs off the ground quicker. I guess that was wishful thinking."

She smiled at him. "There's nothing wrong with wishful thinking. It just shows how important the programs are to you."

"They are. Money problems can lead people to make bad decisions, decisions that will impact them for a long time," he said, thinking of her and Bertice and the sticky situation they'd gotten themselves into with HR Solutions. "If we can help folks stop the self-inflicted problems, there will be fewer of those bad decisions that wreck lives. Programs like the personal finance class can help with preventing problems in the future, but people also need help getting out of today's financial binds."

"I know," she said.

Daniel couldn't help but wonder if she was thinking about her own situation.

"There is good news though," she continued. "While we're prepping for the personal finance classes, we can start a financial support program, but it's going to be tricky to pull off."

"Tricky? How?"

"Well, how do you decide who gets support and how much that support should be?"

He grinned at her. "I supply the money," he said. "You get to answer those tough questions."

She smiled back. "What if we make it a loan program with a forgiveness option? If grantees attend the personal finance class, their loans will be forgiven. If they don't, they have to repay them or do some in-kind service around the church."

"That sounds good," Daniel said, "but there is no way for

us to make folks actually pay if they don't want to. I don't see myself taking anybody to court for nonpayment."

"Well, they don't have to know that."

He grinned at her again. "Now that's tricky. I like the way you think."

"I told you. These programs are going to make Gloria proud."

"Thank you," he said, appreciating her sensitivity.

After what seemed to be a respectful moment of silence for Gloria, Destiny said, "I figured we'd ask Natalie and Gavin, the deacons, and the Sunday school teachers to let us know of people who need financial help. We'd approach them quietly about the program, without making a big deal of it. I'm thinking something like Oprah's Angel Network but done discreetly. No big announcements. Only the recipients will know."

"You're good at this," he said. "I can tell you've thought a lot about it and I appreciate it. Your management and planning skills are shining through. You must be very good at your job. The next time I'm in the market for cosmetics, I'm coming to your counter." When her eyes widened in surprise, he added, "Of course I remembered what you do for a living. You remember what I do, don't you?"

She smiled. "I didn't have to remember. I see you in your work. You've only heard about mine, and only once. You've never seen me in action."

"Is that an invitation to visit you at work?" he asked, amusement dancing in his eyes. "If it is, I'll definitely take you up on it."

"Then consider yourself invited."

He grinned. "Do I need an appointment?"

They were flirting again, she thought, and she liked it. "Only if you want a makeover."

"Do you think I need one?"

"Are you fishing for compliments?"

He laughed. "You can't fault a brother for trying, can you? You know, we have yet to go on an official date. What's up with that?"

She lifted her shoulders in a slight shrug. "I've been wondering the same thing. I may not date much but, if memory serves me well, typically the man asks the woman out for a specified event at a specified time. I don't recall you doing that."

Enjoying their teasing banter, he said, "Okay, you got me. It's on me. Let's wrap up this business first and then plan our first date. On second thought, since you're the better planner, maybe you should plan it. You really are good at it."

"I'm just glad I'm earning my pay, here and at my day job. You should know that this job really came in handy for me. It's not lost on me that I'm a recipient of your largesse. I know the other recipients will appreciate it as much as I do. I especially appreciate being able to work for the money rather just being given a handout."

Daniel understood then that one reason she'd been so good at planning the programs was because she'd put herself in the place of those he wanted to help. It mattered how gifts were given; it wasn't sufficient to just give them. "You're doing a great job."

She smiled. "It's early."

He didn't return her smile. "I can already see one area where you have to improve."

"Where?" she asked.

"You've got to learn to take a compliment. The next time I say something nice about you, just say thank you."

She smiled. "Yes, sir, boss."

He laughed, glad she was comfortable teasing him. "What's next?" he asked.

"Let's see. I'm pretty clear on what I need to do before we meet again." She listed the tasks they'd agreed needed to be done.

"That's a long list. When do you think you'll have all of that completed?"

"I like the idea of meeting at least once a week," she said. "Even if all I can give you is an update."

"Works for me," he said. "So we'll meet here at the same time next week."

"I'll put it on my calendar."

"Good," he said. "Now that work is out of the way, let's talk about our first official date. Have you had a chance to speak to your friend Bertice?"

She chuckled. "Sure did. She had no idea Phil was interested in her. She just thought he was a big flirt, but I got her to thinking a little differently."

"So, Ms. Expert Planner, when are the four of us getting together and what are we going to do?"

She rested her index finger on her chin. "You haven't spoken to Phil recently, have you?"

He shook his head. "It's been a couple of days."

"Well, Bertice decided to call him. They've already made plans to go out. She couldn't make church on Sunday anyway."

"Oh," he said, wondering why Phil hadn't called to update him. "I didn't know. I'd still like to take you out for lunch after church on Sunday, if you'd like to go."

She nodded. "I'd like to go."

He smiled. "Good. I still don't know that much about the best places to eat in Atlanta, so if you have a place you'd like to go, tell me. I don't even want to ask Gavin and Natalie."

She laughed. "I'm with you on Gavin and Natalie. Let's keep this between us for a while. And I'll think about a good place to eat between now and Sunday."

"Good," he said. "Now I have something to look forward to all week." He wanted to spend time with Destiny. Not only because of her involvement with HR Solutions but also because he enjoyed her company. He had liked her when he first met her at the cookout. Learning about her involvement with HR Solutions had sent up some caution flags, but his subsequent interactions with her had eliminated much of his apprehension. She was easy to talk to and he sensed they shared similar, if not the same, losses in their lives. Yes, Sunday was going to be a good day for him.

Chapter 21

Destiny arrived at Beauty Clips, Annie Robinson's salon, on Saturday morning around ten. The salon was located in a strip mall in South DeKalb not that far from her home. While the strip mall itself was nondescript, the salon had a welcoming exterior and entry. A door with three purple and white hair clips that served as the Beauty Clips logo was set in a wall of windows. Chatter and laughter combined with television voices greeted her when she entered. A young college-age woman with a familiar face greeted her.

"Welcome to Beauty Clips," the girl said. "Do you have an appointment?"

Destiny shook her head. "Mrs. Robinson—I mean Annie—invited me to stop by."

The girl snapped the fingers of her left hand. "I thought I knew you from somewhere. You came by the Career Center a few weeks ago."

Destiny nodded, recognizing her as well. "You're the young lady who helped me get set up on the computers."

"That's me," the girl said. "My name is Laura, by the way."

"Nice to meet you, Laura. I'm Destiny. You're a busy young woman. Two jobs?"

Laura grinned. "I don't consider this work. I enjoy it too much."

"What do you do here?"

"A little bit of everything. Mrs. Robinson is helping me get my cosmetology license."

"And you're in school, too? That's a lot."

"It's like Mrs. Robinson says, idle hands are the devil's workshop." She shrugged. "I like keeping busy."

"Is Mrs. Robinson around?" she asked.

Laura nodded. "Let me go find her. I'll be right back. This place can get crazy."

Destiny took the time alone to study her surroundings. It was a fairly large salon with eight hair stations consisting of a chair and counter, much like the setup she had in her basement, lining one wall. Four hair-washing stations, two pedicure chairs, and two nail stations lined the other. She assumed the hair dryers were in the back since she didn't see any out front. The customer waiting area consisted of about twelve chairs, six along the windowed walls on either side of the door. Evidently, the shop did good business because all the stations had clients and all the chairs in the waiting area were taken.

Destiny was about to sit when Mrs. Robinson called her name. "So how do you like my little shop?"

"I like it," she said, "but I wouldn't call it a *little* shop."

"Believe me," she said, "it's small. I'm trying to decide between finding a new and bigger site or knocking out a wall here and expanding this place. Come and let me show you around."

Destiny followed Annie through the main room and on to the back where, as she suspected, were the hair dryers. There was a row of about ten. What she hadn't expected was the canteen-like area complete with vending machine, table, four chairs, microwave, and a full-size refrigerator. Beyond the canteen were three doors marked LADIES, MEN, and LAUNDRY.

"There's a full-size washer and dryer in the laundry room. It's also where we keep our supplies." She opened the door so Destiny could see inside.

"You won't run out of supplies anytime soon, will you?" Destiny asked, taking in the two walls stacked high with product boxes.

Annie chuckled. "I know I need to get a handle on the inventory but I'd rather have too much than not have something when we need it." She eyed her. "I'll bet you know a lot about managing inventory levels."

"Not as much as you think," Destiny said. "At work, we use this computer system that automatically reorders when our stock reaches a certain level. I don't have to do anything at all. When stock hits those levels, an order is automatically generated. Then like clockwork, each Tuesday afternoon I get a new shipment. All I have to do is shelve it."

"I'm sure there's more to it than that," Annie said. "Running this salon is a lot like running that cosmetics department."

"In theory maybe," Destiny said, "but what you have here is a much bigger operation."

"What do you think of it?"

"I like it. Is it always this busy?"

Annie nodded. "Have a seat," she said, pointing to a chair at the table. She opened the refrigerator. "We have Coke and Diet Coke. Which would you like?"

"Diet Coke."

Annie handed her a can of Diet Coke and sat down in the chair next to her in the canteen. "This place is an investment, but it's also my passion."

Destiny nodded. "Laura told me that you were helping her get her cosmetology license."

"She's a gem. She's working as my apprentice and that's how she's getting the hours necessary for her license."

"You're licensed?"

Annie nodded. "You said that you do hair in your home now. Have you thought about expanding that out to a shop?"

Destiny tilted her head. "Are you offering me a station?"

"I'm trying to gauge your interest. You'd need a license to work here. Do you have one?"

Destiny shook her head. "I've thought about getting one, but never got around to it. Besides, I only do my friends' hair."

"That's what you do now, but you can always branch out."

Destiny thought about everything she had on her plate this summer. "There's no way I can go back for my license now that I'm in school."

"You could do like Laura and apprentice with me."

"Why are you offering to do this?" Destiny asked, overwhelmed by the woman's generosity. Was it too good to be true? She was asking herself that question a lot lately.

Annie shrugged. "Because I like you and I see something in you. And as I said before, I see some of me in you."

"I don't know what to say."

"Don't say anything," Annie said. "Think about it. There really is no rush. I know you have a lot on your mind with school and your job."

"I sure do."

"It seems to me that the only way you could reasonably add something else is if you saw it as complementary. For example, if you're still going to be doing your friends' hair, you could change the location of where you do it so that you can get apprenticeship credit for it. Before you know it, you'll have the hours necessary to become licensed and you'll realize you haven't really done any extra work."

This all still sounded too good to be true to Destiny. "What's the catch?"

"There is no catch. Just an opportunity. No hard feelings if you don't take me up on it. Just promise me you'll think about it."

Destiny nodded, her uncertainty still present. "I'll definitely think about it."

Chapter 22

O KAY, TURN THE SWITCH NOW," PHIL HARRIS SAID.
Sitting in his friend's 2006 red Ford pickup, Daniel did as he was told. Nothing.

"Hold on a minute," Phil said.

Daniel sat waiting for his next instruction. He'd never pegged Phil as a wannabe mechanic and he never would have pegged him as the owner of an old red truck that he obviously loved. The recently upholstered interior and fresh paint job told him so.

"Okay, try it now," Phil said.

Daniel turned the switch and this time the truck started. He leaned out the window to look at his friend, who wore a self-satisfied smile. "Whatever you did worked. You really do know what you're doing."

Phil clapped his hands together. "I told you, man. I know my way around automobiles. Next time you have trouble with your ride, holler at me."

"And you'll fix it for me?"

Phil grinned. "Nah, man, I'll just give you enough information to keep the repair shop from ripping you off." He waved Daniel out of the truck. "Get out and wash up. Those steaks are calling my name."

Daniel turned off the truck and got out. "I hear you," he said, heading toward the grill on the patio to the left of the garage and resuming his primary role of cook. He opened the top of the grill. "These babies are about ready."

Phil walked to the sink in the garage and washed his hands. "I'll get the beans and macaroni salad."

Daniel nodded as he flipped the steaks for the last time. He'd enjoyed his afternoon with Phil so far. It was good to kick back and do man stuff. This time with Phil reminded him of why he'd liked him the first time he met him. Then Phil had been involved in a silly pyramid scheme. Fortunately, GDW Investigations had been able to expose the fraud before he lost everything and caused others to lose everything. Phil was a good guy, Daniel thought. His preference for the quick buck just got him into trouble.

"Here you go," Phil said, returning with two bowls. He placed them on the patio table.

Daniel scooped up the steaks and put them on a platter. He took four potatoes wrapped in foil from the grill and placed them on the platter with the steaks. "You got something to drink?" he asked, putting the platter on the table.

"I'm on it," Phil said, heading toward the refrigerator in the garage. "I've got beer, water, and Coke."

"Coke is fine," he said.

Phil laughed. "I should have known," he said. "The Preacher Man doesn't drink, huh?"

Daniel smirked as he took the offered can of Coke.

Phil laughed again. "I still can't believe you're a preacher. Who goes from private investigator to the pulpit?"

Daniel took a gulp of soda. "Life leads us down unexpected roads," he said, thinking about how Gloria's death had led him to this path.

Phil chugged his beer. "That's some road."

"You've traveled some odd roads yourself."

Phil rubbed his fingers down his can of beer. "You can say that again."

"So how did your date go with Bertice?"

Phil looked up at him. "How'd you know?"

"Destiny told me. I was surprised. Why didn't you tell me? You know this was all part of our plan."

Phil shrugged. "That's why I didn't tell you. I didn't want it to be part of a plan. She's a good woman, Daniel. A special woman."

Daniel shook his head. "You've got it bad."

"And I'm not ashamed to admit it. We really had a good time. I took her to a Braves game. She yelled more than I did. Now that's my kind of woman. Beautiful and loves sports."

Daniel laughed. "You don't ask for much, do you?"

Phil grinned. "Just being honest," he said. "But Bertice is so much more. I can't explain it. We just have this connection."

Daniel understood. He'd shared a special connection with

Gloria. With that thought, Destiny's image flashed in his mind.

Phil took a steak and a potato off the platter and put it on his plate. Then he added beans and macaroni salad. "Bertice had quite a bit to say about you and your love life."

Daniel stopped in the middle of cutting his steak. "What?"

"You heard me," Phil said. "She told me about you and her friend Destiny. She filled in the blanks that you failed to mention."

"What did she tell you?"

Phil laughed. "When Destiny first told her that I told you I was interested in her, she thought it was a ruse for you to get next to Destiny." He shot Daniel a knowing glance. "Was it?"

"It was a ruse," Daniel said, not sure he wanted to share his feelings about Destiny with Phil. "Don't forget we're keeping an eye on these two women so they don't get in too much trouble. We need to know the minute any evidence of identity theft occurs."

"Maybe they won't be chosen," Phil said. "Bertice has been involved for more than a year and she hasn't had any backlash like that."

Daniel gulped another swallow of soda. "You're probably right about Bertice. Evidently, she didn't meet the screening requirements for that part of the scam."

"Screening requirements?"

"Yeah," Daniel said. "Our technical staff is putting together a profile of who's selected. Bertice doesn't meet the profile."

"Thank God for that," Phil said.

"Not so fast," he added. "It looks like Destiny does."

"Damn," Phil said.

Daniel felt the same way. "That doesn't mean she will be chosen. It just means she meets the profile we've developed. I hope she isn't."

"We should warn her."

Daniel shook his head. "We can't," he said, even though he wanted to put her on alert. "We just have to be there if she's chosen."

"I still don't like it, man."

Daniel glared at him.

"I know," Phil said. "It's my fault. I got them into this. If I could do it all over, I wouldn't get involved and I definitely wouldn't get Bertice involved."

"Do you really mean that?" Daniel asked, unable to keep his skepticism out of his voice. He'd heard this from Phil before.

"You don't believe me?"

"I believed you when you told me that after the pyramid scheme, but here we are. You've got to stop putting yourself in these situations, Phil. You're going to end up in trouble that you can't easily get out of if you don't. It's only a matter of time."

"I know, man," Phil said. "I'm serious this time. I'm going to stay on the straight and narrow."

Daniel wanted to believe the man, but he knew old habits were hard to break. "You like living on the edge," he said, thinking the man also liked shortcuts but deciding not to use those words. "You need to find another outlet for that energy."

Phil grinned. "Bertice could be that outlet."

Daniel shook his head. "A woman got you into this situation. It's probably not a good idea to look to a woman as your way out. No, you need something that comes from you, not something that comes to you."

Phil frowned. "I don't know what you mean."

Rather than explain it, Daniel decided to give an example. "We're doing a personal finance workshop at church. As part of that we're going to talk about folks finding ways to supplement their incomes. You can be a speaker for us."

"Me, speaking at a church?"

Daniel laughed. "Yes, you," he said. "The church is not going to bite you."

"I don't know, Daniel," Phil said. "Given what I've done, I'd feel like a fraud."

Daniel was pleased that Phil had genuine remorse for the situation he'd put himself in. "It'll be a few months in the future before we'll need you. Hopefully, by then this case will be wrapped up and you can also talk about the pitfalls in trying to take shortcuts."

"You're not asking much, are you?"

"When this is over, you'll need to do something to put it behind you. You strike me as the kind of man who needs to make amends when he does wrong. Sharing with the folks in this program can be a part of you making amends."

"I'll think about it," Phil said.

"That's enough," Daniel said, "for now. And if you really

want a relationship with Bertice when this is over, think what this gesture will mean to her. It may go a long way to showing her that you are truly sorry for the harm you caused."

"I said I'd think about it," Phil said.

Daniel sensed his friend's discomfort. On second thought, maybe Bertice *was* the woman who could change him.

Chapter 23

"Stop!'" Destiny sang along with Natalie and Bertice as they ended "Stop! In the Name of Love" by the Supremes, the last of the three karaoke songs they'd sung tonight.

The audience clamored for one more, but Destiny looked at her two friends standing on the karaoke stage and shook her head as they did. Three was their limit. "That's it for us," Natalie said, continuing her Diana Ross role and speaking for the group. "Thanks, everybody."

The three women made it back to their table amid the applause from the gathering. Before they reached their seats, another would-be crooner took the stage. "Now that was fun," Natalie said, once they were seated.

"It was," Bertice said. "I had my doubts though. Karaoke was not exactly what I was thinking about for a ladies' night out, but it was much better than our original plan to only have dinner."

Destiny leaned into Bertice's shoulder. "Admit it," she said. "You were all over those songs."

"Yeah," Natalie said. "You sang 'Survivor' like you thought you were Beyoncé getting ready to leave Destiny's Child."

Destiny laughed. "Yeah, girl, you belted that one out."

"You can't talk about me," Bertice said. "You thought you were T-Boz on 'Ain't 2 Proud 2 Beg.'"

"What can I say," Natalie said, blowing on her fingers as though she were at a craps table in Vegas. "I got skills."

All three women laughed.

"Gavin married you for your singing voice," Bertice teased. "You know all first ladies have to be able to belt out a gospel tune at the drop of a hat."

"Please," Natalie said. "Gavin married me for more than my singing."

"Tell it," Destiny said.

"No, you didn't go there," Bertice said. "This first lady is coming out of her bag, or should I say, her pulpit."

"Just telling it like it is," Natalie said, not backing off.

"Excuse me, ladies."

Destiny looked up to see the waitress standing at their table.

The young woman inclined her head toward the bar. "Those guys over there would like to buy your next round. What are you having?"

Destiny looked at her friends.

"I'm married," Natalie said, lifting up her ring finger so the men could see it. "It's up to you two."

Destiny and Bertice shared a knowing look. "Tell them

thanks, but we're fine," Bertice said. She lifted her glass toward the men and gave them a smile. Destiny did the same.

"Well, well," Natalie said. "Destiny held true to form, but you surprised me, Bertice. You were supposed to take that free drink."

"Didn't want to give the guy false hope."

Natalie leaned in. "Spill," she said. "You've been holding out on us. You're seeing somebody, aren't you?"

After taking a sip from her soda, Bertice said, "Maybe, maybe not."

"Don't be coy, Bertice," Natalie said. "It's too out of character."

"Give her a break, Natalie," Destiny said, guessing Phil Harris was the man who had changed Bertice's tune. She also guessed Bertice didn't want to discuss him because it might lead to a discussion of their work at HR Solutions, which they still weren't ready to tell Natalie about.

Natalie turned to Destiny with a teasing glint in her eyes. "Okay, we can talk about you then. What's up with you and Daniel?"

Bertice laughed.

Destiny rolled her eyes.

Natalie lifted her arms in frustration. "Well, somebody has to tell me something. Or do I need to share some of my marital wisdom with you?"

"Please don't," Bertice said, holding up her palm toward Natalie. She sighed. "I've started seeing somebody."

Natalie leaned forward. "Do I know him?"

Bertice shook her head. "I don't think so, but Daniel does."

Natalie sat back. "Oh. Now that is interesting. I see some double-dating possibilities here. So who is he and have you asked him anything about Daniel and Destiny?"

"You never give up, do you?" Destiny asked Natalie.

Natalie waved her off. "Hush," she said. "I'm talking to Bertice."

Destiny listened as Bertice told Natalie a little about Phil Harris, praying silently she didn't give her too much information. As she did, she realized the energy involved in keeping her HR Solutions gig a secret. Was it worth it? It might be easier just to tell Natalie everything and try to ease any concerns she might have.

"So have you asked him about Daniel and Destiny?"

Bertice giggled. "You know I have, but it turns out I knew more than he did. I ending up piquing his interest though, so he said he'd feel Daniel out for me."

"Good," Natalie said. She sat back in her chair and looked at her friends. "My babies are growing up," she said.

"Please," Destiny said.

"Let me have my moment," Natalie said. "If you act right, we could have a couples' night out with the three of us. Wouldn't that be fun?"

"Hold on, Miss Matchmaker," Bertice said. "I don't want to scare the man off. Let me get to know him a bit more first before I bring him out for your inspection."

"He'll pass, won't he?"

Bertice nodded. "I think so."

Destiny wasn't so sure.

"He'd better," Natalie said. "My friends deserve only the

best." She glanced at Destiny. "The best has been served to you on a platter. You'd better take him before someone else does."

Destiny laughed. "You're crazy, Natalie. You know that, right? You're talking about the man like he's an item on a buffet table."

"Well," Natalie said, "I've heard some women around the church describe him as delicious. Maybe he's an item on a dessert bar."

"I ought to tell Daniel how you talk about him," Destiny said.

"Please," Natalie said. "He knows how the women talk about him. Gavin makes sure he does."

"Men can be such gossips," Bertice said.

"Hey, that's my husband you're talking about. He's not a gossip. I prefer to think of him as an information provider."

"Yeah, whatever," Bertice said. "He's still a gossip."

When Destiny started laughing, Natalie said, "Don't laugh yet, missy. You still haven't answered my question about you and Daniel."

"There's nothing to tell," Destiny said, deciding not to tell her friend about her and Daniel's plans for lunch on Sunday. Doing so would be like giving red meat to a starving dog.

"Nothing to tell yet," Natalie clarified. "So how's school coming? You can tell me about that, can't you?"

Destiny rubbed her hands up and down her glass of soda. "It's coming a lot better than I thought. I may turn out to be a good student after all."

Natalie bumped her shoulder into Destiny's. "Just say it, Destiny. You like school. Come on, it's not hard to say."

Destiny bumped her friend back. "Okay, I like it, or it looks like I'm going to like it. I haven't been a student but a minute."

"We're happy for you, Destiny," Bertice said.

"Thanks for being such good friends," Destiny said. Then she sighed. "I have a favor to ask."

"Anything," Natalie said. "You know we have your back."

"Yeah, we're here for you," Bertice added. "Just tell us what you need. As long as it's not tutoring help."

Destiny chuckled. "No, it's not tutoring. Mrs. Robinson has been talking to me about getting my natural hair care license and I've decided to take her up on it."

"That's great news, Destiny," Natalie said. "That's the first step to opening your own salon."

"Not so fast," Destiny said. "I'm taking this in steps and only focusing on the license for now."

"How are you going to do it all, Destiny?" Bertice asked. "I know you're Superwoman, but you have a lot on your plate this summer."

"That's where the favor comes in. Mrs. Robinson is willing to let me apprentice in her shop. All the hair I do in the salon will count toward the hours needed for my license."

"Bertice has a point," Natalie said. "When are you going to have time to go to her salon?"

"Easy," she said. "If you two are willing, instead of me doing your hair at my house, I'd do it in the salon. That way,

I'm not really increasing the work I do. I'm just changing the location. What do you think?"

"I think it's a great idea," Natalie said.

"Mrs. Robinson thought of it. I think it's a good idea, too, but it means you two will have to come to the shop in order for me to do your hair. It won't be as convenient for you."

Natalie waved her off. "Please, that is not a problem. We're glad to do it, aren't we, Bertice?"

Bertice nodded. "When you write your Madame Destiny book about how you became rich and famous, just remember to include us and say that we were there from the beginning."

"Count on it," Destiny said.

"We can read the book when you take us to France for our celebratory ladies' night out after it becomes a bestseller."

Destiny began laughing.

"If we're lucky," Natalie said, with a wink, "it will be three couples making that trip to France. You know what they say, France is for lovers."

"You really don't give up, do you?" Bertice asked, shaking her head.

Before Natalie could answer, Destiny said, "Right now the only trip I'm thinking about is one to California to see my kids."

"Are you going to be able to go?" Natalie asked.

"I'm working on it now. The most I can swing is a long weekend because that's all the time I can get off from the store. It's not much time and the trip will be fairly expensive, but it's worth it to me."

Natalie rested her hand atop Destiny's. "Gavin and I would still like to gift you the flight. Please let us do that for you, Destiny."

Destiny shook her head. "It won't be necessary, Natalie," she said. "You've done enough by hooking me up with the job with Daniel."

"But I know how much that pays and it's not a lot, especially not when I know you're also trying to save the money you need to move to Gwinnett."

Destiny glanced at Bertice, a question in her eyes. It was time for them to tell Natalie about their work with HR Solutions. Bertice nodded her agreement.

Destiny cleared her throat. "Well, I was able to get a second part-time job."

Natalie's eyes widened. "Second part-time job? Where? When? Doing what?"

She inclined her head toward Bertice. "One of Bertice's friends runs a temp agency and he found something for me."

"The company is HR Solutions and the friend is Phil Harris, the guy I'm dating," Bertice explained. "I've been working with him for a while now."

Natalie turned to her. "So this is the business opportunity you've been talking about?"

Bertice nodded.

"Why didn't you two tell me?" Natalie asked.

Bertice shrugged, and then turned to Destiny.

"We didn't want you to worry," Destiny said.

"What she means is we didn't want you to worry because of

my track record. I promise you this is not a pyramid scheme. It's perfectly legal."

Natalie's expression said she was skeptical.

"It's a lot of pay for what so far has been a little work," Destiny added, "but it's on the up-and-up."

"So what are you doing?" Natalie asked.

This time Bertice looked at Natalie, who then described their job duties in much the same way that Phil Harris had explained them to her.

"That sure is a lot of money for doing a little work. You know the old saying about something being too good to be true."

Bertice frowned. "This is why we didn't tell you, Natalie. We knew you were going to be negative. Why can't you see the opportunity as a blessing? Do you have to be negative?"

Natalie sat back in her chair. "I'm sorry," she said. "I was just thinking out loud. You know, I'm always happy when good things happen to you two. I love you. You do know that, don't you?"

"We know, but you worry a lot," Bertice said.

"And this time we think the worry is unnecessary," Destiny added.

"I hear you," Natalie said, "but I'm always going to worry about you two."

Bertice nudged Natalie's shoulder with her own. "Maybe it's time you and Gavin start putting out some little Natalies and Gavins. Then you could worry about your babies and not have to worry about us."

Natalie laughed. "Okay, okay. If you drop the baby talk, I'll back off. Gavin and I are practically newlyweds. Babies are still a few years away."

"If you say so," Destiny said. "But babies don't always come according to plan. That I know from experience."

"Speaking of your babies, if this job is going to make it possible for you to visit them, I'm all for it."

"Group hug time," Bertice said.

When they all huddled together, Destiny squeezed them tightly and said, "I love you guys."

"Love you, too," Bertice and Natalie both said.

"So, Destiny," Bertice said, "I'd love to go to California. Do you need somebody to carry your luggage?"

Destiny chuckled. "My mom beat you to it."

"Your mom's going?" Bertice said, eyes wide. "Well, that leaves me out. I guess I'll have to wait on France."

Chapter 24

DESTINY WATCHED AS DANIEL REVIEWED THE PRO-gram materials she had developed since their last meeting. This was the first time she'd seen him since that meeting, as their plans for Sunday lunch had fallen through. She wasn't sure who was more disappointed. He'd already apologized several times and, of course, she'd accepted his apology. He was a minister and there would be times the ministry would come first. Sunday afternoon had been one of those times.

Daniel looked up from the program materials he was reviewing. "As usual, you've done good work, Destiny. The application for the small business development seminar is perfect. I just made a couple of minor changes. Look them over, and if you agree, let's run the application by Gavin and Natalie. After we get their approval, it's ready to be printed."

Destiny took back the application he handed her and glanced at the notes he'd made on it. As he said, they were minor. "I'll make these changes and get the document to Gavin and Natalie. It shouldn't take long for their approval. We should have the application ready for distribution at Sunday services. I hope we can also get a notice in the church bulletin for Sunday. It goes to press on Friday."

"That would be great," Daniel said. "But if we can't, we'll just wait a week. That won't be a problem. I've adjusted my time expectations since our last meeting to something more realistic. 'The race doesn't go to the swiftest, but to him who endures to the end.'"

She smiled at his scripture recitation. "Sounds good to me. Next, we need to make some decisions about the teams we want to send to training to lead our Dave Ramsey personal finance seminar."

"Yeah," he said. "I talked to Gavin about it and he has a couple of folks he strongly wants us to consider. They've been good stewards in the church and they're the kind of people he's comfortable putting forth as examples."

"Makes sense," she said.

"I don't know any of these people personally," he said, handing her a sheet of paper with a list of names.

Looking over the list, Destiny said, "I know four of the eight listed here. Do we have to narrow it down to four or should we send all eight to training?"

"Let's just send all eight," he said. "It's better to have more people prepared than not to have enough."

"Sounds good to me," she said. "Do we contact them or should Gavin do it?"

"He wants us to do it," he said.

Destiny made a note of it. "I'll draft a letter of invitation and we'll both sign it."

"Let's have them meet with us as a group before the training," he said. "That way, we can all get on the same page."

Destiny nodded. "What time frame are you thinking?"

"My schedule is pretty open," he said. He met her eyes. "Maybe Sunday after church. Is that too soon?"

She shook her head. "Not at all. The folks on the list are regular attendees at the Sunday service so it shouldn't be a problem. Instead of a letter, it might be better if you call and invite them. Having one of the pastors call would make it clear how important the church sees the program."

"Good point," he said. "I'll have Doris get their contact information for me and I'll call them tomorrow."

She smiled up at him. "This is going pretty smoothly, isn't it?"

He smiled back. "We're a good team," he said.

"I guess we are."

He leaned toward her. "I really am sorry about Sunday, Destiny. I was looking forward to spending some time with you."

"You don't have to keep apologizing, Daniel. I understand. Really, I do."

"Then can we try it again this Sunday, after we meet with the team?"

She began shaking her head. "I have an even better idea. Why don't we have a luncheon meeting after church on Sunday? We can either provide food here at the church or we can make reservations somewhere."

Daniel nodded. "That's a great idea. I like the idea of providing food here at the church. We can ask Eve to cater it for us. Do you think she'll be able to pull something together on such short notice?"

"I don't see why not. It's such a small group, she should be able to if she doesn't have another event lined up for the weekend. I'll check with her as soon as we're finished here."

"I hope she can do it. Did you know that Eve was the inspiration for the small business seminars?"

She looked up at him. "No, I didn't."

"She brought lunch over for me and Gavin one day and Natalie told me that she was trying to get her catering business off the ground."

"And from that you came up with the idea for the seminars?"

He nodded. "That and the fact that I have some experience starting a small business. I know what it's like to dream about building something and to not be sure that you can pull it off. If I can help somebody else through that maze of insecurity, I want to do it."

"We'll have to make sure that we get Eve in the first small business session. Is there some way you can use her as a case study in the workshop? You know, show the class how to get started by getting her started?"

"You're just full of great ideas today. That's certainly something I can do. We should talk to Eve about it soon. If she can cater the event on Sunday, let's talk to her afterward."

"I'll let her know. She'll be so excited." She met his eyes.

"Daniel, these programs are going to be the answers to so many folks' prayers. Gloria will be so pleased."

"Thanks for saying that," he said. "I hope you're right."

"I know I am," she said, pulling out a sheet of paper from the stack in front of her and handing it to him. "I had the deacons and Gavin and Natalie come up with a list of folks needing help now."

"This is not a lot of money," he said after he'd looked over the list.

"Not to you," she said, "but it is to them."

"You're right," he said. "It's just hard to imagine that so little money can make such a big difference in somebody's life. I say we fund each one. We just have to do it in a way that allows the recipients to keep their dignity."

Destiny was pleased he'd remembered her suggestion from last time. "It'll probably be easiest if everything goes through the deacons. That way, it will still feel like a private matter."

He nodded. "That was easy. Anything else?"

"No more business, but I do have a question."

"Shoot."

"You told me your inspiration for the small business seminars. What was your inspiration for the personal finance sessions and the associated loan program?"

He leaned forward. "You know, this is the kind of conversation we should have had over lunch on Sunday. Again—"

She lifted her palms to him. "If you apologize again, I'm going to be offended. Instead, tell me now about your inspiration."

He released a deep sigh. "The business that I started with my friends was a cybersecurity firm. We handle a lot of cases of corporate fraud. It's been my experience that a lot of the folks who get caught up in those scams do so because they've mismanaged their own finances. While we can't force folks to make the right decisions, we can give them the information they need to make wise choices."

"You have a good heart, Daniel," she said.

He shrugged. "I'm just giving back what I've been given."

"You accused me once of not being able to accept a compliment. You know you're just as bad at it, don't you?"

He smiled. "Maybe that's why we work so well together. We're so much alike."

Destiny fought the need to turn back his praise. "Did you just compliment both of us?"

He laughed. "I think I did. Now that we both agree on how great we are, have we covered all the business for today?"

She looked down at her notepad and then back up at him. "There is one more thing. I'm trying to find some time to take a weekend trip to California so I can visit with my kids. Given how everything is lining up here, school, and my day job, it seems like three weeks from now would be good for me. I need to know if it will be good for you."

"Whatever you need to do, Destiny. Just let me know. Family needs to come first." He met her eyes. "You know, I don't know much about your kids. That's another topic we would have covered over lunch."

"You'd better not be apologizing again."

"I'm not apologizing, but I am expressing regret. Tell me about your kids."

She reached over and picked up her handbag from the chair next to her. She pulled out a mini photo album and handed it to him. "A picture is worth a thousand words."

Daniel thumbed through the album. "They're cute kids. They're six, right?"

She nodded. "Six going on sixteen. They're growing up so fast. Too fast for me."

He handed her back the album. "It's nice that they have such a good relationship with their father."

She nodded. "Our relationship didn't work, but Kenneth has been a good father to the kids. I have to give him that."

"He certainly chose a great vacation spot for them."

"It's more like a work vacation. Kenneth's wife, Mary Margaret, is out there for a summer work project. Kenneth and the kids tagged along since it made for a very inexpensive vacation when you consider their out-of-pocket costs."

He nodded. "I can imagine her company is picking up the tab for most, if not all, of the living expenses."

"You got it. That's why it made so much sense for the kids to join them." She went on to tell him all the activities Kenneth and Mary Margaret had planned.

"I would enjoy a trip like that."

"So would I," she said. "But there was no way I could afford it. The best I've been able to do is take the kids to Disney World in Orlando for a week."

"I bet they enjoyed it."

She smiled. "They had a ball. It's easy to entertain them at their age."

"You're a good mom," he said.

She met his eyes. "I try, but it's not always easy." He'd been open with her about his life so she decided to open up a little to him. "I just want so much for them."

"From the looks of them in those pictures, they're both healthy and happy. Everything is gravy."

"I know," she said, "but I want the gravy."

He chuckled. "I'm getting lost in the analogy. What's the gravy?"

"Right now it's a house in Gwinnett County. That's why I'm working extra jobs this summer."

"You want to move?"

She nodded. "Kenneth convinced me to enroll the kids in a school in his school district. It was the right decision since the school did have a better report card than the school they would have gone to here. But we spend a lot of time traveling between my house, Kenneth's house, and the school. It's a lot for the kids and for me. It would be much easier if we lived closer to the school."

He nodded. "Or the kids could live with their father during the school week. I guess that's not an acceptable option for you."

She shook her head. "No, it's not. Of course, Kenneth has suggested it. I see his point but I don't see my kids living away from me. That makes my best alternative moving to the district. I've already found a little house that's perfect for us. I have until August first to go to contract with the owners."

"Are you going to make it?"

She nodded. "It was touch and go for a while, but with my extra work, I'll be able to swing it."

He met her eyes. "You know, the loan program was made for situations like yours. You're—"

She began shaking her head. "Don't even offer. If I hadn't been able to find extra work, I would consider your offer a godsend. But since I have found work, I couldn't take money that some other family might need." She smiled at him to let him know she wasn't offended by his offer. "I will be one of the first people to enroll in the personal finance workshop though."

"I'm glad," he said. "I ought to enroll myself. It makes sense that we both attend a full session. We can learn something while we're evaluating the session."

"Makes sense to me," she said, jotting down the idea.

He looked at his watch. "It's getting late. Do we have anything else?"

She closed her folder. "No, that's all I have. Unless you have something, I think we're done for the day."

He leaned forward. "I do have one more thing. Given his work at HR Solutions, I spoke with Phil Harris about supporting these programs in some way and he had a great suggestion. He is a member of the DeKalb County Chamber of Commerce and is involved in the Southside Business Council, which includes the community surrounding the church."

She nodded. "I've heard of it."

"Well, they're having an open house and reception next Saturday night that he thinks we should attend. It will be a good way for us to make some connections in the community, connections that might be useful with this program and with the church as a whole. I've already spoken to Gavin about it and he's on board with us going as church representatives." He leaned closer. "I'd like you to attend as my date, not just as the church representative. I'd like to make it up to you for having to cancel last Sunday."

Instead of giving a straight answer, she said, "I guess it's formal."

"I have the invitation right here," he said, pushing it toward her. "It says cocktail attire."

"Cocktail attire," she repeated, mentally going through her wardrobe for the perfect dress.

"So will you go with me?"

She nodded. "I'm looking forward to it."

"Good. Phil and Bertice will be there as well. Phil mentioned going out to a jazz club or something afterward. How does that sound?"

She smiled. "It sounds like we're about to go on a real date. It's sorta scary."

He shook his head. "Nah. It'll be easy. I promise."

Chapter 25

DESTINY HELPED HER MOTHER CLEAR THE TABLE.

"So you've told Kenneth and his wife that I'm coming with you?" her mother asked.

Destiny nodded. "Yes, I told them and I also told them that I wanted to surprise the kids. They agreed not to tell them we were coming."

"That was nice of them. What's on the schedule for the time we're there?"

"We'll hit some local tourist spots that the kids haven't visited yet. They haven't done Disney, so we get to do that with them. Kenneth and Mary Margaret are also trying to get tickets to one of the kids' TV shows filming this summer. I hope we get to take in a taping of one of their favorite shows. It's going to be a short trip, so we won't be able to do a lot. We'll leave here on Friday night and get back on Monday night. Barely just enough time to see the kids and give them a big hug."

"You're right about the short time frame," her mother said.

"I wish we could stay longer. I'd like to make it to one of those game shows myself. Maybe I'll look into it."

Destiny nodded. "Go ahead. It can't hurt and it may work out."

"Would you go with me?"

"Of course I would, Mom. It would be fun."

"I think so. I'll definitely look into it. Is there anything else I need to do?"

Destiny shook her head. "Everything's covered."

"You've already booked the hotel and you're buying the tickets soon?" her mother asked.

"Yes, I'll book them tonight."

"I'm paying you back for everything," her mother said, beginning to wash the few dishes they had used.

"I know, Mom," Destiny said. "I'll put the tickets on my credit card. When I get ready to pay the bill, I'll let you know."

"You'd better, Destiny. I want to pay my way."

Destiny rolled her eyes when her mother wasn't looking. "I'll keep track of everything I spend on you so you can pay me back."

"Okay," her mother said. "Now get a towel and dry these dishes. We should be finished in no time."

Destiny did as she was told.

"I'm glad you came over tonight," her mother said, handing her a plate.

Destiny took the plate and wiped it with the towel. "I told you I was going to visit more."

"But I know you've been busy, so I appreciate your looking in on your old mom."

Destiny wanted to laugh at her mother's reference to herself as old. The woman was anything but.

"How's school?" her mother asked, handing her a pot to dry.

Taking it, Destiny said, "You may have been right, Mom."

Her mother stopped washing dishes and turned to her. "What did you say? Did I hear you right?"

Destiny rolled her eyes again. This time she knew her mother saw her. "You heard me. I said you may have been right. Somewhere along the way I think I turned into a good student."

Her mother turned back to the dishes. "You always had it in you. I've always said so."

Maybe she had been capable back then, Destiny considered. Or maybe she had a different perspective now. Like Mrs. Robinson had told her, having a purpose for her studies made doing the studying much easier.

"How's the job at the church?" her mother asked. Finished with the dishes, she pulled the plug to let the water out of the sink.

Destiny leaned back against the counter and watched her mother clean the counter. "It's going well, too."

Her mother glanced back at her. "So you're working with that new pastor?"

Destiny refused to ask how her mother knew. "Yes," she said simply.

"I hear he's a handsome devil. Single, too."

Destiny knew where her mother was going. "We work together, Mom. That's all," she said, refusing to bring up the open house and reception she and Daniel were attending together next week. She'd hear enough about that from Natalie. She didn't need her mom's two cents. Besides, what she and Daniel were starting was new and fresh and she wanted to keep it between them for a while.

"You're an attractive woman, Destiny," her mom said. "You could have a man if you halfway tried."

Oh no, Destiny thought. Her going back to college was not enough. Now her mom thought she needed a man. And if her mom was true to her nature, she'd harp on this point the same way she'd harped on school. Her mom was never satisfied. "Did I tell you that I'm also going to work on getting my natural hair care license?" she offered as a change in the topic of conversation.

"Natural hair care license? Where did this come from?"

Destiny was able to keep from rolling her eyes this time. "You know I do hair."

Finished with the kitchen cleanup, her mom turned to her. "I know you enjoy doing hair, Destiny, but you need to focus now. Don't bite off more than you can chew."

"I'm not, Mom," Destiny said, realizing that there were few safe topics for her and her mom. They all seemed to end in conflict.

"When do you have time to work on getting a hair care license? You have a full-time job, you're working part-time at the church, and you're going to school. Everything is going well now. I just don't want you to mess it up."

Destiny wanted to believe her mother didn't intend to be negative. It just seemed to always turn out that she was. "It's not going to be too much, Mom. I'm going to work as an apprentice at a shop nearby. I'll continue to do my friends' hair. The only difference is, I'll do it at the salon and get credit toward my license."

"I don't know, Destiny. Are you sure that's going to work? How can you get a license that way?"

"It's going to work," she said.

"Well, I hope you've researched it. I'd hate for you to spend all that time and have nothing to show for it."

"I've researched it, Mom," she said. "Mrs. Robinson, the counselor at the college, told me about it. It's her shop and I'm going to be her apprentice."

"Mrs. Robinson?" her mother asked.

Destiny nodded. "Yes. Annie Robinson. Do you know her? She says she's been at the college for about ten years."

"The name sounds familiar," her mother said. "Then again I'm sure there's more than one Annie Robinson in Atlanta."

"Probably so," Destiny said. "This one has been really nice to me. She helped with my classes and she gave me some tips on how to be a good student. I don't know why, but she has gone out of her way to assist me."

"That's what counselors are supposed to do, Destiny. I wouldn't read too much into it. The woman is only doing her job."

Destiny thought her mother was wrong about Mrs. Robinson. Destiny knew the woman was going beyond what was required in helping her. Natalie and Bertice saw it as God working all these things together for her good. Why couldn't her mother see them that way?

"Well, I hope this woman knows what she's doing. I still think focus is important when you're in school and working two jobs. Nobody can do everything."

"I'm not trying to do everything," Destiny said, wondering what her mother would think if she knew she was working the third job with HR Solutions. "I want to do these things. They're all related anyway."

Her mother folded her arms across her midsection. "I don't see how they are related and I don't see how you can do them all. It's too much."

Destiny thought about trying to explain it to her mother and then decided against it. "You'll have to trust me, Mom, when I say they are."

"It's not about trust, Destiny," her mother said. "It's about wisdom. You have all this on your plate and you're getting ready to take some time off to go to California. Can you even afford to do that given all your commitments?"

"I can afford it, Mom," she said.

"You know I'm not talking dollars and cents," her mother said.

"I've taken care of my responsibilities," Destiny said. "Besides, it's only for one weekend. I'm not going to get behind on anything while I'm away. You really do have to trust that I know what I'm doing."

Her mother didn't look convinced but Destiny was glad she let the matter drop. Grateful for the lapse in conversation, she said, "Well, I should be getting home. I have some homework tonight and I want to read ahead a bit so I don't have to worry about studying when I'm in California."

"Okay, dear," her mother said. "You drive carefully."

"I will," Destiny said, giving her mother a good-bye hug and a peck on the forehead.

"And don't forget to book those plane tickets," her mother called as she walked out the door.

Without looking back, she lifted her hand and said, "I won't, Mom." She couldn't wait until the end of the summer and she and the kids moved into the house in Gwinnett County. Maybe then her mother could see that she was capable of making good decisions.

Chapter 26

Patricia Madison waited patiently for her three-thirty meeting. They had agreed to meet for lunch at a restaurant near the campus. Patricia had chosen the time and place because of the low likelihood they would run into Destiny, who was at work at Marshalls, or any of Destiny's friends. It was important that Destiny not learn of this meeting.

"Hello, Patricia."

Patricia looked up and laid eyes on Annie Robinson for the first time in more than twenty years. "Hello, Annie," she said. "Thank you for agreeing to meet with me. Please have a seat."

Annie looked down at her as if she was going to reject her offer. Instead she sat. "I would say I was surprised when you called, but I'm not. In fact, I've been expecting it."

Patricia nodded. "I can only imagine."

"The last time we met like this you threatened me."

Patricia remembered that day clearly. She'd been so arrogant and full of herself back then. "I was young," she said. "We were both young."

Annie looked as if she were remembering the day as well. Then, as if shaking off the thoughts of the past, she said, "So why did you want to see me?"

"You know why. Destiny told me she met with you at the college. I didn't know you worked there. I didn't even know you were back in town."

"Why would you?" Annie said. "You made it pretty clear that I was never to show my face again. Wasn't that what you said?"

Patricia could only nod. "If I had it to do over, I hope I'd do things differently, but, honestly, I really don't know that I would. I made the best decision I could make at the time."

Annie shot hot eyes at her. "You took my child," she said. "You took my baby."

Patricia shook her head. "I didn't take her. You gave her away. You abandoned her."

"I came back for her."

"She was a baby, not a pet you'd left at the kennel while you went on vacation. You weren't ready to be a mother. You didn't want to be a mother."

"You don't know what I wanted. How could you?"

"I know you wanted my husband," Patricia said coldly. "I know you had an affair with him. And I know you tried to blackmail him with a baby that wasn't his."

Annie looked away. "I made a mistake," she said, "but that didn't give you the right to take my child."

Patricia took a deep breath. "I didn't ask you here to rehash the past. I want to know what you want with Destiny."

"She's my daughter," Annie said. "I want to get to know her. I deserve the chance to get to know her. I did what you asked and I stayed away. I didn't come into her life. She came into mine and I can't turn her away. Don't ask me to turn her away."

Patricia ached at the pain she heard in the other woman's voice. "I'm not going to ask you to turn her away. She needs you."

Annie's eyes widened and Patricia knew her words had surprised her. "Well, we agree on something."

Patricia nodded. She reached in her purse and pulled out a book. Then she handed it to Annie.

"What is it?" Annie asked.

"It's Destiny's life, or a snapshot of it. I've been keeping it for you since she was a baby."

Annie opened the book and began to thumb through her daughter's life. "Why?" she asked, looking over at Patricia. "Why did you do this?"

Patricia shrugged. "You're her mother. I knew you'd come back for her. I expected you to get your life together and come back and fight for her, but you never did. I didn't understand that. If I had been fortunate enough to have a child, I couldn't have left her the way you did and never come back for her. I couldn't have done that. How could you do it? How could you stay away?"

Annie looked out the window. "My life was a mess. If you thought I was in bad shape the last time you saw me, you should have seen me after. You scared me when you threatened to have me locked up. Then I went and did something stupid and ended up locked up just the same. I spent ten years in prison."

"Ten years? What did you do?"

"Does it matter?"

Patricia nodded. "It matters because you're back in Destiny's life and soon you'll be back in the lives of her children. I don't want to see any of them hurt. I won't let you hurt them."

"I'm not going to hurt anybody. I was arrested for fraud, believe it or not, the same charge you threatened to have levied against me. My cheating ways finally caught up with me."

"Have you been back here since you got out of prison?"

She shook her head. "I bounced around a few places first. I've been back here about ten years. I was able to get a job at the college through one of the prison outreach programs. It was the best offer I had when I was released."

"And you never tried to see Destiny?"

"Oh, I wanted to," Annie said. "But prison does something to a person. I didn't feel worthy of a child when I was first released. I had a lot of time to think about how irresponsible I had been. By the time I had forgiven myself and gotten back on my feet, I didn't think it was right to disrupt her life. I did what I thought was best for her. Isn't that what a good parent does?"

Patricia could only nod. This was not the same selfish woman she'd known years ago.

"I forced myself not to look her up. I knew that if I saw

her, I'd not be able to stay away. She was a student at Hillman when I first saw her. She doesn't remember meeting me, of course. And then she comes back into my life a few weeks ago."

"I didn't know it," Patricia said, "but I sent her back to you."

"What do you mean?"

"Destiny had no interest in returning to school but I've been nagging her about it for years and this summer she finally relented."

Annie nodded. "Because her kids are spending the summer in California with their father."

"So she told you."

"We hit it off," she said. "There was an easy rapport between us. It was as though we had a connection."

"You did," Patricia said simply.

"But she doesn't know about our biological connection and she felt it, too. That is what was so magical about meeting her. We may have been separated for all of her life but we were still connected. I guess that's a mother's bond."

"I guess it is," Patricia said, fighting down the resentment she felt toward this woman. She couldn't love Destiny any more if she were her biological daughter, and she knew Destiny loved her, but their bond was strained. There were times she felt distant from her daughter. It wasn't fair that this woman felt a bond with Destiny that she, who'd cared for Destiny all her life, didn't share.

"It's all I have," Annie said. "You had Destiny her whole life, so don't begrudge me this. You have been her mother. You are her mother. I only want to be in her life. I can settle for being her friend. She never has to know who I am to her. I can live with that."

"Maybe you won't have to settle for that. Destiny doesn't know it yet, but she's going to need you."

"What are you saying?"

Patricia took a deep breath. "My cancer has returned, Annie. I haven't told Destiny yet, but my cancer is back."

Chapter 27

DESTINY TRIED TO PAY ATTENTION TO WHAT DANIEL was telling Mr. Crenshaw, the president of the DeKalb County Chamber of Commerce, but her mind kept going back to the look Daniel had given her when he'd picked her up to bring her to this reception. She was used to quick takes, prolonged stares, and even leers from men but there was something more in the look Daniel had given her. She couldn't quite find the words to describe it. It was easier to describe how the look had made her feel. Beautiful. Cherished. Appreciated. Important. Accepted.

"Hey, girl."

Destiny turned at the sound of Bertice's voice. "Hey, yourself," she said, glad for the distraction. She leaned in to give her friend a hug. When she pulled back, she took in the simple deep purple cocktail dress her friend wore and said, "You look great. You're working that purple."

"Thanks," Bertice said. "You're looking spiffy yourself in

that black. I'd say we clean up well. I don't think I've seen that dress before. It's gorgeous. Is it new?"

Destiny shook her head. "This dress has been in my closet for years. I got it on sale somewhere, but I've never had an occasion to wear it until now."

"I'm sure Daniel thinks it was worth the wait. Where is he anyway? We've been looking for you two since we got here." She turned to Phil. "You remember Phil Harris, don't you?"

Destiny nodded. "It's good to see you again, Phil," she said. "Daniel tells me that you're going to be a speaker at one of our personal finance classes."

Bertice turned to Phil. "You didn't tell me that."

Looking down at her, Phil said, "We haven't actually confirmed anything yet. Daniel has only mentioned it to me once."

"Well, you're confirmed in our book, but don't worry about it now. The sessions are a few months away at least. It'll be a while before we can lock in dates and times."

"I guess I'll have to sign up for one of these sessions then," Bertice said to Phil.

He smiled down at her. "You don't have to sign up for a workshop to get advice from me."

Destiny watched as Bertice patted his cheek with her hand and said, "That's nice to hear."

"What are you-all talking about?"

Destiny turned this time to the sound of Natalie's voice. "Hey, girl," she said, leaning in to hug her friend. "I didn't know you and Gavin were coming. He is here, isn't he?"

"Yes, somebody pulled him to the side as soon as we walked in. I decided to look for you. Where is Daniel?"

Destiny glanced around. "He was right behind me. Somebody must have pulled him away, too."

"I see him," Phil said. "I think I'll go join him and leave you women to whatever it is you do when we're not around."

"You have to meet Natalie first," Bertice said.

Natalie extended her hand. "You must be Phil Harris," she said. "I've heard a lot about you."

Phil took her hand and shook it. "All good, I hope?"

Natalie gave him her full smile. "Most of it."

Phil chuckled. "It's nice to meet you, Natalie," he said. "Bertice talks a lot about you and Destiny. I'm glad she has such good friends."

"And we're glad she's met a nice guy like you," Natalie said.

"Did you know that he was a friend of Daniel's?" Destiny asked.

"Yes, I remember Bertice telling me that," Natalie answered. Then she turned her attention back to Phil. "How do you know Daniel? He and my husband go way back. Maybe you know him, too. Gavin Weston."

Phil shook his head. "Daniel and I had a work relationship some years back. I don't think I met your husband though. The name is not familiar to me."

"Well, you'll get to meet him tonight. He's around here somewhere."

"I look forward to it," he said. Then he turned to Bertice. "I'm going to go look for Daniel, okay?"

Bertice nodded.

"After you find him," Natalie said, "have him introduce you to Gavin. Of course, you'll have to find him first."

"I'll do it," Phil said, backing away from them.

Destiny began to giggle. "He couldn't wait to get away from us, could he?"

Natalie grinned at Bertice. "You didn't tell me he was a hottie."

"Hey," Bertice said, "I'm into his mind, not his body."

Both Natalie and Destiny laughed. "Yeah, right," Destiny said.

"You can't talk, Destiny," Bertice said. "Natalie described Daniel as delicious."

Destiny looked at Natalie. "How is it the married woman is the one checking out and rating all the men?"

"I don't check out all men," Natalie said. "Just the ones involved with my friends. I'm married, so I know marriage material when I see it."

"Yeah, right," Bertice said. "What is marriage material?"

Natalie waved her off. "It's too complex to describe. Just believe me when I tell you I have a radar for men who are marriage material. All I need is about an hour with them and I'll know." She looked at Destiny. "It goes without saying that Daniel is marriage material. I didn't even need radar for that one."

"What about Phil?"

"I haven't been around him long enough, but I'm inclined to believe he is. Men who are marriage material tend to hang together. So if Phil's a friend of Daniel's, there's a good chance that he's marriage material, too."

Destiny shook her head. "I don't believe we're having this conversation. Nobody is thinking about marriage. This is the first date for me and Daniel. And Bertice and Phil have only been dating a few weeks."

"I knew it," Natalie said. "Daniel told Gavin it wasn't a date, but I didn't believe him. I dragged Gavin out here tonight so I could see for myself."

"No you didn't," Destiny said.

"Oh yes she did," Bertice said.

Destiny chuckled. "Bertice was right when she said it was time for you and Gavin to have some babies. You definitely have too much free time on your hands."

"When I get pregnant, which won't be for a couple more years," Natalie promised, "you two will be the first ones after Gavin that I tell."

Gavin walked up and put an arm around Natalie's waist. "What are you going to tell and who are you going to tell it to?" he asked, looking down at her.

"Girl talk," she said. "You wouldn't understand."

Gavin chuckled. "Hey, ladies," he said to Destiny and Bertice. "You both are looking lovely tonight."

"You're looking right handsome yourself tonight, Gavin," Destiny said, taking in his basic black suit, tie, and white shirt. He wore it well.

"Natalie deserves the praise. I had to get her okay before I could leave the house."

Natalie slapped him on the shoulder. "That's not true."

Destiny laughed. "I bet it is."

"I know it is," Bertice said.

Natalie looked up at her husband. "See what you've done? You've turned my friends on me."

"I didn't do anything," Gavin said.

"Sounds like you need some help over here, brother," Daniel said, coming to stand next to Destiny. He rested his hand on her waist. "Are these women ganging up on you?" he asked Gavin.

"Something like that," he said.

"Well, Phil and I are here to help you balance the scales."

"Phil is Bertice's friend," Natalie told her husband.

Gavin extended his hand. "Nice to meet you, Phil. I'm Gavin. And this is Natalie, my wife," he adding, pulling her close to him.

"We met earlier," she said. "Did you know he's also a friend of Daniel's?"

Gavin turned to Daniel. "You know Phil?"

Daniel nodded. "We go back."

"Small world, isn't it?" Gavin said.

"It's smaller than you think," Natalie said. "Phil runs the temporary agency that found part-time work for Bertice and Destiny."

"And he's going to be a speaker in the personal finance program we're offering at the church," Destiny added.

"It seems we're a pretty interconnected group," Gavin observed.

Destiny looked up at Daniel when the hand that rested on her waist squeezed. "Phil and I were thinking that we could go down to Peachtree Street for a late dinner and some jazz. How does that sound?" he asked.

"Sounds good to me," Destiny said.

"Me too," Bertice said.

"What about you two?" Daniel asked Gavin and Natalie.

"We wouldn't miss it," Natalie said.

When Destiny and Bertice laughed, Daniel asked, "What's so funny?"

Destiny shook her head. "It's a female thing," she said. "I'll explain later."

Chapter 28

DANIEL AND DESTINY WALKED HAND IN HAND UP HER walkway from his car to her townhouse-style apartment. "Did you enjoy yourself tonight?" he asked.

"I had a great time," she said. "It was a perfect evening."

He shook his head. "Not perfect, but close to it."

"What was missing?"

"Nothing was missing," he said. "There were just too many people for it to be perfect. Perfect would have been just you and me. We'll have to do that soon."

She chuckled. "The way we're going, we may be destined for group dates only."

"I'm not going to claim that," he said. "In fact, the next time we go out, it will be just you and me. I claim it. Now. In Jesus's name."

"Now you're being silly."

"Just a little," he admitted. "All kidding aside, there is something affirming about being out with a group of friends who know both of us."

When they reached the courtyard near the front door, Daniel stopped. "Do you have to go in?" he asked.

She shrugged. "You're welcome to come in with me," she said.

He shook his head. "It's such a beautiful night that I'd rather sit out here in your courtyard. That swing is calling my name. What do you think?"

She smiled. "I think my couch might be more comfortable, but the view of the night is nowhere near as good as it is out here."

"Then come and sit with me," he said, leading her to the wicker glider that was the centerpiece of the courtyard. After they were seated, he stretched out his legs, leaned his head back, pulled her close, and put his arm around her shoulders. "Now this is more like it," he said.

She kicked off her shoes, folded her legs on the glider, and leaned closer to him. Smiling into his shoulder, she said, "It's not bad."

He lifted his head and peered down at her. "Not bad?"

Her smile grew broader. "All right. It's nice. Very nice."

"That's more like it," he said, leaning his head back again.

It was nice sitting here with him listening to the quiet of the night.

"You're not falling asleep on me, are you?"

She shook her head. "No way."

"I thought you said you lived in an apartment," he said.

"This is a townhouse-style apartment. It's the only community I've seen that's like it. It's perfect for me and the kids."

"But you're going to move away?"

She sighed. "I don't want to, but I have to for the kids. Kenneth is right. We can't keep shuttling them across town next year the way we did this year. It's too much and it's unnecessary."

"What's your schedule for moving?"

"I wanted to be settled in before the kids get back from California. The move and the house will be my surprise for them. I want them to know that their mom was thinking about them when they were away. I've already decided how I'm going to decorate their rooms. They're going to love them."

He squeezed her shoulder. "I'm sure they will."

She looked up at him. "What are you thinking about?" she asked.

Looking down at her, he said, "You. Us."

She swallowed. Hard.

"And this," he said, lowering his head until his lips touched hers. The kiss was soft and so very sweet. When he lifted his head, he said, "I've been wanting to do that since I picked you up."

"So have I."

He moaned and then he lowered his head for another kiss, a kiss that was deeper and longer than the first one. When he lifted his head this time, he gave her a satisfied grin and then leaned his head back again.

She giggled.

"What are you laughing at?"

"I'm just happy," she said.

She felt him smile. "So am I."

Chapter 29

Are you all settled in?" Annie asked Destiny as she completed the setup of her station for her first day at the salon.

"Almost," Destiny said. "All I need now is a customer."

"Do you have one scheduled?"

Destiny nodded. "My friend Bertice is coming in. I'm leaving for California on Friday and I needed to get her and my friend Natalie done before I fly out. Natalie was coming today but something came up. I still hope to get her in before I go."

Annie nodded. "Sounds good. Just let Leslie know your schedule each week. If you're around, you may be able to pick up a walk-in or two. You don't have to, but it's an option."

"Thanks," Destiny said. "I mean that, Annie. Thanks for everything."

"Don't thank me," Annie said. "Just make me look good by doing well both here and at school."

"I'll try," Destiny said. "I really will."

"I believe you."

"There's my friend," Destiny said, looking over Annie's shoulder and toward the front of the salon. "I want you to meet her." Lifting her arm, she waved her hand to get Bertice's attention and then beckoned her over. "I'd like you to meet Mrs. Robinson," she said to Bertice.

"Mrs. Robinson, this is Bertice Brown, a longtime friend."

"Nice to meet you," Bertice said. "Destiny talks of you often."

"All good, I hope."

"Definitely," Bertice said. "We consider it a miracle that Destiny met you. Look at how things are working out for her since then. You're her good-luck charm."

Mrs. Robinson smiled. "I believe more in hard work than in luck," she said, "but I know what you mean. I'm glad our lives intersected also. We have a lot in common."

"Maybe Destiny was switched at birth and you're her real mom," Bertice teased.

Mrs. Robinson laughed. "How in the world did you come up with that?"

"Bertice teases a lot, Annie. Don't take her too seriously."

"I know it's all in good fun," Mrs. Robinson said. She turned to Bertice. "It really was nice to meet you. Destiny's friends are always welcome here. I hope we'll see you again."

"As long as my girl Destiny is here," Bertice said, "I'll be here."

"Then I'll see you next time," Annie said, making her way over to greet the woman who'd just sat in a station two chairs down.

"She seems as nice as you said," Bertice said to Destiny.

"She's special." Destiny patted the back of her chair. "Take a seat so we can get started." After Bertice sat in the chair at Destiny's station, Destiny ran her fingers through Bertice's hair. "When was the last time you washed it?"

"A little over a week ago."

"Hop up then. Let's go to the back so I can wash you."

Destiny led Bertice back to the shampoo bowls.

"This place isn't bad," Bertice said, taking a seat in front of the first shampoo bowl. "It's not your house, of course, but it's still not bad. Do you like it?"

Destiny adjusted the water temperature in the bowl. "I don't not like it," she said. "Today is my first day; I haven't been here long enough to have any kind of opinion. It seems as though it's going to work out for me."

"I'm glad to hear it. You know I'm proud of you, don't you, Destiny? Things are looking up for you both professionally and personally. Where are things with you and Daniel?"

Destiny used the sprayer to saturate Bertice's hair with water. "They've been going well," she said. "We've been seeing each other a couple of times a week since the reception, not counting the time that we spend working together. If you count those and when I see him at church, I'd say we see each other four or five times a week."

"It sounds like things are getting serious with you two. Is it? You're certainly spending a lot of time together."

"I know, but it's only because of work and church," Destiny said as she began rubbing shampoo into Bertice's hair.

"We're both excited about where things are going but we're still really taking things slowly. Neither one of us is in a rush."

"That sounds about like me and Phil. I really like him, Destiny. You like him, too, don't you?"

Hearing the uncertainty in her friend's voice, Destiny said, "Of course I like him. Why wouldn't I? He's a nice guy, Bertice. The work he found for me has been a godsend. And Daniel likes him, too. I think he even won Natalie over, and you know what a coup that was."

"I think so, too. It started the night of the reception but I think he really sealed it last Sunday when we showed up at church."

Destiny chuckled. "I think you're right. How did that happen anyway?"

"I invited him," Bertice said. "As much time as you, Natalie, and I spend together, I figure it's important that the men in our lives get along. Even better, that they like each other. We can plan one of those couples' nights out when you get back from California. We had a nice time together the night of the reception. We should try it again soon."

"Sounds good to me. After I get back will be great."

"Are you excited?" Bertice asked.

"Eager to see my kids," she said. "Even with all I'm doing while they're away, I still miss them like crazy. I can't wait to get on that plane."

"Are you all packed and ready to go? Do you need me to take you to the airport?"

Destiny shook her head. "It's a short trip so I didn't have

much packing to do, and Daniel's going to drive me and Mom to the airport."

"I should have known," Bertice said. "I wouldn't be surprised if Daniel was going to California with you."

Destiny chuckled. "We're not that serious."

"Yet," Bertice added.

"Yet," Destiny agreed.

"Well, is there anything else I can do?" Bertice asked. "Do you want me to check on your house while you're gone?"

"If you don't mind. That would be great. You still have your key, don't you?"

"Sure do," Bertice said. "I may go rummaging through your stuff while you're away. That'll keep me busy."

Destiny rolled her eyes. "You rummage while I'm home, so you don't have a need to do it while I'm gone."

Bertice chuckled. "You've got a point."

Destiny cut off the water, grabbed a towel, and squeezed the water out of Bertice's hair. When she was done, she wrapped the towel around her friend's head. "You can get up now so we can go back to my station."

After Bertice was seated at her station, Destiny removed the towel from her head and fluffed out her hair. Then she took out her blow dryer and began to dry it. "Do you and Phil have plans for this weekend?"

"We had planned to go to church again on Sunday," Bertice said, "but I'm not sure what else we're doing."

"Is something wrong?" Destiny asked, detecting a hint of concern in her friend's voice.

"To be honest, I don't know," Bertice said. "Things are

going well with me and Phil but I'm beginning to feel some distance. I can't put my finger on it and he says there's nothing wrong but I can't shake this feeling."

"What kind of feeling? Do you think he's seeing somebody else?"

"Nothing like that," she said. "But Phil's dealing with something that he's keeping from me."

"You don't have any idea what it could be? Maybe it's the business. He could be having financial trouble of some kind."

Bertice shook her head. "I don't think that's it. I don't know. Maybe I'm blowing this out of proportion. I shouldn't look for trouble, should I?"

"No, you shouldn't. Sometimes you create trouble for yourself by looking for it when it doesn't exist."

Bertice chuckled. "That makes no sense, but I fully understand it. I think that means we've been friends too long."

"Nah. It just means that we understand each other."

Chapter 30

DANIEL EXPERIENCED A NEW LEVEL OF DISCOMFORT AS he drove to Destiny's house. Though he'd visited her home several times since that fateful night of the reception, today's visit was different because he was meeting Destiny's mother for the first time. After they ate lunch, he was driving them to the airport. Destiny had hinted that lunch was her mother's idea. And he knew enough about mothers to understand the woman wanted to check him out. He didn't mind though. It was only natural that a mother would want to meet the new man in town who was dating her daughter and was also her boss. Well, sort of her boss.

No, his uneasiness did not come solely from concern about meeting Destiny's mom. Much of his uneasiness was based in the half-truths he'd told Destiny, from his relationship with Phil to what he knew about what was going on with HR Solutions. If what was growing between them was to have any chance at all, he needed to come clean with her.

He'd decided to wait until after her return from California so that she could enjoy her trip without the cloud of what he had to tell her hanging over her head. And while she was away, he'd make a quick trip to Memphis to have a strategy session with George and William. He'd also have to get on the same page with Phil. The man was as anxious to come clean with Bertice as he was to come clean with Destiny. They both were being led by their hearts.

As he pulled his car into Destiny's driveway, he said a quick prayer for guidance and courage, knowing he needed both in order to do what had to be done.

Destiny greeted him at the door after he rang the bell. "You're right on time," she said when she opened the door. "Thanks for offering to drive us to the airport. You really didn't have to do it."

He leaned in and pressed a kiss on her cheek, effectively cutting her off. When he pulled back, he said, "I'll take any excuse to see you."

She smiled, but before she could speak, her mother called out, "Is that your friend?"

She smiled again and reached for his hand. "Come on," she said. "I hope you're ready for this. Patricia Madison is a special kind of force."

He squeezed her hand. "She'd have to be to have a daughter like you."

She chuckled. "You're pretty good at this," she said.

"Just calling them like I see them," he said.

When they reached the kitchen, the older woman who had to be Destiny's mother was mixing a salad. When Destiny called out to her, she turned toward them. Daniel looked for Destiny in her mother's features, but he didn't see her. She must look like her dad, he thought.

"Mom," Destiny said, "I'd like you to meet Daniel Thomas." She looked at Daniel. "Daniel, this is my mom, Patricia Madison."

Daniel took a few steps to close the distance between them. "I'm honored to meet you, Mrs. Madison." Then he leaned in and pressed a kiss on her cheek.

"It's nice to meet you, too, Daniel," she said, when he pulled back. "I've wanted to meet you for a while now. Thank you so much for being willing to drive us to the airport and pick us up when we get back. I really don't like the hassle that comes with parking and getting to and from the terminal."

He glanced at Destiny. "I'm glad to help out," he said. "Besides, it gives me one last chance to spend some time with Destiny before she leaves. I've gotten used to seeing her beautiful face."

"I'll be back before you start missing me," Destiny said, but he could tell by the light in her eyes that she was pleased with his words. "Monday will be here before you know it."

Daniel noticed Mrs. Madison was smiling as well. He was glad to have made a positive first impression. He hoped the rest of their time together continued that impression.

"We'd better eat," Mrs. Madison said, "if we're going to get out of here and not have to rush to the airport." She tipped her head toward the dining room. "Daniel, why don't you wash up and take a seat at the end of the table."

He smiled down at her. "You're not putting me on the hot seat, are you, Mrs. Madison?"

The older woman chuckled. "Not me," she said, feigning innocence.

He gave her a quick grin in return, and then headed to the bathroom to wash his hands. Destiny said something to her mother. Though he couldn't make out the words, her chiding tone told him that she was warning her mother about making him uncomfortable. He'd have to let her know that he was enjoying himself and not being made uncomfortable at all. When he made his way to the dining room, Destiny and her mother were seated on opposite sides of his chair at the end of the table. "I could get used to this," he said, taking his seat. "Beauty and charm on either side of me. I'm going to get spoiled."

"You're a charmer, aren't you, Mr. Thomas?" Mrs. Madison said.

Daniel picked up his napkin and put it in his lap. "No, ma'am," he said. "I'm merely making an honest observation."

Mrs. Madison raised her glass to him. "I think I like you, Daniel Thomas."

He glanced at Destiny. "I hope you do," he said, "because I'm really enjoying getting to know your daughter. She's smart and charming." He turned back to the older woman. "And now I know where she gets both."

"You're a charmer yourself, Daniel," Mrs. Madison said, a twinkle in her eyes. "Destiny's lucky to have a boss, and friend, like you."

Daniel laughed. Not much got by the older woman. "Destiny's been a great help with getting a couple of programs off the ground at the church. No way could I have done it without her."

Mrs. Madison turned to Destiny. "I'm not surprised. She's always had a good head on her shoulders. I'm glad to see others recognize it."

"Mom," Destiny said, and Daniel knew that while her mother's words pleased her, she was also a bit embarrassed by them.

Seeing her discomfort, he turned the conversation. "Has Destiny told you about our project?"

"A little," the older woman said. "But I'd love to hear more."

Daniel took that as his cue to take over the conversation, so he did. After he finished describing both programs, he said, "A lot of folks will be helped by these programs. Lives will be changed. And none of it would be happening without Destiny's help."

"I wouldn't go that far," Destiny said. "You would have pulled this off without me. I'm quite sure of that."

He shook his head. Then he spoke directly to Destiny. "I'm not so sure. We would have had the programs, but they wouldn't be the same programs. I firmly believe that God puts people together for a reason. Our meeting each other and working together are no coincidence."

"You and I think alike, Daniel," Mrs. Madison said. "There are no coincidences with God." She looked at her watch. "I'm going to go freshen up before we have to head for the airport. I'll leave it to you young people to clear the table."

"Will do," Daniel said as she got up to leave.

"Don't say I didn't warn you," Destiny said, after her mother left the room. "She means well."

Daniel reached out and covered her hand, which was resting on the table, with his. "She didn't say or do anything that requires an apology. She's as charming as you are."

Destiny threaded her fingers through his. "I'm glad you see it that way."

"There's no other way to see it," he said, lifting their folded hands to his lips. "I really am going to miss you."

"I'll be back before you have time to miss me," she said.

He eyed her. "Does that mean you won't miss me?"

She smiled. "How can I miss you if I'm going to be talking to you every day?"

"So you're going to call me every day that you're gone? I'm not sure I believe that. You're going to be too excited about being with your kids."

"You're right about that. I miss them something fierce. Kids. They drive you crazy when they're around and they drive you crazy when they're away. It's not fair."

He gave her fingers a light squeeze. "I don't think fairness has anything to do with the parent-child relationship. It just is what it is," he said, thinking both of her relationship with her kids and her relationship with her mother. He'd save further discussion of the latter until she returned from her trip. "So I'm going to let you off the hook. I'm not going to expect you to call me every day. If you find some time, please do call, but don't let calling me get in the way of your time with your kids. You're only going to be there a short time and we'll have plenty of time to catch up when you get back."

"I appreciate your understanding," she said, "but I'm sure I'll find time to call you."

"Just know there's no pressure."

"I know," she said. "I'm going to just relax and enjoy myself and my kids. No worries at all."

"That's my girl," he said, wishing he wouldn't have any worries. But he would. He'd have them until he was able to sit down and tell her the full truth about his involvement with HR Solutions. "Hey, we'd better get moving. I don't want your mom getting mad at me for making her have to rush to the terminal."

Chapter 31

DESTINY'S HEART RACED AS SHE WATCHED HER KIDS run down the beach back toward the leased beachfront house Mary Margaret's company had rented for the summer. She'd been a bit irritated when they first arrived and she learned that Mary Margaret's mother was visiting the same weekend that she was. She hadn't come to California to socialize with Charlotte Wells. She'd come to spend time with her kids. She'd feared that she'd be stuck making nice with the adults but her fears had been misplaced. Her kids had saved the day for her when they'd invited her to join them on their nightly walk on the beach. She'd been so happy to spend time with them that she hadn't minded Kenneth's presence.

When they entered the house, Mary Margaret asked, "Did you guys have a good time?"

"Kenae tried to make Mom walk into the waves but she wouldn't do it," KJ said. "She was scared, wasn't she, Dad?"

"I wasn't scared," Destiny said to her son. "I didn't want to get wet."

"Mary Margaret likes to go in the water," KJ offered. "Don't you, Mary Margaret?"

"I sure do, KJ," she said. "The ocean feels wonderful. You have to try it before you leave, Destiny."

"That's right, Mom," Kenae said. "You can spend the whole day on the beach with us."

"Okay," Destiny said, willing to do whatever her kids wanted to do. "You've convinced me. A full day on the beach it is."

"You, too, Grandma," KJ said.

"A day on the beach sounds great to me. I brought my Kindle so I can read while everybody else swims."

Kenae rolled her eyes. "I can't believe people in this family don't like to swim. You're missing out."

"Enough, kids," Destiny said, feeling magnanimous now that she'd had some time with her kids. "Why don't you go to your rooms and let the adults talk for a while. I'll be in to say good night."

"Sounds good to me," Kenae said.

"Come with us, Mom," KJ said. "You said you wanted to see the video I shot."

"It's late, KJ," Kenneth said. "We don't have to do everything in one day. Your mom is going to be here until Monday, so save something for tomorrow."

"But—" KJ began.

Destiny tapped her son on his head. "No buts. Your dad's

right. If we do everything today, there won't be anything left to do for the rest of the trip."

"But—" KJ started again.

"Give it up," Kenae said. "Nobody wants to watch videos tonight. Besides, I thought you were supposed to be Skyping with Walter Grimes tonight."

"I forgot," KJ said. He turned to his mother. "So we'll watch the videos tomorrow?"

"I can't wait," Destiny said.

"Neither can I," Patricia chimed in. "Now when you become a famous moviemaker, I'll be able to say I saw your first works."

"Aw, Grandma," KJ said.

"Him?" Kenae pointed at her brother. "You haven't seen the videos yet, Grandma."

Kenneth rocked his hip into his daughter's side. "Stop teasing your brother. He wouldn't be the first person to get that Hollywood fever. You'd better be nice to him so that when he's rich and famous, he'll be nice to you."

"That's right, Kenae," Patricia said.

Kenae just rolled her eyes and put her earphones in her ears. "I'm going to my room," she said. "Don't leave without saying good-bye, Mom."

Destiny pulled her daughter close and pressed a kiss against the top of her head. "Never, sweetheart."

"Why don't you and Grandma stay here, Mom?" KJ asked. "We can make room."

"No, Grandma and I are staying in a hotel down the road,"

Destiny explained. "If it's okay with Mary Margaret and Kenneth, you and your sister can come spend a night or two with us before we leave. This beach house is pretty fantastic though, so if I were you, I'm not sure I'd want to leave it to go stay in a hotel room." She turned to Mary Margaret. "This is a great house and the location is perfect. Even a person who doesn't swim would appreciate waking up to the sunrise on the beach."

"I agree, but I didn't have anything to do with picking it out. The staff at work did everything."

"They did a great job."

Mary Margaret just nodded.

Charlotte Wells cleared her throat. "Speaking of hotels, I should probably head out to mine."

"Don't rush off, Mrs. Wells," Destiny said, turning to Mary Margaret's mother. "Forgive us for barging in like this. You all seemed to be engaged in a lively discussion when we walked in. We shouldn't have interrupted the way we did. My kids usually have better manners and so do I."

"I was enjoying talking to your mother," the older woman said. "But like you told the kids, we don't have to cover all the ground today." She turned to the kids. "It was nice meeting you, KJ and Kenae. I'm sure we'll see each other again before I leave." Then she turned to Destiny and Patricia. "And I'm sorry it's taken us so long to meet. I fear that's my fault."

"It's nobody's fault," Patricia said. "We all lead busy lives."

Charlotte just nodded. She turned to Mary Margaret. "Where are my keys?"

"No way are you driving," Mary Margaret told her mother. "You've been drinking."

"Not that much. I can still drive."

"You're not supposed to drink and drive," KJ said. "You could have an accident."

"That's enough, KJ," Destiny said. "You two should say good night to Mrs. Wells and head off to your rooms. I'll check in on you before I leave."

"All right, Mom," both kids mumbled.

"Good night, Mrs. Wells," they said, and then they headed off to their rooms as their parents had directed them.

Mary Margaret turned back to her mother. "I'll drive you," she said. "Kenneth can follow in our car and bring me back home."

"That's not necessary, Mary Margaret," her mother said.

"Yes, it is," Kenneth chimed in. "There's no way I'm going to let my wife's mother behind the wheel of a car tonight. So you may as well get with the program. We either take you back or you spend the night here. There are no other options."

Charlotte sighed. "I have an early morning, so I really do need to get back tonight."

"That settles it then," Destiny said. "Mom and I will stay with the kids until you get back."

"Thanks, Destiny," Mary Margaret said. "Her hotel is not that far away. We'll be back in about an hour or so."

"No problem," Destiny said, with a chuckle. "Like I told KJ, this place is much nicer than our hotel."

Chapter 32

DESTINY GLANCED OVER AT HER KIDS AS THEY PLAYED in the arcade area of the beachfront restaurant where they were having lunch. "They're growing up, Mom," she said. "I don't think they missed me anywhere near as much as I've missed them."

Patricia chuckled. "They miss you enough," she said. "Stop feeling sorry for yourself and start appreciating that you've raised independent children who feel as safe and comfortable with their dad as they do with you. It's a blessing, Destiny. Trust me."

"I hope you're right," she said, "because I don't like this feeling."

Their waitress returned to the table and said, "I hope you enjoyed your meal. Would you like anything else?"

"Not me," Destiny said. "How about you, Mom?"

"No, I couldn't eat another bite. The shrimp was delicious."

"Thank you," the waitress said. "I'm glad you enjoyed it."

"We'll take the check then," Destiny said. "The kids don't need anything either."

The waitress reached in her pocket and pulled out the check and a pen. "Take your time," she said. "I'll be right back to pick it up."

Destiny nodded. After looking at the check and making sure it was accurate, she opened her purse, pulled out her credit card, and placed it on top of the receipt.

"So I guess I don't have to ask if you're enjoying your vacation as much as I am." Her mother leaned closer. "Tell me what you thought of Charlotte Wells."

Destiny shrugged. "I can't get a read on that woman. Mary Margaret and Kenneth have been married for four years and that was my first time meeting her. Obviously, she and Mary Margaret don't have a close relationship."

"Yeah, I sensed tension between them. Did you know that she's a surgical oncologist and Mary Margaret was accepted to medical school?"

Destiny caught the eye of their waitress, who made a quick trip to the table to pick up the credit card.

"I had no idea," she said to her mother.

"I don't think the woman ever got over the disappointment of her daughter not becoming a doctor," her mother continued. "She probably took Mary Margaret's rejection of medical school as a rejection of her."

"That doesn't make a lot of sense."

"Just like it doesn't make sense for you to feel threatened by the relationship Mary Margaret and Kenneth have with KJ and Kenae? Parental feelings don't have to make sense. You know I'm right."

"Excuse me." Destiny looked up to see the waitress. "I'm

sorry," she said, handing Destiny back her credit card. "But there was a problem with your card. Do you have another one?"

Destiny frowned. "No problem," she said. She reached in her purse and pulled out another card. "This one should work. I guess I'll have to call the credit card company about the other one. It should have worked, too."

"We ran it twice," the girl said, taking the new card.

"Thank you," Destiny said.

"What was that about?" her mother asked. "Please tell me that you're not over your limit or some such nonsense."

"Of course not, Mother," Destiny said. "All my credit card accounts are up to date. I checked all the available balances before I left for this trip. There must be some mix-up. I'll call the credit card company tonight."

"Be sure you do," her mother said. "You have to keep on top of your finances, Destiny."

"I know, Mother," Destiny said, praying her mother wouldn't begin to lecture.

"Here comes the waitress," her mother said. "Sign that receipt so we can get out of here."

"I'm sorry," the waitress said when she returned to the table, "but that card doesn't work either."

"What?" Destiny asked. "There has to be some problem. Are you sure there's not anything wrong with your credit card machine?"

The young woman shook her head. "All the other cards are processing correctly." She cleared her throat. "Uh, we also take cash."

Destiny felt a flush of embarrassment flood her face. "Of course," she said. When she opened her wallet, she realized she had only twenty dollars in cash. She turned to her mother.

"I'll take care of it," her mother said, clearly exasperated with her and embarrassed to be in this situation. She handed three twenty-dollar bills to the waitress. "You can keep the change."

"And I'd like my card back," Destiny added.

"I'll be right back," the girl said.

"I thought you told me you had enough money for this trip, Destiny. I offered to help out but you said you didn't need my help. What's going on?"

Destiny shrugged. "I have no idea. I'll have to call the credit card companies to find out. This has not happened to me since I was in college."

"It shouldn't be happening now. I'm glad that the kids were occupied and didn't get to see it."

Destiny glanced over at her kids, who were still at the arcade. "I'll get it straightened out as soon as we get back to the hotel. It has to be a computer glitch."

"Here comes the waitress again," her mother said. "Let's get your card and get out of here."

"I'm sorry again, Ms. Madison, but the manager would like to see you in his office."

"For what?" Destiny asked. "I'd just like my card back."

"I'm sorry, ma'am," the waitress said. "I'm only telling you what I was told to tell you."

"What are you talking about?" Destiny asked.

The girl leaned closer and whispered, "I'm sorry, ma'am. When the second card failed, an alert was sent to the police. An officer is waiting in the back to speak with you. Please don't make a scene. Just follow me to the manager's office and no one will be the wiser. If you don't come, the police are going to come to you."

"I don't believe this," Patricia said. "We have rights. What's going on here?"

"It's all right, Mom," Destiny said. "I'll go see what they want. You stay here and watch the kids."

"No, I'm going with you."

Destiny shook her head. "No, I need you to stay with the kids. I'll update you as soon as I know something. Keep your cell on. I'll call or text if I need you."

"I don't like the idea of your going back there alone. I'm calling Kenneth. He can take the kids."

"Don't do that, Mom. It's probably nothing."

"If the police are involved, it's not nothing."

"Calm down," Destiny said. "I'll be right back."

Destiny felt a bit of trepidation as she followed the waitress to the back of the restaurant. She'd never been in trouble with the police before, never even had occasion to go to a police station. Her anxiety rose with each step. As they made their way through the kitchen, she saw a man standing at the end of a short hallway. His hands rested on his hips and he had what looked like a badge clipped on his belt. She took a deep breath.

When she reached the man, he pulled his badge off his belt and held it up for her to see. "I'm Detective McCoy.

Why don't you come in here," he said, pointing to the room to his left. "My partner and I have a few questions for you."

Destiny's mind raced. All those episodes of *Law & Order* came flooding back to her. How did she know these were real police? What if this was a trick of some kind? Did the police really show up for mere credit card problems? She didn't think so.

Her musings must have run long, for the detective said, "We can do this here and let you get back to your family, or we can do it at the station. It's up to you."

Destiny said a silent prayer, shook off her fears, and walked into the room, where another detective, this one a black female, was seated in a chair near the desk. The woman stood. "Thanks for agreeing to talk to us, Ms. Madison." She pointed to the other chair in front of the desk. "I'm Detective Armstead. Please take a seat."

"What's this all about?" Destiny asked, as she did what she was told and sat down.

The female detective glanced up at the male detective, who stood by the door, before retaking her seat. While Destiny waited for her answer, the woman flipped through the notepad she had in her hand. "Do you recall where you were on the first Monday of last month, the fifth?"

"Not really," Destiny said. "Why is that date important? Do I need a lawyer?"

"At this point, we're just asking questions," Detective McCoy said from his station by the door. "You don't need a lawyer unless you've done something wrong."

Destiny had seen just enough *Law & Order* to make her

nervous. The one thing she'd learned was that the suspect was always better off with a lawyer.

"So where were you on the fifth of last month?" Detective Armstead asked again.

"I told you I don't remember," she said.

The female detective glanced over at the male detective again. "When was the last time you were in Denver, Colorado?"

Destiny looked from one detective to the other. "What is this about? I've never been to Denver."

"What about Sioux Falls, Iowa?" Detective Armstead asked.

"What about it?" Destiny asked, growing agitated now. Why were they treating her this way over a simple credit card error? It didn't make sense.

Detective Armstead met her gaze. "When was the last time you were in Sioux Falls, Iowa?"

"I've never been to Sioux Falls," Destiny said. "What do all these questions have to do with my credit cards? I'm not answering another question until you tell me what this is about."

Detective McCoy left his perch near the door and came to stoop down next to her. "We want to work with you, Ms. Madison, but you aren't doing your part to help us out. Why don't you tell us about your involvement with HR Solutions?"

Destiny's apprehension escalated. "HR Solutions? It's the temporary employment agency that I work for in Atlanta.

Why are you asking me about HR Solutions? What do my credit cards have to do with HR Solutions?"

"We're asking the questions here, Ms. Madison," Detective McCoy said. "It's in your best interest to answer them. We'd hate to have to drag you out of here in cuffs, but we'll do it if you don't cooperate. Now tell us about your involvement with Phil Harris and HR Solutions."

"I told you. It's a temporary employment agency in Atlanta that I work for. I don't know what else you want me to say."

"What kind of work do you do for them?"

"Marketing and consumer research," she said, her apprehension growing. "Why are you asking me these questions?"

"Do you want to get arrested, Ms. Madison?"

"No, I don't want to be arrested," Destiny said. "I just want to know why you're asking all these questions."

Instead of answering her questions, the two detectives stepped away from her and consulted with each other. When they were finished, Detective Armstead returned to her side. "Destiny Madison," she said, "you're under arrest for suspicion of credit card fraud, bank fraud, wire fraud, and identity theft."

Chapter 33

Daniel sat in his old office at GDW Investigations in Memphis and read through the latest intel on the HR Solutions case. The IT team had made great inroads in tracking this scam back to its ringleaders. They had more than enough information to take to the authorities and begin the process of shutting down the entire crime syndicate.

"What do you think?" his old partner and friend George Campbell asked from his chair in front of Daniel's desk.

"I think the team has done a great job. Have you scheduled a meeting with the authorities?"

George nodded. "Because this fraud spans state and national borders, we've arranged a joint meeting with the assistant U.S. attorney from the Western District of Tennessee and a special agent from the FBI's Memphis division. We've had some preliminary, off-the-record talks with them already. This meeting is to formalize our complaint and develop a strategy to arrest the guilty parties. We've done a good job here, Daniel, and you played an important role."

"I don't know about that," Daniel said. "I'm just glad this is about to be over. Some folks I care about are involved and I need to let them know what's going on. I feel like I've been lying to them for too long."

"But you did it for a good reason. We had to let the scam continue to play itself out. As you can see, we've identified many of the affected people, and one of the goals of the meeting with the Feds is to decide how to deal with them. We're not interested in seeing them prosecuted and neither are the Feds. They'll all probably get off with a slap on the wrist if they cooperate the way Phil has done."

"That's good to hear," Daniel said, thinking specifically about Destiny and Bertice. "What about the folks who have been targets of identity theft?"

"Our plan is to get all those cases expedited so they can be resolved quickly. It's another item on the agenda for the meeting with the Feds."

"I'm glad to hear it," Daniel said. "Now my life and the lives of my friends can get back to normal."

"It sounds like you're talking about more than Phil here. Don't tell me Gavin somehow got caught up in this?"

Daniel shook his head. "Not Gavin," he said. "Two of Natalie's friends."

"Oh man, I hate to hear that."

"And I hated to find out about it. When I learned about their involvement, it was hard not to warn them about what was going on. I'm relieved that now I can be honest with them. I hope they'll understand."

"They should," George said. "You've helped them more than harmed them."

"That's true for one of the friends but not the other. One has been involved for over a year but the other one only became involved after I moved to Atlanta. She's come to be special to me, George. Very special. And I've been lying to her for quite a while now."

"Well, it's about time," George said. "Gloria would be happy that you've found somebody. I know I am. I worried that you'd never let another woman in."

Daniel shrugged. "Maybe I shouldn't have. Not this woman. Not at this time. And definitely not under these circumstances. I hope she understands when I explain everything to her."

"If you don't mind me asking, how did she get involved with Phil in the first place?"

"Through a friend of hers, who's also a friend of Natalie's," Daniel said. "This friend is dating Phil and is the reason he was compelled to come to us." He shook his head. "It's a convoluted mess of relationships, George, a real mess."

"And this woman, the one you're interested in, she didn't know what she was doing wasn't on the up-and-up?"

"You know how it works. I think her initial reaction was that it was too good to be true. But she needed the money, so she let herself be convinced that it was all legal. Phil is a good salesman. He does a masterful job of addressing those initial fears."

"Are you sure you're not making excuses for her because you care about her?"

Daniel shrugged. "Maybe a little, but she's a good person, George. I know her heart. I've only known her for a short time, but there's something about her. Finding out she'd gotten herself involved with Phil didn't make those feelings fade. If anything, I became protective of her. Sure, I was disappointed that she'd let herself be exploited, but seeing a victim of this scam helped me to decide to do a little something to reduce the helplessness that leads some people to become victims."

"That doesn't surprise me," George said. "What did you do?"

Daniel told him about the financial programs he was starting at church. When he was finished, he added, "Destiny, that's her name, is working with me on getting them started. We've been spending a lot of time together. I hate that I haven't been totally honest with her."

"You're worried she's not going to react favorably when she learns what you've been up to?"

Daniel gave a dry laugh. "You know what's funny? Phil told me that the reason he came clean was because of Bertice, the other one of Natalie's friends. He'd fallen for her since getting her involved and knew he had to do something to make it right. We've both been lying to women we care about. Lying for a good reason, but lying just the same."

"And you never know how women are going to react to that, do you?"

"They're funny creatures when it comes to their hearts.

Trust is hard to gain but very easy to lose. I don't want Destiny to regret trusting her heart to me. She's been through enough disappointment when it comes to men. I don't want to be that guy."

"You won't be," George said. "You'll sit her down next week and tell her everything. She'll probably be more embarrassed than anything. If she's half the woman you think she is, she'll understand why you kept her in the dark."

"And if she doesn't?"

It was George's turn to shrug. "Maybe she's not the woman for you."

Daniel didn't want to let his thoughts go down that road. It wasn't lost on him that his relationships with both Gloria and Destiny had ties to his work at GDW Investigations. What did that say about him? What did it say about them? Before he could begin to ponder answers to those questions, the cell phone in his pocket began to vibrate. "Let me check to see who this is," he said, pulling out the cell phone. "Destiny went to California where her children are vacationing and I don't want to miss a call from her." When he looked at the caller ID, he said, "It's her. I need to take this."

"No problem," George said. "I'll be in my office."

Daniel shook his head. "No, don't leave. I'd like to finish this conversation. Let me tell her that I'll call her back."

Daniel turned his chair so that he faced away from George and out the windows behind his desk. "Hello, Ms. California," he said. "I'm glad you haven't forgotten me."

Instead of giving him back the playful banter he expected, she murmured, "I'm in trouble, Daniel."

Daniel jumped up from his chair. "Trouble? What kind of trouble? Are your children all right?"

"The children are fine," she said, her voice shaking. "It's me. I'm in trouble."

"What happened?"

"I'm at the L.A. police station," she said. "It started with a rejected credit card at a local restaurant and now I'm being held for questioning."

"For what?" he asked, his voice rising. "Surely not for a declined credit card."

"I don't know why," she said. "They've been asking odd questions, not about the rejected credit cards, but about Phil and HR Solutions."

"Don't answer anything," he said. "Sit tight and I'll round up an attorney for you. This whole thing doesn't sound right."

"Don't hang up," she said. "I'm scared, Daniel. Why are they asking about Phil and HR Solutions? What have I gotten myself involved in?"

Daniel's heart beat faster with each of her questions. He wished he were there to help her. "Everything will be fine," he said. "Don't worry. You're not going to jail. Do you know which precinct you're at?"

"Yes," she said, and gave him the precinct number.

"Sit tight," he said again. "I'll have an attorney down there within the hour."

"Thank you," she said. "I need to get out of here. They arrested me when I was at a restaurant with Mom and the kids. I need to see my kids."

"Don't worry," he said again. "I've got this. I need you to trust me. I've got this."

She took a deep breath. "It was awful, Daniel. They put me in handcuffs at the restaurant." Her voice began to break. "What if my kids had seen me like that? It would have scarred them for life."

Daniel wanted to throttle the cops who'd mistreated her but he was three thousand miles away and there was nothing he could do. "Look," he said. "Don't hang up. I'll get on another line and contact an attorney. Don't hang up."

"I won't," she said.

Daniel turned to George, who had rushed to his side. "What's going on?" George asked.

Daniel put the phone on mute. "The L.A. police have taken Destiny to the station and they're asking her about HR Solutions."

"Damn, damn, damn," George said.

"I feel the same way," Daniel said. "Can you round up one of your L.A. contacts and get a lawyer down to the jail and get her out?"

"Consider it done," George said.

"And have Anika book me on the next flight out to L.A."

"You're going out there?"

"I have to," Daniel said. "She's scared. Besides, I want to be there when she learns the truth." He sighed deeply. "I definitely didn't want her to find out this way."

George clasped him on the shoulder. "It'll work out," he said. "You have to believe that."

"I'm trying," Daniel said, "but she's so scared. I can hear the fear in her voice."

"Okay," George said, "you get back on the phone with her and try to keep her calm. I'll get an attorney down there ASAP, the same on the flight arrangements. We're going to make this right for her, Daniel. I promise."

"Thanks, man," Daniel said, though he wondered if that were possible. When George headed toward the door, he unmuted the phone and went back to Destiny. "I'm back," he said. "We're getting in touch with the attorney now. I'll stay on the phone with you until he gets there. If we get disconnected or they force you to hang up, know that I'm still here for you. I'll always be here for you."

Chapter 34

DESTINY LET THE CALMING WARMTH OF THE SHOWER soothe her tired spirit. She still couldn't believe that she'd been handcuffed and taken to the police station. Thank God, Daniel had contacts in California who'd been able to get her released. That she hadn't been booked or officially charged didn't make the incident any less harrowing.

When the water began to grow chilly, Destiny knew her shower time was coming to an end. She wrapped herself in a towel and stepped out of the shower. Catching herself in the mirror above the bathroom counter, she was surprised that the horror she'd endured today wasn't reflected in her appearance.

Destiny pushed away the negatives of the day and tried to focus on the positives. Fortunately, she had some things for which she could be grateful. She was grateful her kids hadn't seen her handcuffed. The police hadn't been particularly nice to her but they had honored her request to take her out the back so her kids wouldn't see. She was also grateful they'd let her call her mother and let her know what was going on. That's where her gratitude toward the police ended. According to the attorney Daniel had found for her, they should never have handcuffed her and taken her to the station in the first place. He'd made noises about a civil suit against the department, but she figured that was only posturing to get her released faster. Whatever it was, she was glad it had worked and she was now back at the hotel.

She exhaled deeply. She'd put it off long enough. She had to face her mother. The woman deserved some answers. Unfortunately, Destiny didn't have many. Her attorney told her only that the police were interested in HR Solutions and Daniel would give her the details when he arrived. Why did he have to come all the way to California to tell her? Why couldn't he tell her over the phone? Had he spoken to Phil? What was going on?

"Destiny," she heard her mother call. "You can't hide in there all night. You're not the only one who has to use that bathroom."

Destiny sighed. Then she pulled open the bathroom door. "The bathroom is yours, Mom."

"It's about time," Patricia muttered. "You're not the only one who had a rough day. How do you think I felt sitting in that restaurant waiting for you, only to learn that you'd been taken to the police station? I was terrified. I didn't know what was going on. I still don't know what was going on."

"You know as much as I do, Mother."

Patricia huffed. "I know that's not true. Are you're going to tell me everything before we leave to see those kids?"

"We can talk later tonight," Destiny said. "All I want to do now is drive out and say good night to the kids."

Patricia began shaking her head. "You may want to wait until tomorrow to see the kids though. I told you that Kenneth was pretty angry when he picked them up at the restaurant."

It didn't matter how upset Kenneth was. She needed to see her kids. They were the most important parts of her life and she felt like she'd come close to losing them today. She needed to see them to reassure herself that hadn't happened. If she had to bear Kenneth's wrath, so be it. "I'm going, Mom. It's up to you whether you go with me or not."

"I'm going if you're going," her mother said, though her tone told Destiny she'd be going grudgingly.

"Don't do me any favors, Mom."

Patricia sat down on the side of the bed. "I was so afraid, Destiny. I didn't know what was happening with you. I've never felt so helpless in all my life."

Destiny sat down next to her mother, full of compassion for her. "I'm sorry you were worried, Mom, but as you can see, I'm fine. Nothing happened to me."

"How can you say that, Destiny? Something did happen. You were taken to the police department and I want to know why. Was it about the credit cards?"

"I'm not sure."

"What do you mean you're not sure? What did your attorney say? Where did you find the attorney in the first place? You don't know any lawyers out here, do you?"

The fear and concern in her mother's eyes caused Destiny

to relent. Even though her mother was a tough taskmaster, she was her mother and she loved her. She didn't want her to worry and she didn't want her afraid. She started with the easy question. "Daniel found the attorney for me. He has friends with contacts out here."

"When did you talk to Daniel?"

"I called him from the police station."

"Why him? Are you two that serious? I would think this kind of incident would squelch a new relationship. What man wants this kind of drama?"

Her mother's words stung even though Destiny knew she didn't mean them to. She was only stating what she thought was obvious. "He's my friend, Mom. I trust him. He was the first person I thought of, so I called him."

"Why did they arrest you? What are you not telling me, Destiny?"

"Honestly, Mom, I'm not sure yet. According to the attorney, Daniel will give me the details when he gets here."

"Daniel's coming to Los Angeles?"

"He may already be here. His attorney friend is picking him up. They have the information that the police wanted from me."

"You're talking in circles, Destiny. Just tell me."

Destiny looked away from her mother. "Honestly, Mom, I don't know the details. All I know is that it has something to do with HR Solutions."

"What is HR Solutions?"

"It's a temporary agency in Atlanta that I've been doing some part-time work with."

"Since when? I didn't know you were working a temp job. When do you work? What do you do?"

Destiny thought her mother's questions sounded much like the ones the detectives had asked. "I did market and consumer research from home on the computer."

"Well, if the police were asking about it, there must have been something fishy about it. If you had focused on school the way I asked, you wouldn't be in this mess. I told you that all these little jobs wouldn't amount to much. Now this one has landed you in jail. What were you thinking?"

Destiny bit her tongue to keep from screaming. When she was calm, she said, "Kenneth thinks hauling the kids between my house, his house, and school every day is too much for them. He wants them to live with him and Mary Margaret during the school week since his house is closer to their school."

"When did he tell you this? Why didn't you tell me?"

"I'm telling you now, Mom."

"Why did you wait so long to tell me?"

She met her mother's gaze. "I wanted to wait until I had an answer for you. I wanted to solve the problem myself. I didn't want you to solve it for me."

"I would have helped, Destiny. The kids don't have to live with Kenneth."

"I know," she said. "Since I didn't like the option that Kenneth presented, I had to come up with another one."

"So what did you come up with?"

"I decided that the kids and I needed to move into the school district so the school would be closer. I started looking for places a few months ago, but the apartments are priced higher and they're much smaller than what we have now. I couldn't find anything that worked for us until I started looking at houses."

"You've been looking at houses?"

Destiny nodded. "I found one that's perfect for us. The owners, a retired couple moving to Florida, offered me a great lease-purchase option. So I found a part-time job that would yield me the money I needed. Unfortunately, the offer was rescinded a couple of weeks before I was supposed to start. Then things got even more complicated when Kenneth decided to cut his child-support payments in half for the summer months because the kids were with him. So I took on the extra jobs because I needed them. It's just that simple."

"Why didn't you come to me, Destiny? I could have helped you out. You didn't have to resort to criminal activity."

"I didn't do anything illegal, Mom."

"Well, I'm not a genius," her mother said, "but if the police picked you up, I'd guess whatever it was must have been illegal."

She knew her mother was right. "It certainly seems that way, but I don't really know. According to my attorney, Daniel will give me the details when he gets here."

"Why would Daniel know anything?"

"All I know is that he's friends with the guy who runs HR Solutions."

"This is an awful situation, Destiny."

Destiny could only nod her agreement. "Go take a hot shower, Mom. You'll feel better."

"I think I'll lie down first," her mother said. "I'm too tired to think about a shower now."

Destiny's heart ached with the knowledge that she had caused her mother's fatigue. "I'm sorry, Mom," she said.

Her mother patted her shoulder. "I know you are, sweetheart. Just let me rest for a little while. I'm so tired."

"You're still going with me to see the kids, aren't you?"

Her mother shook her head. "Not tonight," she said. "Tell them I'll see them tomorrow. Tonight I need to rest."

Destiny got up from the bed and watched as her mother slid under the covers. Though Destiny still looked the same after her ordeal, it seemed her mother had aged several years. Destiny despaired that she was the cause.

Chapter 35

DANIEL PACED THE CONFERENCE ROOM OF HIS BUSINESS suite while he waited for Destiny to arrive. Malcolm Winters, the attorney who had gotten Destiny released from jail, sat at the conference table going over the notes from their earlier meeting with the police. Daniel silently thanked God again that GDW's investigation had been complete by the time this happened. Otherwise, Destiny would be in a world of trouble. As it was, the local police were willing to fall in line with the Feds when it came to HR Solutions and the related fraud. Turned out that HR Solutions wasn't the only firm involved.

"You're wearing out the carpet with all your pacing," Malcolm finally said. "There's no need for you to be nervous. Your girl got the best possible outcome. You should be celebrating, not pacing."

"I hear you," Daniel said, hoping the man was right. Sure, Destiny was going to be all right in this mess, but would their budding relationship survive? He'd learned one thing during the long flight from Memphis to Los Angeles: he wanted their relationship to work. They both deserved a chance to see where it would go.

Malcolm chuckled. "You may hear me, but you don't agree. And I can't figure out why."

Daniel stopped pacing. "I'm sorry, man," he said. "I have a lot on my mind. I do appreciate what you've done for Destiny. I'll never be able to repay you for the way you quickly stepped in and got her released. I owe you."

"It wasn't a problem at all," Malcolm said. "George has helped me out numerous times. It was only right that I return the favor. Besides, it's turned into some solid work for me."

"How's that?"

"George has tapped me to be the local intermediary between the Feds and the fraud cases here in the Los Angeles area. Apparently, there are several victims of this crime in the city. Many of them have become victims of identity theft, like Destiny. They need help extricating themselves from the fraud and navigating through the demands the Feds will have for them. I'll represent their interests."

"How will you get paid? I don't imagine these victims have the money for the fees you normally command."

"That's the beauty of it. I'll be paid out of a fund the Feds establish from the money they confiscate from the crime ring. Between your IT experts at GDW Investigations and the IT experts at the Justice Department, they were able to find an account where much of the money was stashed. They hope they'll find others, but what they've found already is more than enough for us to get started helping people."

"And that's how you'll be paid for helping Destiny?"

"Exactly. Normally an attorney in the Atlanta area would do her case, but since her problems surfaced here, I'll handle it. I know she was scheduled to return home on Monday. I suggest she stay a couple of days longer so we can get all the necessary paperwork filed. The travel costs for her and her mom will also be covered by the fund. Like I told you, she has the best outcome possible. She'll be fine."

When he heard a knock at the door, Daniel said, "That must be her." He opened the door without asking who it was and was not surprised to see Destiny standing there. Her sad countenance told him that she'd had a rough day. Instead of asking how she was, he just pulled her into the room and into his arms and held her close. She collapsed against him and began to weep.

When her tears subsided, she said, "What have I done, Daniel? Please tell me what's going on."

He wiped at her tears. "It's nothing that we can't fix," he said, guiding her over to the table where Malcolm sat. "Sit here and let Malcolm tell you what's going to happen next."

She nodded a greeting to the attorney. Then she turned to Daniel. "You're going to stay, aren't you?"

"Of course," he said, pulling out the chair next to hers and sitting down.

Destiny turned to Malcolm. "I know I've said it before but I need to say it again. Thank you so much for everything you've done for me. I really appreciate it. You haven't mentioned money yet, but I want you to know that I don't expect your time to come free. I'll pay. I probably won't be able to use a credit card or a check, but I'll pay. Somehow."

Malcolm began shaking his head. "Don't worry about money," he said. "You were the victim here so I'll be paid out of the victims' fund."

Destiny's eyes widened. "A victim?" She turned to Daniel. "I don't understand."

"Malcolm will explain," he said.

She turned back to her attorney.

"You were a victim of identity theft," he told her. "That's why the police were asking about your credit cards. Several credit accounts have been opened in your name. A woman, using your credit information, purchased a car in Sioux Falls, Iowa. Somebody else bought a house in Denver. Those are just a few of the accounts. I'm pretty sure more will pop up over the next three months. By that time, your credit will be ruined and the scammers will be on to their next victims. That's how identity theft works."

"So that's why my credit cards were rejected at the restaurant?"

Malcolm nodded. "They're all over the limit. Somebody's been buying high-end electronics."

"And it hasn't been me. How did they get my information? Did I do something wrong?"

Her attorney cleared his throat. "That's where HR Solutions comes in. The company was acting as a front for an international bank fraud network. The work you were doing for them was an elaborate form of electronic money laundering."

"Money laundering?"

He nodded. "Money was wired into your account. When you took your cut and wired the rest into another account, you were turning the dirty or illegally gained money into clean or legal money."

She shook her head. "I can't believe I was so gullible. I knew in the beginning that job was too good to be true. I should have listened to my first instincts."

"Don't beat yourself up too badly," Malcolm said. "You're not the first person to get caught up and, unfortunately, you won't be the last."

"It was a very sophisticated scheme, Destiny," Daniel added. "Phil did a good job of knocking down each of your concerns. That was his primary role in the fraud and he was good at it."

Destiny clearly remembered her first session with him. He had done a masterful job of addressing all of her questions and skepticism. "So Phil was in on this from the very beginning?"

"I'm afraid so," Daniel said.

"Does Bertice know about his involvement?"

He shook his head. "Not yet."

"I'm sure she didn't know what he was up to. She never would have involved me if she had. If she knew, she would have told me."

"She didn't know," Daniel said. "Phil never told her."

"I can't believe Phil used us like this. I thought he was a nice guy. Poor Bertice. She was falling in love with him."

"It's not all bad," Daniel said. "Phil has been working with a security firm to shut down the network for the last year. His work is part of the reason Malcolm is going to be able to help you."

"That's something," she said. "But how is this related to the identity theft?"

"They used information from the application you submitted to HR Solutions. It's another angle to the fraud. They set you up as an electronic money mule and then they steal your identity and ruin your credit. It's a one-two punch. The good news is that the fraud had been unraveled by the time your identity was stolen."

"I guess you could call that good news."

"Believe me," Malcolm said, "it is. Now where were we?"

"You were telling me about the victims' fund."

"Oh yes," he said. Then he went on to explain the fund to her in much the same way he'd done earlier with Daniel.

"Well, that's nice to know," she said. "Exactly what do I have to do?"

Malcolm laid out the terms she had to agree to in order to get consideration from the Feds. The consideration included immunity from prosecution for any crimes related to the HR Solutions fraud and access to monies from the victims' fund. In return, she had to supply the Feds with a signed statement of her involvement with the fraud. The Feds specifically wanted to know what she knew and when, who else she knew was involved, and what damage had been done to her as a result of her involvement.

Malcolm handed her a sheet of paper. "This outlines the terms as they relate to the statement. We won't start working on that tonight. Over the next couple of days, I want you to try to think through answers to the questions on that sheet. Write them down. When we next meet, we'll take your answers and turn them into a formal statement. Any questions about that?"

Destiny shook her head as she scanned the sheet.

"Okay, next we have to deal with the identity theft. I have several standard documents for you to sign that I will have sent to all your financial institutions and the credit bureaus. We can't stop the fraud that has already happened but we can prevent anything else from happening."

Destiny nodded. "Will all my credit cards be suspended?"

"Yes, it's best to start with a clean slate. We'll have a couple of the companies send replacement cards with new numbers so you'll have them for the remainder of your trip."

"So that's all I have to do to clear up the identity theft and any resulting fraud?"

Malcolm shook his head. "Those are only the first steps. Once we pull your credit report from the three bureaus, we'll have to identify the fraudulent accounts, close them, and notify the creditors that you were a victim of identity theft. Fortunately for you, the creditors will believe you because of the backing of the Feds and the short window of time during which you were subject to identity theft. Normally, people have a much more difficult time proving they were victims. The Feds have named you a victim so they have taken care of that for you. And since you've been involved with HR Solutions for less than six months, we have a short window of possible fraud actions. I'm not teasing when I say you have friends in high places. Your case will probably be the simplest one that comes across my desk."

She gave a dry laugh. "I don't know how simple it is. I did end up handcuffed and taken to the police station."

"And I told you, and the police chief, that was a gross overreach by those officers. There is no way they should have gone to those lengths. We may have a good case for a civil suit, but the Feds are going to want to include indemnifying the police in the terms of their deal with you."

"What does that mean?" Destiny asked.

"It return for consideration, you can't file suit against any governmental entities for actions related to the frauds."

Daniel cleared his throat. He had kept quiet until now. "Isn't that asking a lot of her? Personally, I'd like to see her sue the LAPD. Like you said, they were way out of line."

Malcolm tapped his pencil against his chin. "At this point, I'm not sure it's worth it." He turned to Destiny. "Depending on how you look at it, the police actually helped you by letting you know you had been a victim of identity theft. We could counter that you would have found that out anyway, but the timing does matter. If you want me to pursue this further I can, but I'd have to charge my fee for doing that work directly to you because the fund won't cover it. You don't have to decide now. Think it over and you can let me know when we meet in a couple of days." He looked at Daniel. "Any more questions?"

He shook his head. "Not right now."

Malcolm then turned to Destiny. "Are you all clear on what you need to work on over the next couple of days?"

She nodded.

"Good," he said. He slid one of his business cards toward her. "If you have any questions, don't hesitate to call my office."

"Thank you," she said. "I can't seem to say it enough."

Malcolm chuckled as he began picking up the scattered papers from the table and putting them in his briefcase. When he finished, he said, "I'm going to head home. I just may get there in time to kiss my kids good night before they go to bed."

Destiny stood. "I hope you make it. I want to see my kids tonight as well."

Daniel extended his hand to Malcolm. "Thanks, man. You've been a great help and we appreciate it."

After Daniel walked Malcolm to the door, he returned to where Destiny was still seated at the conference table.

"What's on your mind?" he asked.

She looked up at him. "I need to see my kids. I really need to see my kids."

He nodded. "Then we'll go see your kids. I'll drive."

"You don't have to do that," she said. "I can drive myself."

"You're emotionally exhausted, Destiny, so you don't need to get behind the wheel. I'll drive you and wait in the car while you say good night."

"Wait in the car?"

He nodded. "I don't want to meet your kids or your ex under these circumstances. We can plan for me to meet them if, and when, the time is right for both of us."

"Are you sure?"

"I'm positive," he said. "Do you have everything you need or do you have to go back to your room for something?"

"I really should check on my mom," she said. "What happened with the police today upset her badly. I think it would ease her mind to know that everything has worked out."

He nodded. "Makes sense to me. I'm sorry she was worried."

Destiny sighed. "You have no need to be sorry. This has been nothing but another case of me letting her down by not living up to her expectations."

"Don't be so hard on yourself."

She shook her head. "I have to be. Even though things have worked out well for me, I made a reckless decision that landed me in this situation. I need to own that. My mom saw as clearly as I did what I almost lost."

"Your kids?"

"That's right. They're more important to me than anything and I made a decision that could have separated us for a very long time. It's going to be a while before I forgive myself for that, and it's going to take a while for my mom to forgive me. I thank God that I won't have to explain anything to my kids."

"Cut yourself some slack," he said. "We all make mistakes."

She gave a weak smile. "And I made a whopper of one. I knew something wasn't right with HR Solutions from the very beginning. I heard the still, small voice but I ignored it. That's all on me."

Daniel's esteem for Destiny grew as he listened to her assessment of her actions. She'd needed to accept full responsibility for what she'd done, and now she needed to forgive herself and move on. He was committed to helping her do just that. "I'm proud of you, Destiny," he said. "And your mom will be, too, once she gets past her fear of what could have happened and begins to focus on what actually happened."

"I hope so," she said.

"I know so." He tapped her on the nose with his finger. "Now how long do you think you'll be with your mother? Should I meet you downstairs in the lobby in about thirty minutes or so?" he asked.

She shook her head. "You've done so much already that I hate to ask this, but can you come up with me to talk to my mom? The details will be more credible coming from you."

"Of course I'll go and explain things to her. Should we head out now?"

Destiny nodded. When he reached to open the door, she placed her hand on his. "Thank you," she said, "for everything. Your support has been more than I could have imagined. I want you to know that I appreciate the kind of friend you've been to me. You're a special man, Daniel Thomas."

Daniel could only smile down at her, hoping his guilt did not show on his face. She still didn't know of his full involvement in the investigation. He'd planned to tell her as soon as Malcolm left, but if he were honest with himself, he was glad her need to talk to her mother and visit her kids forced him to delay his confession. He'd tell her tomorrow, he told himself. She needed a good night's sleep tonight. He ignored the small voice that told him he was only delaying the inevitable.

Chapter 36

DESTINY HAD BEEN RIGHT ABOUT HER MOTHER. THE older woman had brightened considerably after hearing Daniel's explanation of the day's events and what was going to happen as a result. She'd visibly relaxed when she heard that Destiny had been a victim of identity theft. That was a much better outcome than having her daughter arrested for fraud. Of course, she was still disappointed in Destiny for getting involved with HR Solutions in the first place, but she no longer worried about Kenae and KJ being taken away. Destiny watched her now in lively conversation with Mary Margaret's mother and Daniel, looking like her old self and not the haggard and aged woman she'd been earlier this evening.

Destiny smiled at Daniel. Patricia had quickly nixed the idea of him waiting for them in the car. Given what he had done for Destiny today, he was the man of the hour in her eyes. "It's been some day," Patricia said. "Destiny finds out she's a victim of identity theft and then Charlotte and Daniel reconnect."

"This woman was a godsend when my wife was sick," Daniel said, looking at Charlotte. "I can't thank you enough for what you did for Gloria."

"I wish I could have done more," Charlotte said softly. "Gloria was a special woman."

Daniel nodded.

"More special than you know," Destiny added. "I never met her and I've been touched by her."

Daniel glanced over at her, his eyes thanking her for not going into detail about the programs they were starting at church. "You and Gloria would have been fast friends, Destiny," he said. "You—"

Before he could finish, KJ bounded into the room and said, "It's time for our walk on the beach. Who's going?"

Under other circumstance Destiny would have chastised her son for interrupting adult conversation, but they'd needed his interruption tonight. The conversation had been about to turn somber.

"I think I'd like to go," her mother said. "After all that's happened today, I want to get out and feel the night air."

"Yay, Grandma's going!" KJ chimed in.

Patricia turned to Charlotte. "Come with us. It'll be nice."

Charlotte smiled. "Well, I don't see why I shouldn't."

"Kenae," KJ called out. "We're heading for the beach."

Destiny shook her head, wondering why KJ felt the need to yell for his sister. She shouldn't have been surprised though since he did it often. She'd scold him tomorrow; tonight all she could do was take joy in being with them.

As Destiny was getting up to join the group, Kenneth said, "You guys go on. Mary Margaret and I need to talk to your mother. We'll catch up."

The look on Mary Margaret's face told Destiny this need to talk was news to her. The questioning looks on the faces of Patricia and Charlotte suggested they had the same reaction. Destiny had a feeling she knew what Kenneth wanted, so she asked Daniel to wait with her.

After the oldest and the youngest among them had left, Kenneth said, "Now tell us what really happened. There's more to it than you're saying. What are you hiding?"

"Kenneth—" Mary Margaret warned.

"It's all right, Mary Margaret." She turned to Kenneth. "I don't know what you want me to say. You should be happy it was only identity theft. That's bad, but not anything that can't be resolved."

"My concern is my children. Seeing you carted off to jail could have damaged their psyches."

The thought of it made her shiver. "But that didn't happen. My attorney has cleared up everything with the police and he's working on the identity theft. It's taken care of, Kenneth. Let it go."

"I don't like having my kids put in bad situations."

Destiny heard the indictment of her mothering skills in his words. "I'm a good mother, Kenneth, and you know it."

He met her eyes. "I'm a better father."

Destiny's head jerked as if he had struck her. "What do you mean by that?" she asked, fire building in her chest.

Mary Margaret cut a hard glance at her husband. "He didn't mean anything by it," she said. "It's been a tough afternoon for us. We didn't know what was going on with you at the police station and we were worried. As you can imagine, all sorts of negative thoughts went through our minds."

Destiny heard the "our" in Mary Margaret's words but she knew it was Kenneth who'd had the negative thoughts. How had she even put herself in a situation for him to question her mothering skills? She'd gotten off easy with the authorities but she wasn't sure Kenneth would be as accommodating. "If you have something to say, Kenneth, just say it."

When Kenneth only glared at Destiny, Daniel spoke up. "Why don't we all take a few minutes and calm down." He turned to Destiny. "Now is a good time for that walk on the beach. Are you ready?"

She shot a hot glance at Kenneth. "Let's go," she said to Daniel. "Apparently, Kenneth didn't have anything to talk about after all." With those words, she turned and followed Daniel out of the house and down to the beach.

Chapter 37

Did you hear what Kenneth said to me?" Destiny asked. "I can't believe his nerve."

"I heard it," Daniel said, "but I wouldn't read anything into it. Like his wife said, this was a difficult day for all of us. I'm sure it crossed Kenneth's mind that if anything happened to you, he and Mary Margaret would be left to take care of the kids."

"That's exactly what he wants. Well, he'd better get rid of those thoughts. I'm the custodial parent and that's not going to change."

Daniel stopped and tugged on her arm, forcing her to stop as well. "Give him a break, Destiny. He's had a rough day, too. I can only imagine the thoughts that went through his mind when he got the call from your mother to come get his kids."

Destiny exhaled slowly. "I came too close to losing everything important to me. I can't believe I was so reckless. And when I think of the lives that could have been harmed—"

"Be grateful none of that happened."

She turned and looked at him. "I need to call Bertice and let her know what happened to me. She needs to take precautions so it doesn't happen to her. I need my cell."

When she turned to head back to the car where she'd left it, he stopped her. "You don't have to worry about Bertice. She'll be fine." He pointed to some beach chairs nearby. "We have to talk. Let's sit over there."

As Destiny followed him to the beach chairs, her anxiety rose. Whatever Daniel was going to tell her, she wasn't going to like. She was sure of it. After they sat, Daniel folded both of his hands around both of hers. "I want you to know that I had your best interests in mind the entire time."

"What are you talking about?" she asked, her apprehension rising. What had Daniel done?

Daniel sighed deeply. "Let me start at the beginning. I told you before that I started a cybersecurity firm with a couple of friends from college."

She nodded. "I remember."

He rubbed her fingers. "That firm, GDW Investigations, has been investigating HR Solutions since before I moved to Atlanta."

She heard his words but they didn't make sense to her. "What? How?"

"Phil contacted them and reported the fraud that was going on. He felt people were being hurt and he wanted to get out. He felt particularly responsible for one person."

"Bertice?"

He nodded. "He'd come to care for her, and knowing

what he'd gotten her into began to weigh on him. He was looking for a way out for him and her. The parameters of a deal have been in place for them for a while now. You don't have to worry about either of them."

She met his eyes. "And you know all this because?"

"Because when my friends at GDW learned that I was moving to Atlanta, they asked me to help them out."

She pulled her hands away from his. "Help them out how?"

"Phil was getting nervous. They'd warned him it would take time to gather the information they needed to shut down the crime ring, but he was feeling more and more guilty each day. He didn't like lying to Bertice. He didn't like that he'd gotten her involved and then moved on to getting her friends involved. My job was to see that he stuck to the plan."

"To make sure he didn't tell Bertice what was going on?"

"That's right."

"So you've known HR Solutions wasn't on the up-and-up since before you came to Atlanta?"

"I only learned the day before I was to come here. I am no longer involved in the day-to-day activities of the company. This was to be the last case I worked on for them. I only agreed to do it because my friends convinced me I was the best person for the job."

"Why?"

"Why was I the best person for the job?"

She nodded.

He shrugged. "There were several reasons. Phil and I had history from another case in the past so they felt he'd be comfortable with me. It helped that I am a pastor, so if anybody was watching Phil, they wouldn't think anything about my presence in his life."

"So you were undercover?"

"You could say that."

"Did Gavin and Natalie know?"

He shook his head. "No. I've worked cases like this before. The best way to run them is to keep everything on a need-to-know basis. Even though a part of me wanted to, I couldn't tell Gavin, Natalie, or you about my involvement. I couldn't tell you for the same reason Phil couldn't tell Bertice. The only way we could track the electronic footprint of the illegal transactions was to make sure the pipeline continued."

"You found out I was involved, didn't you?"

He nodded. "I learned about Bertice first. It's such an odd name that I suspected she was the same Bertice who had captured Phil's heart."

"And a woman who was also involved in his illegal activities."

"Yes, I knew that, too."

She was glad it was dark. She looked out at the ocean. "When did you find out I was involved?"

"The day after the cancer walk. I confirmed with Phil that your Bertice was his Bertice and then I asked about you."

"And yet you never said anything to me. Never tried to warn me."

"It was too late. By the time I found out, you were already involved. You'd already submitted your application. Once you were in their system, you had to stay in. We didn't want the ringleaders to suspect anything was wrong. You have to catch these criminals in the act. If they had suspected we were on to them, they could have shut the whole thing down."

"What would have been so bad about that? Isn't it what you wanted anyway?"

He shook his head. "No, they would have shut it down with Phil and HR Solutions and just started up with some other person in some other company. We wanted to shut it down for good, not just give them a reason to move on to the next target. The only way to do that was to keep the pipeline flowing."

Destiny wasn't sure she agreed with him, but she knew he believed what he was saying. "When did you learn that identity theft was a part of the fraud?"

"I knew from the beginning, but I couldn't be sure who would be a target. Bertice has been involved much longer than you and there is no evidence of identity theft related to her. You fit the profile, but I honestly didn't think you'd been in long enough to be a target."

"Profile? You had a profile and you still didn't tell me?"

"I didn't tell you, but we were keeping track of you. I really didn't think you would be a target."

"But you were wrong."

"Yes, I was wrong. It never should have come to this. The L.A. police overreached. That situation at the restaurant should have ended with the declined credit cards. It was a case of one authority not knowing what the other was doing. I do apologize."

She looked at him, his face, clear in the moonlight. "So all of this that happened today could have been avoided if you'd told me what was going on."

He reached for hands again. "Maybe or maybe not," he said again. "Once you submitted that application and did the first job for HR Solutions, they had you. Telling you after the fact would have only made you aware and may have resulted in you being subject to criminal charges. You have to believe me. From the day I learned of your and Bertice's involvement, I've worked to make sure you were protected."

"Well, you didn't do a very good job, did you?"

"I know you don't see it now, but things could be a lot worse. By wiring that money from your account to the designated HR account, you broke several federal laws. This was a very serious situation, Destiny."

Destiny looked down at her hands. "I really messed up, didn't I?"

"Yeah, you did, but it's nothing that can't be fixed."

She looked up at him. "You must think I'm an awful person."

He shook his head. "I don't think that at all. This isn't the first case like this that I've worked. I've learned that you really can't judge the people who get involved. In your case, you felt you didn't have many options, so it was fairly easy for Phil to convince you the job he offered was on the up-and-up."

"I think they call that willful ignorance or something like that."

"It doesn't matter what they call it. It's over now and you can move forward."

"But it's not over," she said. "You heard Kenneth. Because

of what happened today, he's threatening to take custody of my kids."

"I wouldn't read too much into what Kenneth said tonight. Give him a day or so to cool off and then talk to him again. He's running on fear right now."

"I don't know," she said. "He wants custody of the kids. He's been angling for it since they started going to school in his district." She chuckled, but it wasn't from joy. "It's ironic, isn't it? I took the job with HR Solutions so I could move to Gwinnett and put a stop to Kenneth's efforts to take custody of the kids, and now the job with HR Solutions may give him the very ammunition he needs to gain custody."

"You can't think like that, Destiny."

"I'm scared, Daniel. I can't lose my kids."

"You won't."

"You can't be sure."

He tilted her chin up. "We'll get through this, Destiny. I promise you."

When he pulled her into his arms, Destiny didn't resist. She needed the comfort right now. Everything else would have to wait until tomorrow.

Chapter 38

Mary Margaret sat up in the bed, trying to read a budget outlook for one of her entertainment projects. She couldn't really focus because her mind kept wandering back to the events of earlier in the evening. Kenneth had crossed a line tonight. No way should he have drawn her into an argument with Destiny about who should have custody of the twins. If Kenneth was even considering making a move like that, they should have discussed it together. And, frankly, it was not something she wanted. She loved Kenneth's kids and enjoyed having them around. If anything happened to Destiny and they had to take custody, she would willingly and gladly do it. She wouldn't even mind if the kids stayed with them during the week when school was in session so they could get to and from school more easily. What she couldn't do was strip the kids away from their mother on a whim from Kenneth. It wasn't right on a lot of levels.

She looked up when the bedroom door opened and Kenneth walked in. "Don't ever do that again, Kenneth."

"Don't do what?" he asked, kicking off his shoes.

Mary Margaret leaned over and placed her unread report atop the nightstand on her side of the bed. "Drag me into a discussion with Destiny and then blindside me."

"I don't know what you're talking about."

"I'm talking about what you did tonight, threatening to take custody of the kids from Destiny. We haven't discussed anything like that."

"I didn't mean anything by it," he said. "I was angry about what happened today. I still believe there is more to it."

"Well, she says there wasn't, and I think we should believe her. She has done nothing in the past to make me question her parenting of the kids, so she deserves the benefit of the doubt."

"If you say so," Kenneth said.

Mary Margaret didn't like his noncommittal attitude. "I'm serious, Kenneth. You can't threaten to take custody of the twins without talking to me about it first."

Kenneth came and sat next to her on the bed. "I won't lie, Mary Margaret. Since the kids started going to school in our district and spending so much time at our house, I've thought a lot about becoming the custodial parent. Haven't you enjoyed having them with us this summer?"

Mary Margaret didn't like where this was going. "Of course I've enjoyed them. I always enjoy having them around. You know that."

"Don't you see?" he said. "The next logical step is for them to live with us. We can give them a more stable home, where they'd have both a father and a mother."

Mary Margaret began shaking her head. "You're wrong for even thinking about doing this."

"I'm not wrong. I love my kids and I know that we can provide a better home for them than Destiny can. What's wrong with wanting them to live with us?"

Mary Margaret took a deep breath. "You're living in a fantasyland, Kenneth. You can't just take the kids from their mother on a whim. It wouldn't be fair to them or to her. She's the custodial parent and she should remain so until she does something that shows she's not fit."

"Maybe she has and we just don't know it yet," he said. "I'm going to be watching her more closely from now on."

Mary Margaret just shook her head. "You're going down a dangerous road, Kenneth. If you continue on this path, you may find yourself somewhere that you don't want to be."

"What are you saying?" he asked.

"I'm just thinking of the old Mahalia Jackson adage: *If you dig one ditch you better dig two cause the trap you set just may be for you.*"

Chapter 39

DESTINY THOUGHT THE DRIVE BACK TO THE HOTEL would never end. As the conversation between her mother and Daniel swirled around her, her thoughts moved from one dire consequence to another. Despite Daniel's attempts to calm her fears about Kenneth's threat to seek custody of the kids, she still felt threatened by the possibility. She'd concluded that she needed some legal advice.

Then there was Daniel. When she'd left Atlanta, she'd been so hopeful about where their relationship was going. That her first thought when she was in trouble was to call him showed just how much he'd come to mean to her in a short time. On the surface, his response showed that she'd come to mean a lot to him as well. But below the surface was the fact that she had been a person of interest in an undercover operation he was running. As a result, she couldn't be sure if his response was out of his feelings for her or his duty to his job. Even more complicated was the idea that it was some convoluted combination of each. She had really screwed up this time. And she wasn't sure how she was going to fix it.

When Daniel finally pulled the car up to the front of the hotel, Destiny resisted the urge to jump out and run yelling into the night. Her mother's presence forced her to stay seated and say, "Thanks for the ride, Daniel."

"Yes, thank you," her mother added, opening the rear passenger car door so she could get out. "You really came through for Destiny today. I still can't believe that you flew all of the way out here to support her and get that police mess cleaned up, but I'm glad you did. We needed you today."

"I'm glad I was able to help," Daniel said. He reached for her hand. "Destiny is very important to me."

"I'll see you upstairs, Destiny," her mother said, getting fully out of the car.

"Okay, Mom, I'll be up shortly."

Alone in the car with Daniel, she looked down at their joined hands and then back up at his face. She searched his eyes for some hint of a change in his feelings toward her but saw none.

"Feeling any better?" he asked.

"I don't know how I'm feeling," she said. "The words that come to mind are *unsettled*, *uncertain*, and *unstable*. I feel as though I've lost my footing."

He squeezed her fingers. "It's natural. You went through a major ordeal today. Things will look a lot better tomorrow."

She met his eyes. "I wish I could believe that."

"Believe it," he said.

But faith without works is dead, she thought. "I think I'd

feel better if I could talk to an attorney about Kenneth's custody threat. Do you think we could get Malcolm to come over in the morning?"

Daniel nodded. "I'm sure we can. He's not a family law attorney but he may have some insights that will help ease your mind."

"That would be great. If he can't help me, maybe he can recommend somebody back in Atlanta. I don't want to be blindsided if Kenneth decides to go through with his threat."

"I'm sorry for all of this, Destiny," he said. "All I've tried to do this whole time is help you and protect you. Your getting arrested was never even a consideration."

She sighed again. "I know," she said. "It's not your fault. In a way, I wish I could blame somebody else, but the only person to blame is me. This is all on me."

"What can I do to help?" he asked.

She gave him a sad smile. "You've done more than enough already. You don't have to stay out here and babysit me. I'll be fine."

"I'm not babysitting you, Destiny," he said. "You're my lady and I'm supporting you. That's the way relationships work."

She met his eyes. "But ours is not a normal relationship."

"How do you mean?"

She lifted her shoulders in a slight shrug. "It's not wise for undercover cops to get involved with their targets, is it?"

"That doesn't apply to us because I'm not a cop and you're not a target."

"Not technically, but it's close enough." She looked directly at him. "How much of your concern for me is because of the case and how much is because of your interest in me? Were we spending so much time together because you enjoyed my company or because you wanted to keep watch over me?"

"Why can't it be all those things?"

"It can, but it makes everything complicated. You see, I know how I feel about you, but I'm not sure you know how you feel about me."

"So now you know my feelings?"

"I'm not trying to be offensive, Daniel. I'm just being honest. When I left Atlanta, I thought I knew where we were as a couple. Tonight, I have no idea."

"Those are your insecurities," he said. "Not mine."

"Maybe they should be."

"What are you saying?"

She released a deep breath. "I think we both need to take a step back and reevaluate our relationship. I need to reconcile the Daniel I left in Atlanta with Daniel the investigator. He's still a great guy but I don't know him well."

"There's only one Daniel."

"That's easy for you to say but not so easy for me. I'm just asking for a little time, Daniel. I'm not running away and I'm not pushing you away. I just need some time not just to figure out how I feel about you but to also figure out how I feel about myself. According to Malcolm, I need to stay out here a few extra days. I see now that I need that time to get recalibrated."

"And you can't do that with me here?"

"I could, but I don't think that's best for us in the long run. You need to get back to your life and rethink how I fit in it, and I need to do the same with you."

He began shaking his head. "I don't need to rethink anything," he said. "I know how I feel about you. I—"

She pressed her fingers to his lips. "Don't say it," she said. "If it's true tonight, it'll be true when I get back to Atlanta. Emotionally, I'm not prepared to hear anything more. Not tonight."

He pressed a kiss against her fingers. "Even though I don't want to, I'm going to honor your request and get a flight back to Atlanta tomorrow. But I want you to know that I'll be waiting for you to come home to me."

"I'm counting on it," she said. After pressing a soft kiss against his lips, she got out of the car and headed into the hotel. She didn't bother to look back though she knew in her heart that Daniel was waiting for her to do so. They needed a clean break, if only for tonight. For both their sakes, she kept facing forward.

Chapter 40

WHEN DESTINY WALKED INTO THE LOBBY OF THE hotel, she was surprised to find her mother waiting for her. "I thought you were going to the room," Destiny said.

"Is everything all right between you and Daniel?" her mother asked, rushing toward her. "You two aren't fighting, are you? He's a good man, Destiny. Whatever he has done couldn't be bad enough to make you overlook everything he did for you today."

Destiny didn't want to get into a deep discussion with her mother. "I'm tired, Mom," she said, continuing on toward the elevators with her mother on her heels. "I thought you'd be in the room by now."

Stepping on the elevator behind her, her mother said, "I was worried about you and Daniel. What happened when we went for that walk on the beach? Before we left, we were all getting along well and enjoying ourselves, but by the time we got back, everything had changed. What happened?"

Destiny took a deep breath. She'd known her mother long enough to know that she was not going to give up until she got the answers she was seeking. "Do we have to do this now?" she asked. "Can't you at least wait until we get back to the room?"

Her mother frowned, but she didn't say anything more as the elevator doors opened and they got off and headed to their room. The silence ended as soon as they entered the room and closed the door behind them. Her mother dropped down on the end of the bed. "Now tell me, what's going on with you and Daniel?"

Destiny wiped her hands down her face. "The problem is not really me and Daniel. It's Kenneth. When you-all went walking on the beach with the kids, he lit into me about what happened today and threatened to take custody of KJ and Kenae."

"What are you talking about?" her mother asked. "Kenneth wants custody of the twins?"

Destiny sat next to her mother. "Yes, he does. Though he hasn't come right out and said it until tonight, he'd been making noises. It started with his suggestion that the kids live with him during the school week. Now he's using what happened today as an example of bad parenting on my part."

Her mother began shaking her head. "I feared something like this might happen, but I thought, or hoped, that Daniel coming here and clearing everything up with the identity theft would put an end to it."

"Well, Kenneth thinks there's more to it than the identity theft."

Her mother sighed. "And he's right, but there is no way for him to know for sure. You're right. Kenneth had to have been thinking of getting custody of the kids long before now. He's just using this incident as an opportunity to do what he's always wanted. I don't know why I'm surprised, but I am."

"Well, I can't let him do it. I'm going to call Malcolm, the attorney, in the morning, so I can see where I stand legally."

"That's a good idea," her mother said. "I just wish you hadn't gotten involved in all of this in the first place. It really wasn't worth it. I hope you see that."

Since Destiny agreed with her mother's assessment, she wasn't offended by it. "I see it all right, Mom. I made a mistake, a big mistake, one I won't make again, but it was a mistake. It shouldn't be something that Kenneth can use to take my kids."

Chapter 41

AFTER A SLEEPLESS NIGHT, DESTINY HAD STARTED THE day with a renewed sense of purpose. Kenneth's threat to take custody of the kids had triggered an instinct that she hadn't known she had. There was no way he was going to take her kids and there was no way she was ever going to do anything again that would make him think he even had a chance at doing so.

She owed a lot of her good spirits to her late breakfast meeting with Malcolm. He'd relieved many of her concerns about losing custody of her children. According to him, had she been convicted, or even charged, with a felony, Kenneth may have had a case for a custody hearing. Given that she wasn't even arrested, there was really no case for Kenneth to bring related to the L.A. police incident since the case was being adjudicated as an identity theft case in which she was the victim. Malcolm further advised her to get her custody and child-support agreement with Kenneth recorded by the courts. He'd even given her the name of a good family law attorney in Atlanta who would help her and she'd already scheduled an appointment.

With her primary concern alleviated, she needed to clear up one more matter before she left California. She refused to spend her remaining extra days at odds with Kenneth, and by extension, Mary Margaret. They needed to clear the air, which was why she was waiting at the beach restaurant for the two to arrive. It was no coincidence that she had chosen the restaurant where she'd had the police encounter. She wanted Kenneth and Mary Margaret to see that she had no reason to run and hide.

She waved to the couple when they entered the restaurant. As she watched them weave their way through the crowd and to her table, it occurred to her that she hadn't planned her outfit today as a dig at Mary Margaret. She realized she was not in competition with the woman, not when it came to her kids or when it came to Kenneth. She'd bet some folks would call that personal growth. "Did the kids get off okay?" she asked when they reached the table.

Mary Margaret nodded. "They should be at the mall now. Your mother got to the beach house about thirty minutes ago and my mother was pulling up when we left. She's going with them. She and your mom have become fast friends."

"That's good to know," Destiny said, referring both to the kids and to her mother's budding relationship with Mary Margaret's mother. "And thanks to you two for joining me. I know this was short notice."

"I'm glad you called," Mary Margaret said as she took the chair that Kenneth pulled out for her. "We didn't like the way things ended last night, did we, Kenneth?"

Sitting next to his wife, Kenneth said, "I could have handled it better."

Destiny could only smile. "Do you know why I chose this restaurant, Kenneth?"

He smirked. "You wanted to come back to the scene of the crime?"

She chuckled, in no way offended by his smirk or his words. "That's part of it, but the primary reason was so that you could see that I'm not afraid to show my face here. I would even feel comfortable bringing the kids back. They enjoyed themselves in the arcade."

"I'm not sure what point you're trying to make, Destiny," Kenneth said.

She drew a deep breath. "I don't want you to question my parenting of the twins or to threaten to take custody from me. I want you to respect me as their mother as I respect you as their father and Mary Margaret as their stepmother. We've done well coparenting the last few years and I don't want that to change."

"Neither do we," Mary Margaret said. "Yesterday was a bad day all around, Destiny. We were worried."

Destiny tilted her head in Kenneth's direction.

"Okay, I was worried," he admitted. "Hell, Destiny, I was more than worried. I was terrified. I had no idea what was going on with you and the police."

"I understand," she said. "And I apologize for giving you

cause to worry. I want you to know that I appreciate you for rushing down here to get the kids so my mother could come to the police station and be with me. I wanted her to stay with the kids and not bother you, but she wanted to come be with me."

Kenneth shook his head. "Your mother did the right thing by calling me. I would have been angry had all this gone on and I had not known about it. You can't keep things like that from me. If it concerns the kids, I need to know. And this concerned the kids because of what could have happened."

Destiny nodded. "I can respect that, Kenneth, and I'll continue to keep you in the loop where they are concerned, but I also need something from you."

"Like what?"

"I need you to trust me," she said. "It was unfair of you to challenge my parenting because of what happened. It was cruel to even suggest that you would challenge me for custody. That can't happen again."

"I was angry, Destiny," he said. "You would have been angry, too."

She shook her head. "The anger I understand. The threat to take the kids, I don't. Is becoming the custodial parent of the kids something that's on your mind? If it is, I need to know."

Destiny noted the quick glance Kenneth shot at Mary Margaret. "I've thought about it," he said. "We love having them with us. Seeing them every day after school has been great and so has the time we've spent together this summer. We enjoy having them with us."

"I would never begrudge any time that the kids spend with you and Mary Margaret," she said. "And I understand how important it is to the kids' well-being that you're a concerned and caring father. I want you to have a strong relationship with them. That said, I don't plan now or in the future to yield custody of them to you."

"Not even during the school year?" Kenneth asked. "You want to keep hauling them back and forth across town?"

She shook her head. "That's not what I want at all. I had planned this as a surprise for the kids, but I'll let you in on it. When the kids return from their summer vacation, I'll already have us moved into a house in their school district. There will no longer be a need to drag them back and forth across town."

"You're moving?"

She nodded. "I listen when you make a point that's for the benefit of the kids. I listened when you suggested they would be better off at a school in your school district. And I listened when you observed the burden all the back-and-forth put on them. I love our kids, Kenneth, and every decision I make, I make with them in mind. I'll probably make a mistake every now and then, but it won't be because I wasn't thinking of them."

"I don't know what to say," Kenneth said. "I had no idea you were planning to move."

"You didn't know because I didn't tell you and I didn't tell you because I wasn't sure I could make it work."

"I guess congratulations are in order," Mary Margaret said. "Welcome to the district!"

Destiny gave Mary Margaret what she guessed might be her first sincere smile. "Thanks, Mary Margaret."

"And for the record," Mary Margaret added, "we are not planning to challenge you for custody of the kids."

Destiny looked at Kenneth for confirmation.

When Kenneth slowly shook his head, Destiny wondered who had made this decision, Kenneth or Mary Margaret. "Things are working well the way they are now," he said. "I don't see any need to change. I was upset last night and said some things that I shouldn't have." He glanced at Mary Margaret before turning back to Destiny. "I apologize for that."

"I don't need an apology but I accept yours in the spirit you gave it." She looked between him and Mary Margaret. "I appreciate you both and what you provide emotionally and financially for the kids. I don't want you to think that I take you for granted, especially you, Mary Margaret. We haven't always had the best relationship, but I think we're in a good place."

Mary Margaret nodded. "So do I, Destiny, and I want to keep it that way." Mary Margaret glanced at Kenneth, then added, "As we think about expanding our family, family harmony will be even more important."

"Expanding your family?" Destiny asked.

Kenneth nodded. "We're thinking of giving KJ and Kenae a little brother or sister. How do you think they would react?"

Destiny felt her mouth drop open, and she quickly closed it. "They'll be happy," she said. "I'm even more glad now that they've had this summer to spend with you two. As long as they're confident about their place in your lives, I think they'd welcome a younger sibling. They really are good kids."

"You've done a good job with them," Mary Margaret said. "I hope I do as well with our little ones."

"I didn't do it by myself," Destiny said. "You and Kenneth played a big role."

Kenneth started laughing. "We should consider having our own reality show. We could call it the 'Blended Family Experiment.' On second thought, that wouldn't work since we get along so well. We may need to create some drama."

Destiny began shaking her head and she noticed Mary Margaret did, too. "Our goal is to be drama free, and to that end there is one more thing I want to discuss with you two. I'd like to sit down with a family law attorney and draw up a child-custody agreement."

"I thought you were happy with the child-support arrangement as it is."

"I am," Destiny said. "I'm not asking for more money or trying to give you less time with them or anything like that. I just think we need a legal record for the protection of the kids."

"I don't see anything wrong with that," Mary Margaret said. "What about you, Kenneth?"

"I don't see why we need to involve lawyers if we've done so well ourselves."

"Having a formal agreement keeps things clean between us, Kenneth. The little problem we had about the child support this summer would not have occurred had we had a formal agreement. The document will help us take the emotion out of our decisions about the kids. Will you at least think about it?"

"I'll think about it," Kenneth said.

"That's all I ask," Destiny said.

Mary Margaret picked up her menu. "If we've covered everything, I think we'd better order," she said. "If we don't, all three of us may end up in the back room in handcuffs."

Destiny knew their talk had been a success when all three of them laughed.

Chapter 42

DANIEL LOOKED AT THE STACK OF LOAN APPLICATIONS on his desk and thought about Destiny. Trying not to think about her was a futile activity. In a short time, she'd come to touch every aspect of his life. He looked again at the stack of applications. She had been right to go through the deacons and other church leaders to identify families who might be helped by a loan. The quickness with which the applications had been returned was a testament to how much the loan program was needed. He only wished he could focus on them. He'd probably been through the stack twice. Why did he even bother? He was going to fund them all anyway.

Now that that was settled he let his thoughts freely go to their chosen destination: Destiny. He hadn't liked the way he had left things between them in California. At first, he'd thought he should have fought harder to stay out there with her and help her work through whatever she had to work through about their relationship. Now though he recognized the wisdom in her decision.

"How was Memphis?"

Daniel looked up at the sound of Gavin's voice. "Hey," he said, welcoming the interruption. "Come on in."

Gavin walked fully into the room. "So how was it? Did the trip help keep your mind off Destiny?"

Daniel looked up at his friend. "That wasn't the purpose of the trip."

Gavin only grinned. He took a seat in the chair in front of the desk. "It was either that or you were avoiding Natalie."

"Why would I avoid Natalie?"

Gavin chuckled. "Because she'd hound you for an update on your relationship with Destiny. We've noticed that you two have been seeing a lot of each other. Don't worry, I'm not going to hound you about it. I'll leave that to Natalie. I want to hear about Memphis and the guys."

Daniel looked at his friend and knew that it was time to tell him the truth. "I misled you about the reason I went to Memphis, Gavin. It wasn't a social visit, it was work."

"What work? Were you doing something related to the financial programs you're planning?"

He shook his head. "Not that kind of work." He sighed deeply. "There's something I need to tell you. I wanted to tell you when I first got to town."

"Tell me what?"

"About the case I've been working on for GDW Investigations since I've been here."

Gavin leaned forward in his chair. "Case? I thought you stopped that work when Gloria became ill."

"I did, but George and William asked me to take on one last case when I came to Atlanta. It was a fraud investigation involving a temporary services business. A lot of good people have gotten caught up in the scam. They were offering high-paying jobs as a cover for a money-laundering and identity-theft crime ring."

"Sounds serious, but why all the secrecy?"

"This is a wide-reaching scam and George and William were concerned that some members of your congregation might be involved."

Gavin's eyebrows shot up. "I know George and William. Are you telling me they thought I was involved?"

"Not really," Daniel said. "They were more concerned that you might know people involved or that you or Natalie would somehow tell the wrong person about my investigation. It was safer all around to keep you and Natalie in the dark."

"Since you're telling me now, I assume you've wrapped up the case."

"Almost," Daniel said. "There are still a few loose ends that have to be tied up. I'm telling you now because you and Natalie know a couple of people who got caught up in it."

Gavin sat back in his chair. "Are you trying to tell me that some people from the church are involved?"

Daniel nodded. "It's even worse. It's a couple of people who are close to both you and Natalie."

"Who?"

Daniel let out a deep breath. "Destiny and Bertice."

"Destiny and Bertice?"

Daniel nodded.

"How did they get involved?"

Daniel shrugged. "They were both having money troubles and the opportunity presented itself to make some easy money. They couldn't walk away from it. It's a scam and a lot of good people fall for scams. Even though the whole thing was too good to be true, they let themselves be convinced that it was all on the up-and-up."

"Man, I hate this. How much trouble are they in?"

"It's a long story."

"This is important," Gavin said. "I can make the time. Tell me."

Daniel told Gavin everything, starting with Phil Harris's initial involvement, his recruitment of Bertice and Destiny, and his decision to reach out to GDW for help to get out.

"I don't believe it," Gavin said. "I thought Bertice and Destiny were smarter than that."

"Scams wouldn't work if smart people didn't fall for them."

"But still—"

"Don't judge them too harshly, Gavin. They're not going to be prosecuted but they will have to pay." He eyed his friend. "In fact, Destiny has already paid."

"Explain."

Daniel took a deep breath. "I didn't only go to Memphis this weekend. I also went to Los Angeles."

"Los Angeles? You went to see Destiny?"

"Not exactly," Daniel said. Then he explained how Destiny had ended up at the police station. "Somebody stole her identity and then used it to commit credit card fraud."

"That must have been pretty scary for Destiny. I'm sorry to hear it happened. How is she?"

"Overall, she's fine," he said. "She's angry at herself for getting involved with HR Solutions. And she's angry that the whole mess landed her in the police station. Being taken to the police station was traumatic for her."

"I'll bet it was," Daniel said. "Are you sure she's all right? I can't believe she didn't call Natalie but I find it very interesting that she called you. Sounds to me like you two have developed a close relationship in a short time."

"Before she left, I would have agreed with you. I'm not sure where we are now. She thinks we need to reconsider our relationship in light of the new information we have about each other."

"In other words, she's a little upset that you kept the secret from her?" Gavin asked.

"That's part of it."

"Well, I think you made up for it after you went all the way to Los Angeles to help her out of a legal mess that she created by her own reckless actions."

"You're being too hard on her, Gavin."

"And you're letting her off too lightly. She should be holding on to you with both hands and both feet."

"Of course I agree with you, but she says she needs time to reconcile her feelings for the Daniel she knew before she left town and the Daniel she met in Los Angeles. I think she likes both of us, but she's unsure what the future holds. She's also worried that my feelings for her may be complicated by her role in the case. It's a mess."

Gavin shrugged. "Women can be unpredictable. You both have got to put yourself in the other's shoes. That's relationship rule number one. It seems you've forgotten it."

Daniel pondered Gavin's words long after his friend had left him alone in his office. As he sat there, his thoughts turned to Gloria. GDW had brought the two of them together and it had almost torn them apart. Was that history repeating itself with Destiny?

Chapter 43

DESTINY BOARDED THE PLANE FOR ATLANTA FEELING good about her trip. Yes, there had been a few bumps, but things had turned out well. As she looked ahead, the life waiting for her back in Atlanta looked pretty promising. She'd have her kids, her house, and school, and if things worked the way she wanted, she'd also have Daniel. "Which seat do you want, Mom?" she asked when she reached their assigned row. "Window or aisle?"

"I'll take the window," she said.

Destiny stepped back and let her mother enter the row first. After she was settled in, Destiny took the aisle seat. "Comfortable?" she asked her mom.

"I'm fine," she said. "How about you?"

"I'm good," Destiny said. "We had a long day today, so I'm glad for the rest."

Her mother chuckled. "I know what you mean. Despite the drama that led to it, I'm glad we were able to spend a couple of extra days here."

Destiny agreed. "I wish we could have stayed even longer, but I have to get back to my responsibilities."

Her mother looked at her. "I don't know if I've told you this, Destiny, but I'm really proud of what you're doing with your life this summer."

"Proud?" Destiny repeated. Given that entire police and HR Solutions fiasco, Destiny hadn't expected to hear the word *proud* from her mother for a very long time.

"Yes, proud," she said. "I know you think I'm too hard on you, but all I've ever wanted was for you to live up to your potential. I always saw it in you, but you never saw it in yourself. I could never understand why. Sometimes I blame myself for your lack of confidence. I think things would have been different if your father had lived. Two parents balance things out. I could be the taskmaster when your dad was there to be the nurturer. After he was gone, I didn't do a very good job of combining our roles. It was just easier for me to stick with what I knew. I was so afraid when your dad died."

"Afraid? You never seemed afraid."

"Of course I had to put on a strong face for you, Destiny. All I wanted you to see from me was strength. Then I had the first breast cancer occurrence when you were about the age that KJ and Kenae are now and I was terrified you'd end up an orphan. I think that's why I was so hard on you. I needed you to be prepared for life without both of your parents. I guess I still do."

"I didn't know that, Mom. I wish you had told me."

"It's hard to talk to you, Destiny. You take every word I say as criticism."

Destiny looked over at her mother. "You do criticize me a lot."

"That's not how I see it, so we'll have to agree to disagree. That's why I want to go on the record and let you know that I'm proud of you."

"You certainly picked a strange time to tell me. A couple of days ago I was hauled off to a police station. You didn't seem too proud of me then. You seemed more disappointed than anything."

"I was disappointed," she said. "What mother wouldn't be? Why can't I be both?"

"Because they're contradictory emotions, Mom."

Her mother shook her head. "That's not true. I can be proud of you, in a general sense, but disappointed about a specific act. Yes, I'm disappointed that you felt you needed to take a shortcut to get money this summer. I thought I'd raised you better than that."

"You raised me fine," Destiny said.

"Maybe. Maybe not. But we're getting off track. I need you to hear that I'm proud of you. Do you hear me?"

"I hear you."

"What do you think I'm proud of?"

Destiny shrugged. "You're proud that I'm going back to school to get my degree."

Her mother nodded. "And I'm proud that you're doing it while working at Marshalls, planning those financial programs with Daniel at the church, and doing an apprenticeship at the salon. And I'm especially proud that you're working to move you and the kids into a house closer to their school."

Destiny eyed her mom. "I thought you were worried I was doing too much."

"You are," she said, "but I realized that most mothers, especially single mothers, end up doing too much. It's our lot in life."

"I guess it is," Destiny agreed.

"But I'm even more proud of the way you handled yourself this weekend," her mother continued. "You faced some adversity, self-inflicted adversity, but adversity just the same, and you didn't let it beat you down. Kenneth hit you with a low blow when you were already staggered by the police, but you didn't give up or give in. You stared him down and got him to back down. If something happened to me tomorrow, I know you'd be okay."

"Don't even think like that, Mom. Nothing is going to happen to you."

"I'm a two-time breast cancer survivor, Destiny. Nothing is promised to me. Every day is a gift. I don't want to leave you, but it gives me comfort to know that you can take care of yourself and the kids."

Destiny turned to her mother. "What are you trying to tell me, Mom? Have the doctors told you something?"

Her mother took her hand and squeezed it. "I have good news and bad news."

Destiny closed her eyes briefly and prayed a silent prayer for her mom to be okay. "Tell me," she said.

Still holding her hand, her mother said, "The bad news is that the cancer is back. The good news is that Charlotte, Mary Margaret's mother, told me about a clinical trial that will be starting in a couple of months. She thinks I'm a good candidate and she's practically guaranteed me a spot in it."

Destiny felt tears well up in her eyes. "How long have you known about this?"

"Not long," her mother said.

"Why didn't you tell me?"

"Because I didn't want to upset you," her mother said, using her fingers to wipe away Destiny's tears.

Destiny covered her mother's hand with her own. "You still should have told me."

"I know, sweetheart, but I needed time to come to grips with it first. And I wanted to better understand my treatment options. Charlotte did a good job of making those clear to me. She's a really nice woman, once you get beyond that harsh exterior. We're a lot alike. I think it's because we're both single mothers. You've got that same toughness. It was just simmering there below the surface waiting to be activated."

"What are you talking about, Mom?" she asked, though she really wanted to discuss her mother's treatment options. She just didn't think this airplane was the place to do it. No, she'd hold off until they were home. And she'd make it a priority to be at her mom's next doctor's appointment.

"You handled your business like a woman," her mother continued. "Kenneth's threats, both of them, scared you. I know they did. But the fear didn't paralyze you. No, it sent you into action. You started looking for a house closer to the kids' school after the first threat and after the second you sought legal advice. Then armed with that advice, you called for a sit-down with Mary Margaret and Kenneth. I just wish I had been there to see you in action."

"There was nothing to see. We had an adult conversation."

"Exactly," her mother said. "You handled your business like a woman and Mary Margaret and Kenneth had to take notice. You fought for yourself and your kids and you fought the right way."

"I don't know what to say. What else could I have done?"

"Nothing. That's the point. You did the right thing and you did it the right way. At least, you did with Kenneth. I'm not so sure about Daniel."

"What are you talking about?"

Her mother shot a glare in her direction. "You know what I'm talking about. It was nice to see you start a new relationship. I don't like to think of you old and alone. You deserve someone to love you and share your life—the good times and the bad. I was hoping Daniel was that special man for you."

"He still might be."

"Then why did you send him away?" her mother challenged.

Destiny thought about her last conversation with Daniel. "I needed to think about what I wanted from him and I needed him to think about what he wanted from me. Daniel knows the worst of me, Mom. He's had a front-row seat to my moral failures. I can't hide from him. That's pretty scary."

"But wonderful if he knows all that and still wants to be with you."

She nodded. "That's right. I know what kind of man he is and he knows exactly what kind of woman I am. There's no hiding with us. We're either going to move forward together full force or we're going to go our separate ways. That's just who we are. I guess I'll find out which way things will go when we meet next Tuesday."

Chapter 44

THANKS FOR THE RIDE, BERTICE," DESTINY'S MOTHER said as she turned to open the front passenger door so she could get out of Bertice's car.

"No problem, Mrs. Madison," Bertice said. "I was coming over to Destiny's as soon as she got in anyway. I couldn't wait to hear all about her trip. Picking you two up at the airport just gave me a head start on getting all the news."

"And you don't know the half of it," Destiny heard her mother murmur as she got out of the rear passenger seat.

"Will you get my bags for me?" her mother asked when they both stood outside the car.

"I don't know why you didn't let Bertice drop you off at home, Mom," Destiny said, heading to the rear of the car so she could get her mother's suitcase out of Bertice's trunk. "I could have brought your car to you later this afternoon."

Her mother began shaking her head. "That's not necessary. You must be as tired as I am. You get some rest. That's exactly what I plan to do when I get home."

"Then let me drive you," Destiny said, following her mom to her car, suitcase in hand.

When they both stood at her mother's open trunk, the older woman said, "I'm fine, Destiny. You don't have to worry. I can drive myself home."

"You're not fine, Mom," Destiny said, closing the trunk.

Her mother gave a slight frown. "Yes I am."

Destiny raised a brow. "Did you forget what you told me on the plane?"

"No, I didn't forget," her mother said as she moved toward the front passenger door of her car. "This is why I didn't tell you earlier. You worry too much."

Holding the door open for her mother, Destiny said, "No, you should have told me as soon as you found out. I need to know what's going on with you. What are the doctors saying? What are the treatment options that you mentioned? I need to know, Mom."

Her mother leaned up and pressed a kiss on her cheek. "Stop worrying."

Destiny began shaking her head. "That won't happen until I get some more information."

Her mother sighed. "Okay," she said. "Charlotte's going to review my case files. I'm supposed to call her office to set up an appointment for us to discuss them. You're welcome to come."

Destiny nodded. "I'll be there. Just let me know when."

Her mother eased behind the steering wheel. "I'll call you as soon as I know."

Destiny closed the door after her mother was seated and

leaned through the open window. "I love you, Mom," she said.

Her mother smiled. "I love you, too."

Destiny stepped back from the car. "Drive safely and call me when you get home," she said.

"I will. And I need you to do something for me."

"What?"

"Call Daniel."

"Stop worrying about me and Daniel," she told her mother. "I told you that I would see him next Tuesday and I still plan to do that."

Her mother frowned. "Don't wait that long. I'm serious, Destiny. Work this out with him before it gets blown out of proportion."

Destiny couldn't help but smile. Her mother was still her mother. "I hear you, Mom," she said.

"Good," her mother said. Then she began backing the car out of the driveway.

After her mother pulled away from the house, Destiny made her way to the townhouse, where Bertice was waiting for her. Her friend had used her key to let herself in. Destiny found her in the kitchen, standing before the open refrigerator. "There's nothing in there," she told her friend.

"You're telling me," Bertice said. She closed the refrigerator door and turned to Destiny. "Do you want to go out to get something?"

Shaking her head in the negative, Destiny walked to the adjacent family room, pulled off her shoes, and dropped down on the couch.

"Tired?" Bertice asked.

"More than tired."

Bertice sat down beside her. "What's going on with you and your mom? It took you a long while to say bye to her."

Destiny closed her eyes and then quickly opened them. "Her cancer is back."

Bertice reached out and placed a hand on her friend's shoulder. "I'm sorry, Destiny. What's the prognosis?"

"I don't really know. Mom didn't want to talk about it. She just dropped the news on me when we got on the plane to come back home. This is her third occurrence, Bertice, so it can't be good, can it?"

Bertice rubbed her shoulders. "We don't know that," she said. "Your mom is a fighter. She's beat this thing before, twice before, and she can beat it again. We have to believe that she'll beat it again."

Destiny wanted to believe her friend was right, but she knew enough about breast cancer to know that the disease was unpredictable and varied from woman to woman. *Help her, Lord.*

"Hey, how are you holding up? You've had more than your share of drama these past few days."

Destiny sighed. "You can say that again." She turned to her friend. "They can't have been easy for you either. How are you doing?"

"I've been better," Bertice said. "Phil and I are done. I dumped him right after I went off on him. I don't think I've ever been as angry with anyone as I was with him."

Destiny squeezed her friend's hand. "I'm sorry. There was no way you could work through it?"

"Work through it? Please. That man almost ruined my life. I could have ended up in jail."

Destiny huffed. "Like me."

"I blame myself for that, Destiny. I hate that I got you involved. I'm sorry."

Destiny shook her head. "It's not your fault. I'm a grown woman and I'm responsible for my actions. I don't blame you."

"I appreciate you for saying that, but you know it's my fault."

"Don't be so hard on yourself. You didn't know it was a scheme."

"Well, I knew it was a very good gig. I could have looked closer, asked more questions."

"So could I. Looking back doesn't help anything. I'm just grateful things turned out the way they did. They could have been a lot worse."

"You can say that again. Daniel really saved our behinds. I can't believe that he has been investigating HR Solutions the entire time he's been in Atlanta. Did you have any idea?"

Destiny shook her head. "None whatsoever. I thought Phil was just somebody from his past."

"Are you okay with how everything went down?"

Destiny shrugged. "It's complicated. Daniel's most attractive feature is his heart. He cares about people, not only with words, but with his actions. Everything he did is consistent with the man I know him to be."

"I hear a *but* in there somewhere."

Destiny smiled at her friend. "Not really. It's just that since he's such a high-character guy, can he really be content in a relationship with me, given what I've done and what happened as a result?"

"There's more to you than that one incident. If Daniel is the man you think he is, he'll see that. If he doesn't, then he's not the man you think he is and you're better off without him."

"That's easy to say, but it'll break my heart if he wants to end things. I really felt we had the beginnings of something good between us."

"Well, don't give up on him yet."

Destiny looked at her friend. "Like you gave up on Phil?"

"That's different."

"They're similar enough. Phil made a mistake, a big one, but there's more to him than that mistake. Daniel told me that you were the reason he blew the whistle on the whole fraud scheme in the first place."

"What?"

She nodded. "He told Daniel that he was falling for you and he didn't want to see you hurt. He regretted his actions, Bertice, and tried to make things right. He really did."

"I didn't know," she said. "I thought he was playing me." She looked over at Destiny. "He told me that he thinks he's in love with me."

"How do you feel about him?"

Bertice shrugged. "I don't know how I feel. A part of me wants to put the whole situation, including him, behind me and move forward. That would be the smart thing to do." She paused and then she grinned. "But when have I been known to do the smart thing?"

Destiny chuckled. "Whatever you decide, I'll support."

"We're quite the pair, aren't we?" Bertice said.

"Friends forever." She turned to Bertice. "Have you spoken to Natalie?"

She shook her head. "She's called a couple of times, but I haven't had the courage to call her back. Turns out she was right about me and my schemes. Do you think Daniel told her and Gavin everything?"

"Yes, he told them. I spoke to her briefly before I left Los Angeles. We should go see her. You know how she worries."

"That she does," Bertice said, standing up and extending her hand to Destiny. "Get up."

Destiny took her hand. "Where are we going?"

"To raid Natalie's refrigerator, if she's home."

"Good idea. We've made her wait long enough."

Chapter 45

I'M GLAD DR. WELLS AGREED TO JOIN YOUR CARE TEAM, Mom," Destiny said as she placed the bowl of salad on her mother's dining room table. "I'm feeling a lot better after talking to her."

"You can tell she's a teacher," her mother said, taking a seat at the table. "I appreciate the way she clearly presents the information to you and encourages questions. Not all doctors like questions."

Destiny sat next to her mother. "And I asked a lot of them, too."

After she blessed their meal, her mother said, "You sure did. And they were good questions, too. You worry about me but you also worry about Kenae, don't you?"

Taking a bite of her lasagna, Destiny nodded. She'd felt relieved after learning that her mother's cancer was noninvasive, but the mere fact that her mother was experiencing her third bout of breast cancer made her concerned for Kenae. "I worry about her the way you worried about me. You know, I did that genetic testing when you had your second occurrence back when I was in college. I was relieved when the tests came back negative."

Her mother scooped some salad from the serving bowl into her salad bowl. "Kenae's much too young for such testing, so that's one thing you don't have to worry about. I'm glad Dr. Wells made it clear that you shouldn't even think about testing her until she's at least eighteen."

Actually, Dr. Wells had said those ages were the recommendations given the current standard of care, but given the rapid advancements being made in the medical field, the standard could change. "It's still hard not to worry."

Her mother put down her fork. "There's something I have to tell you, Destiny, and I guess now is as good a time as any."

Destiny's heart jumped at her mother's statement. Please, God, she prayed silently, don't let anything else be wrong with my mother. "What is it, Mom? Did the doctor tell you something that she didn't tell me?"

Her mom reached for her hand. "It's not that," she said. "This is something I should have told you years ago."

"Years ago. Does it have something to do with Dad?" Destiny didn't have any memories of him since he died when she was four and her mom rarely talked about him. As a child, she'd thought they didn't talk about him because it was so sad. As she grew older, she began to think that her parents hadn't had a good marriage.

"It does have something to do with your dad, but what made you think so?"

Destiny shrugged. "I don't know. Maybe because you mentioned him when we were on the plane coming back from L.A. So what did you want to tell me about my dad?"

Her mother sighed. "He had an affair before you were born."

"That explains why you don't talk about him. Were you pregnant when he cheated on you?"

Her mother shook her head. "At one point, I thought he was going to leave me for her, but he chose to stay with his family."

"Why are you telling me this now, Mom? He's long dead and this happened before I was born."

"I'm trying to set the stage so you'll understand." Her mother paused for a moment, as if she were trying to organize her thoughts. "One day his lady friend came to visit me and she brought me a gift."

"Well, she had some nerve. What made her come here?"

Her mother sighed. "Since your father wouldn't leave me, she wanted me to leave him."

"I hope you threw her and her gift out of the house."

Her mother gave a dry laugh. "I threw her out," she said. "But I kept the gift."

Destiny took another bite of lasagna. "What was it?"

"A baby. Her baby."

Destiny stopped eating and looked at her mother. "A baby?"

Her mother nodded. "A baby she said was fathered by your father."

It was Destiny's turn to reach for her mother's hand. "I'm so sorry, Mom. I can't believe she brought a baby here. What did Dad say?"

"Your father wasn't home at the time. The baby's mother said that since I had the man, I should also have the baby. Then she left, leaving the baby with me."

"She left her baby? What did you do?"

"I didn't know what to do," her mother said. "I started to call your dad and give him a piece of my mind about his woman coming to my home, but I didn't."

"He deserved it, Mom," Destiny said. "You should have done it."

"Well, I didn't do it because I got distracted by the most beautiful and perfect baby girl that I've ever seen." Her mother gave a soft smile and Destiny knew she was remembering that day. "I know this makes no sense at all, but I literally fell in love with that baby the moment I looked at her."

"It was a girl. Does that mean I have an older sister somewhere?"

Her mother shook her head.

"Oh no, did she die?"

Her mother shook her head again.

"Then where is she?"

Her mother met her eyes. "Right here," she said. "That baby is right here. You are that baby."

Destiny thought she had misunderstood her mother. "What did you say?"

"You are that baby, Destiny. Your birth mother brought

you to me when you were six weeks old. You've been my baby since that day."

Destiny started shaking her head. "This makes no sense. Are you saying you didn't give birth to me?"

Her mother nodded. "That's exactly what I'm saying."

"I don't know how I'm supposed to respond. Why are you telling me this now?"

"Because I don't want you to worry about Kenae and breast cancer. I don't know of anyone in your birth mother's family who's had breast cancer."

Destiny sat back in her chair. This conversation was going too fast for her. "So you knew the woman?"

"I didn't know her until she showed up at the house, but I learned who she was then."

"And you've kept up with her family?"

"Not really," her mother said. "But I did meet with her after this last diagnosis."

"Mom, this is sounding crazy to me. You need to stop with these one-sentence comments and give me some information. None of this is making sense to me."

"I'm sorry, Destiny. Let me go back to the beginning. After your birth mom left, it was just you and me until your father came home from work. Of course, the first thing he did was ask about the baby. I told him what had happened and his reaction was to take you and go confront your birth mother. I still can't believe what I did next."

"What did you do?"

"I told him he could go wherever he wanted to go, but he wasn't taking my baby anywhere." Her mother chuckled.

"He looked at me like I was crazy, but when he left, he didn't take my baby."

"Your baby?"

"From that day on, you were my baby. Your dad and I had been married about four years at the time and we hadn't been able to conceive. I knew the moment I looked at you that you were God's gift to me. I knew it then and I've never doubted it since."

"What happened after Dad came back?" Destiny asked, still trying to wrap her mind around the story her mom was telling.

"Well, he found your birth mother. She essentially told him that she wanted him and his baby, not just his baby. You see, she thought I would leave your father because of the baby and then she'd get them both. What she didn't know was that I would have given her your father, but she was not going to get my baby."

Destiny smiled because she could imagine her mother saying just that to somebody. "So what happened?"

"After your dad came home, we talked and decided that we would raise you as our own."

"And you never saw my birth mother again?"

"No, she came back a couple of years later, but by then I wasn't giving you up. All three of us decided it would be best if she gave up her parental rights. To be honest, I strongly suggested that she do so. In all honesty, *coerced* might be a better word than *suggested*."

Destiny stared at her mother, taking in her every feature. Over the years, she'd looked for pieces of herself in her mother and had not found them. As a result, she'd assumed that she was more like her father. Turned out she'd been right. "I still can't believe this. I don't know what to say."

"This is a lot to hear. I'm sorry I waited so long to tell you. I really should have told you when I had the last recurrence and saved you the genetic testing and associated worry, but I didn't have the courage. It's been me and you for so long that for stretches of time I forget that I'm not your birth mother."

The woman who raised her was not her birth mother. Destiny couldn't make sense of it. She knew she'd have a thousand questions over the next few days, but right now she had none.

"I know it will take a while for you to digest all this, so take all the time you need. I just hope you get a little relief by knowing that Kenae is not predisposed to breast cancer because of me. You've had so much come at you recently. You don't need that worry."

Destiny knew her mother meant well. While she appreciated not having to worry about Kenae and breast cancer, her mother had given her a whole new set of reasons to worry. She asked the only question she had at the moment. "Who is she, Mom? Who is my birth mother?"

Her mother looked her directly in the eyes. "Annie Robinson."

Chapter 46

DESTINY HADN'T GOTTEN MUCH SLEEP LAST NIGHT AS her mind played the conversation she'd had with her mother over and over. It was such an incredible story that she wouldn't have been surprised to get a call from her mother this morning saying, "April Fool." Only it wasn't April. And her mother had not been joking.

Destiny had told herself that she would wait until after work to go see Annie at the salon. Yet here it was, almost two P.M., and she was walking through the Career Center doors. Even though she'd needed to catch up at work for her extended weekend away, she hadn't really been able to focus on her given tasks. It seemed best to deal with Annie since she couldn't stop thinking about her.

"Hey, Destiny," Leslie called when she reached the reception desk. "I didn't expect you today. Are you here to see Mrs. Robinson?"

Destiny nodded. "Is she here?"

"She sure is. You can go on back."

Destiny thanked the young girl and headed back to Mrs. Robinson's office. She stopped just before she reached the door, realizing she had no idea what she was going to say. Well, she was here now, she told herself, she had to go in.

"Hi, Destiny," Mrs. Robinson said as she entered the door. "I've been expecting you."

"I should have known my mother would call you," Destiny said, searching the woman's face for a likeness.

"Have a seat," she said. "Yes, your mother told me about your conversation last night. She thought you might drop by today. She knows you well."

"That she does," Destiny said.

Mrs. Robinson cleared her throat. "I know you have questions, Destiny, so feel free to ask me anything. Before you get started though, I want you to know that I never intended to intrude on your life any more than I already have. You have a mother, a good mother. I'd consider it an honor if you could call me a friend."

Destiny didn't want to think about what she should call this woman. "Why didn't you tell me who you were when we first met?"

"It wasn't my place. Your mother and I made a deal when you were a baby and I've abided by it. Back in those days, I didn't keep too many promises, but I kept that one. It was best for all of us, especially you."

Destiny nodded like she understood, but she didn't. Not really. "Why did you leave me with her in the first place?"

"Because I was young and stupid, and too smart for my

own good." She gave a self-deprecating laugh. "I wanted your father and I was determined to have him. I thought you would be my ticket to a life and family with him, but I was wrong. Very wrong. Your father was not going to leave your mother for me, baby or no. He made that very clear."

"But he cheated on her with you."

"He did, but he ended it before your mother found out. She never would have found out had I not showed up at her house with you."

"That was cruel and you had some nerve."

She shook her head. "It was a desperate move by a desperate woman. I'm sure I hurt your mother, but that was not my intent. She was a nonentity to me. I saw her only as an obstacle between me and the man I wanted. I was pretty selfish back then."

"Why didn't you come back for your baby?"

"Oh, I did, when I realized my little game was not going to turn out the way I wanted. But your mother is a formidable woman. She let me know, in no uncertain terms, that I was not taking her baby."

"But she was your baby, not hers."

Mrs. Robinson shook head. "No, in all the ways that mattered, she was your mother. I was the outsider."

"I still don't understand how you left your baby. My kids are in California with their dad for the summer and I was just out there to visit. No way could I go two to three months without seeing them."

Mrs. Robinson gave a sad smile. "You're trying to make

sense of a situation that was senseless. I wasn't a very good person back then, Destiny. For more than a few years, my life consisted of an ongoing series of bad choices. Every time I had two options, I seemed to pick the wrong one. If I could tell the truth or tell a lie, I told the lie. If I was good at anything, it was making bad decisions. I had that down to an art form."

"I don't know what all that looks like," Destiny said. "What exactly did you do?"

She took a deep breath. "So you want specifics? Well, the biggest lie I told was telling your mother and father that your father was your father."

"What? My father wasn't my father?"

"I'm sorry, but he wasn't. I wanted him to be. I prayed that he was. But I knew he wasn't. He ended things with me because I wouldn't stop seeing other men. I didn't realize how much I cared about him until he dumped me."

"Does my mother know my father was not my father?"

Mrs. Robinson nodded. "Both of us had to give up our parental rights in order for you to be adopted. But who your birth father was didn't matter to your mother. She still loved you."

"So who was my father?"

Mrs. Robinson gave her a name that she had never heard before.

"Tell me something else about you and your life."

"I guess the major markers in my life are having a baby, going to jail, getting the job at the school, and opening the salon. The first two markers represent the height of my bad decision making, while the last two mark the beginnings of good decision making."

"So why did you go to jail?"

The older woman met her eyes. "Fraud."

Destiny gave a dry laugh. "Must be in the genes."

"What do you mean?"

Destiny explained what she'd been through with HR Solutions.

"Unfortunately, that sounds exactly like something I would have done," Annie said. Then she explained the series of cons she'd run, most of them involving men. "I'm not proud of my past, but I don't run from it either since remembering it helps me to not repeat it."

"It's hard for me to believe that was you. It's not the person I've come to know and like very much."

Annie smiled. "That's because you've only known Good Annie. I'm glad you never knew Bad Annie. Your life is better for it, believe me."

Destiny sighed. "I do."

"How do you feel about all of this, Destiny?"

"I don't know," she said. "It's almost like I'm learning about somebody else's life, not my own. I think I need more time to process it."

"Take all the time you need. Nobody's rushing you. I do hope you'll continue to work at the shop though. I've meant every word I've said to you, Destiny. You do believe that, don't you?"

"I believe you," Destiny told the older woman. "I'd like to continue coming to the salon."

"That's good," Annie said. "Things between us don't have to change unless you want them to. I'm more than content being your mentor and friend."

Destiny thought Annie was right. She couldn't think of Annie as her mother, as that role was filled quite well. But she definitely had room in her life for a mentor and friend.

Chapter 47

DESTINY WAS APPREHENSIVE AS SHE WALKED TOWARD Daniel's office at Faith Community Church. She hadn't seen or talked to him since he'd come to rescue her in Los Angeles, but she had thought a lot about him. When she reached his office, she stopped outside the door and said a quick prayer before walking in.

Daniel sat at his desk, head down. "Working hard or hardly working?" she called out to get his attention.

He looked up. When he saw it was her, he smiled broadly before wiping the smile off his face, as if he'd caught himself doing something wrong. She knew his uncertainty with how to greet her was her fault.

"Working hard," he said. "I hope that will change now that you're back. It certainly is good to see you."

"It's good to see you, too," she said, sitting in one of the chairs near the desk they had shared in the past. "I'm glad to be back."

"Your trip ended well?" he asked.

She nodded. "Malcolm and I filed all the necessary paperwork related to the case, so that's out of the way. I guess I'm all set on that front. And three extra days in Los Angeles with my kids was icing on the cake. All in all, I really can't complain."

"It's great you got to spend some extra time with your kids. I'm glad some good came out of everything you went through."

"So am I." She leaned forward, toward him. "Daniel, I have to thank you again for everything you did to help me and Bertice. I couldn't see it all clearly as it was happening, but it's very clear now. You've been like a guardian angel to both of us, watching out for us when we didn't even know we were in trouble."

"I'm glad I was able to help," he said simply. "But I don't think you should put me up there with guardian angels. In case you've forgotten, you did end up in police custody."

She chuckled. "I remember," she said. "That was my first thought, too, but you know what I finally realized? Guardian angels don't keep you out of trouble that's the result of your own actions. They merely protect you as you're going through that trouble. And that's exactly what you did."

He got up, walked around the desk, sat in the chair next to hers, and turned to her. "Does this mean you're no longer angry with me?"

"I was never angry with you."

He met her eyes, challenging her words.

She gestured with her thumb and forefinger. "Maybe just a little," she said.

"You sent me away."

"It wasn't anger that made me send you away. It was fear."

He sat back in his chair. "Fear? I don't understand. What were you afraid of?"

She looked down at her hands. "That you'd realize I wasn't good enough for you. That you'd see I couldn't live up to your moral standards. You had proof. I had given it to you by my actions."

He tipped her chin up with his hand so that she looked at him. "I thought you knew me better than that. Do you really think I would sit in judgment of you that way? Do you think I think less of people who get caught up in these types of scams?"

"Some people would."

"Then shame on them." He stroked his finger down her cheek. "I never told you how Gloria and I met, did I?"

She shook her head.

"She was a client of GDW Investigations," he began. "She came to us because some fast talker had conned her out of money that belonged to the nonprofit that she ran. The guy had convinced her that he could get the group, which was always short on funds, some outrageous return on their money. Of course, he had no intention of doing so. He took the money and she never saw him again. I still remember how embarrassed she was as she told me the story. She could barely look at me."

"I had no idea," she said.

"Wait, it gets worse. She made the decision to let this guy invest the money without the approval of her board of directors, so technically what she did was embezzlement."

"Were you able to help her?"

He nodded. "We got back some of the money, but not all of it. And she had to confess to her board what she had done, which was hard for her because she loved that non-profit and she was afraid she would have to step down from her position. To their credit and her relief, they didn't make her resign."

"I never would have guessed."

"I know," he said. "But she was no different from you. She did the wrong thing for a good reason and she had to suffer the consequences. It didn't make her a bad person or a person of low character. It just made her a fallible human being, which is what we all are, including me."

Destiny knew he was sharing all this with her because she knew how much he had loved Gloria. "Thank you for telling me, Daniel."

"Thank Gloria," he said. "It was a story she told often herself. It had a lot of lessons she learned, and she wanted to share those lessons with others."

"I already thought she was a special lady, and now even more so," she said, wondering how any woman could take Gloria's place in Daniel's heart.

"So where do we go from here?" he asked. "Is gratitude all you feel for me? Do you see me only as some guardian angel watching over you?"

She kept her eyes focused on his. "I don't know what I feel," she said honestly. "Because my emotions are every-where, but I do know what I want."

"And what is that?"

"I want to continue what we started before I left for Los Angeles. I thought we were on the road to somewhere nice and I want to see where that road takes us." When he opened his mouth to speak, she pressed her hand against his lips. "Before you say anything, you have to know that my life is complicated and seems to be growing more complicated every day."

He removed her hand from his lips and kissed her fingers. "Are you trying to scare me away?"

She shook her head. "But I do want you to understand what it means to be involved with me. No surprises."

"I know what you're trying to do, Destiny, but life doesn't work that way. You could list all the complications in your life today and another unforeseen one can come up tomorrow, or next year, or in the next ten years. And my life could end up with more complications than yours. That's why it's called life. We have to live it day by day. I can only tell you that I'm willing to work with you through any complications we face, that I want to walk along this relationship road with you."

"It sounds good, but—"

He sat back in his chair and folded his arms across his chest. "Okay," he said. "Tell me your complications and I'll tell you if I can handle them."

"I'm being serious," she said.

"So am I. Give me your complications."

"You know my kids are my main priority," she said. "For their sakes, I still need to move this summer, which becomes complicated because I no longer can count on the money from the HR Solutions job to do it."

He shrugged. "I mentioned this before and you shot me down, but I really do think you need to take the money from the funds we're using for the short-term loan program. It's the best solution."

She wouldn't disagree with him this time. "I came to the same conclusion myself. I'll put together a funding application and submit it to you for approval. I don't want special treatment."

He smiled at her. "Okay, but you do know I'm approving everybody, right?"

She frowned. "Well, yes, there is that."

"Now that complication wasn't so complicated after all. What's next?"

She slapped him on his forearm to remind him to take her seriously. "It's not lost on me that you started these programs about the same time that I submitted my application at HR Solutions. If I had waited a little longer, even a couple of weeks, I would have had another option. Instead of waiting on God to send me a solution, I acted out of desperation and made a bad choice. Lesson learned."

"Stop beating yourself up about it," he said. "Now what's your next complication or have you run out of them already?"

She took a deep breath. She knew what she had to tell him next would bring back sad memories. "My mom is about to undergo treatment for another bout of breast cancer."

Daniel reached for her hand and squeezed. "I'm sorry, Destiny," he said. "But she can fight this. I'll be right there with you giving you all the prayer and support I can. What are the doctors saying?"

"Charlotte Wells has agreed to join her care team. We met with her the other day and she presented us with several treatment options. We're deciding among them now."

"I trust Charlotte's judgment. She was great with Gloria."

"We feel the same way." She met his eyes. "Given what you went through with Gloria, are you sure you're ready to deal with breast cancer again, if only peripherally? I'd certainly understand if you weren't."

"Life happens, Destiny. All we can commit to is to be there for each other through its challenges. We can't pick the challenges we want. As people of faith, we just have to believe that God can bring us through those challenges, maybe even send a guardian angel or two to watch over us. Agreed?"

She smiled. "Agreed."

"Now is that your last complication or do you have another one?"

"One more," she said. "Turns out my mother, the woman who raised me, the woman you met, is not my biological mother."

"What? You're adopted?"

She nodded. "I told you my life was complicated."

He sank back in his chair. "I'm stunned, but you seem to be handling this well. How long have you known?"

She smiled. "Since yesterday. I was sharing the concerns I had about breast cancer possibly being in Kenae's future. Mom told me about my birth mother so I wouldn't worry so much about Kenae and breast cancer."

"I don't know what to say. How are you doing?"

"I don't know if it's sunk in yet. And, oh yeah, I know who my birth mother is."

"You do?"

She nodded. "In fact I've met her. Her name is Annie Robinson. She's the counselor who helped me get enrolled in school, and who is letting me apprentice under her in order to get my natural hair care license."

His mouth dropped open. "Okay, I admit it. This is a complication."

She gave a dry laugh. "Yes it is. But if I'm really honest about it, being adopted somewhat explains the connection I felt with Annie when I first met her, and it even explains some of the disconnect that I sometimes feel with my mom. My immediate concern though is how and when to tell the kids, about Annie and about their grandma being ill. It's going to be a lot for them."

He reached for her hand again. "Whatever you need from me, just ask, okay?" After she nodded, he said, "Bring on the next complication."

"That's it," she said. "Here you have me with my short-comings and complications laid bare before you. Are you ready and willing to go on this road trip with me, with all the detours that may be required along the way?"

To answer, he leaned toward her, pulled her close, and pressed his lips against hers. When he pulled back, he said, "Does that answer your question?"

She smiled at him. "Perfectly."

Epilogue

DESTINY SAT IN THE HILLMAN GYMNASIUM WITH THE other graduates waiting to be awarded their bachelor's degrees. Her journey to get here had been long, and sometimes rocky, but it had always been worth it. She'd taken charge of her life, made good decisions and bad ones, and lived through the consequences of both. Her future and her outlook on life were on the upswing.

She looked up in the stands in the general direction of where her family and friends were seated. She spied the wildly flailing arms of KJ and Kenae first. She couldn't help but grin at their antics.

She turned her attention from the twins to her mother and Daniel, who sat on either side of them. She thanked God that her mother was present and that her cancer was again in remission. She was grateful that the protocol from Charlotte Wells's clinical trial had given her and her mother time to build on what they had started two summers ago on that fateful flight from L.A. back to Atlanta. She and her mother were closer today than they had ever been.

Kenneth, Mary Margaret, and three-month-old baby Kendra were seated a row above the others. As usual, baby Kendra was in the arms of her doting grandmother Charlotte. As she had expected, KJ and Kenae had fallen in love with their baby sister and showed no signs of jealousy.

Bertice, Phil, Natalie, and Gavin sat on the next row up. She was glad Bertice and Phil had been able to patch things up. They'd been talking about marriage for the last year, but hadn't announced a formal engagement yet.

Destiny's attention returned to Daniel. Their financial seminars had been a big hit with the church, so much so that they were made standing events on the church calendar. She and Daniel had worked magic with them and found magic with each other. If anybody had told her years ago that she would one day be on the verge of becoming a pastor's wife, she would not have believed them, but that's exactly where she found herself today.

Destiny's focus returned to the graduation when the procession attendant gave her row the signal to stand. As directed, she rose from her seat and followed her group to the left of the stage. As she stood waiting for her name to be called, she looked into the stands again. This time her eyes locked with Annie's and they shared a private smile. Annie, her friend and mentor, had enriched her life in many unexpected ways. Not only had she helped Destiny get her natural hair care license, she had also made her a partner in the salon. They were looking to expand with a second salon, which Destiny would manage, in the coming year.

Destiny turned her attention back to the graduation exercise as the time for her name to be called drew near.

"Destiny Madison."

When Destiny heard her name, she began her walk across the stage, leaving the Summer of Me behind.

Acknowledgments

The process of writing a novel is a long and, many times, arduous journey. Along the way, the writer needs lots of support. I'd like to acknowledge three of the many people who supported me through the writing of *The Summer of Me*.

I cannot fully express the gratitude I owe to my editor, Erika Tsang, for the way she labored with me as I struggled to finish this book. She forced me to move out of my comfort zone, and as a result, caused me to grow as a writer. Thank you, Erika.

My agent, Natasha Kern, was also wonderfully supportive. Good agents do more than their fair share of listening to a writer's woes and helping them find workable solutions to life problems that affect the writing process. Thank you, Natasha, for being a good agent.

Finally, I'd like to acknowledge my husband, George. The only thing more difficult than being a writer on deadline is being the husband of a writer on deadline. George was a true partner throughout the entire process. I could not have written this book without his willingness to pick up the slack in our home and with our family. Thank you, George.

About the Author

ANGELA BENSON is a graduate of Spelman College and the author of fourteen novels, including the Christy Award–nominated *Awakening Mercy,* the *Essence* bestseller *The Amen Sisters, Up Pops the Devil,* and *Sins of the Father.* She is an associate professor at the University of Alabama and lives in Tuscaloosa, Alabama.

KS BY ANGELA BENSON

THE SUMMER OF ME
A Novel

As a single mother, Destiny makes sacrifices for her children—including saying good-bye for the summer so they can spend time with their father and stepmother. Though she'll miss them with all her heart, the time alone gives her an opportunity to address her own needs, like finishing her college degree. But Destiny's friends think her summer should include some romance.

DELILAH'S DAUGHTERS
A Novel

An inspirational family drama set against the backdrop of the music industry. Delilah Monroe and her husband, Rocky, always dreamed of their three daughters making it big in show business. After Rocky's death, Delilah's determination is even stronger. However, her daughters aren't so sure.

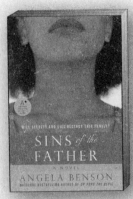

SINS OF THE FATHER
A Novel

Sins of the Father is a powerful story of a house bitterly divided—a wealthy black entrepreneur with two families and the catastrophic consequences when they both collide. It blends romance, drama, inspiration, and intrigue in an unforgettable tale of redemption and, ultimately, of love.

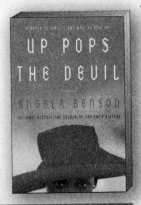

UP POPS THE DEVIL
A Novel

Two hard years in prison have changed Wilford "Preacher" Winters for the better. He did his time, now he's going to "do the right thing." But the women in his life have other ideas. With his world about to explode all around him, Preacher is going to need every ounce of his newfound faith to remain strong. Because it takes a lot to become a new man, sometimes even a miracle.